D0406023

The Guardian Stones

Books by Eric Reed

The Guardian Stones

The Guardian Stones

Eric Reed

Poisoned Pen Press

First Edition 2016

10 9 8 7 6 5 4 3 2 1

Library of Congress Catalog Card Number: 2015946347

ISBN: 9781464205019 Hardcover
9781464205033 Trade Paperback

Poisoned Pen Press
6962 E. First Ave., Ste. 103
Scottsdale, AZ 85251
www.poisonedpenpress.com
info@poisonedpenpress.com

Printed in the United States of America

Cast of Characters

Edwin Carpenter, retired American professor, widower, visiting Noddweir to study its stone circle

Grace Baxter, daughter of former village constable George Baxter, member of the Women's Voluntary Service

George Baxter, Grace's father, recently left the village to join the military

Martha Roper, Grace's maternal grandmother, a "wise woman" knowledgeable about herbal preparations, folk cures, and magic

Polly, Martha's apprentice

Isobel (Issy) Chapman, missing child, daughter of Jack Chapman

Jack Chapman, blacksmith, widower, father of Isobel (Issy)

Duncan and Meg Gowdy, proprietors of the village pub, parents of Violet

Tom Green, Special Constable sent to replace Grace's father

Constable Harmon, from nearby Craven Arms

Joe Haywood, conscientious objector, works on the Wainman farm

Emily Miller, village shop proprietor, good friend of Susannah Radbone

Susannah Radbone, retired schoolteacher, houses an evacuee

Harry and Louisa Wainman, farmers who house several evacuees

Timothy Wilson, vicar of Saint Winnoc's Church

Brothers Mike and Len Finch, evacuees, tough city boys

Bert Holloway, evacuee, friend of Violet Gowdy

Reggie Cox, evacuee, wears leg brace due to polio

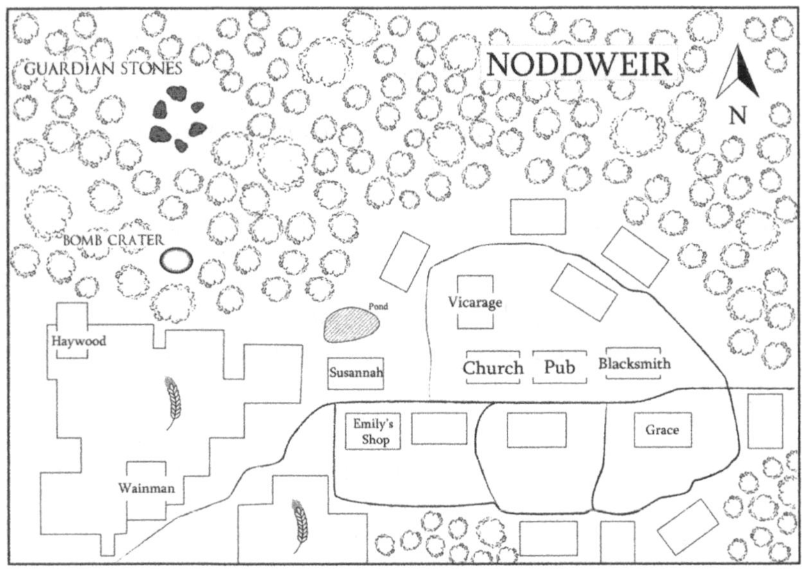

Chapter One

Thursday, June 12, 1941

"Don't look behind you, said Death, but we're being followed." The stout, elderly woman sounded breathless as she labored up the forest slope, her walking stick repeatedly searching for purchase in the thick ferns.

"What do you mean, Miss Miller?" Edwin Carpenter, twenty years her junior and considerably thinner, was more winded. He stopped and the thick lenses of his eyeglasses steamed up instantly in the humid air. He polished them slowly with his handkerchief, giving himself a moment to rest.

"It's just a local saying, Professor Carpenter, but in fact, we are being followed." Emily waved her stick toward a gap in the trees where a flash of red moved below. "That's Grace Baxter's jacket." She thrust her stick back into the ferns and resumed climbing.

"Oh." Edwin gasped. He wanted to tell her to call him Edwin rather than professor but he couldn't find the breath. It was all he could do to force himself to follow. He feared falling as he waded through knee-high ferns, stumbling over hidden rocks and roots. He never realized how dark a forest could be even in daytime, and it was fast approaching dusk. A big brown mongrel trotted along behind his mistress, tongue lolling and tail wagging, delighted with the game.

Unfortunately it wasn't a game. Nearly every adult in Noddweir had spread out through the forest covering the mountains around the village seeking the missing girl. Shouts back and forth in the distance, the sound almost swallowed by surrounding trees, marked their progress.

Edwin started to regret he'd volunteered to help. Maybe he should have stayed back at the house and unpacked, after all. As the younger and more able-bodied searchers vanished into the trees, Edwin found himself left behind with Emily Miller, the village shopkeeper.

He barely avoided being left behind by her until, through the trees ahead, he finally glimpsed the crown of what locals called Guardians Hill. He had seen the hill earlier as he approached the village along the dirt road leading into the valley. A wooded knob, bald on top, rose above Noddweir, solitary as if abandoned when its fellow mountains retreated across the Welsh border. He grabbed at branches to keep upright and struggled the last few yards to where the trees ended.

Edwin had come to southwest Shropshire to study the circle of standing stones at this very place. He never expected his first visit to be under such circumstances.

Entering a clearing of limestone outcroppings and gorse, he was surprised to see a man and a young woman in a red jacket waiting at the summit. There was obviously more than one path up the hill and Edwin's guide, he thought ruefully, took him the long way around.

The man accompanying Grace Baxter was in his mid-twenties, bulky but soft. He stared suspiciously at Edwin, who was naturally a stranger to him, having arrived in the village only hours before.

"We know each other," Grace told the man. "We met, briefly, before I had to rush off. Professor Carpenter's my new lodger." She looked Edwin up and down, narrowing her eyes. "You really should have stayed at the house and rested."

Edwin offered a wan smile.

"Just as I told you. A perfect view of the village from here, Professor," Emily panted. "In the daytime, at least."

"That's as may be," said the young man, "but we've no time to chat. Right now we have a missing child to find."

Emily planted her stick in the ground and leaned on it. "Issy Chapman's always causing trouble, she is. What makes you think she's come to grief, Constable?"

Edwin thought she put undo emphasis on the word "constable."

"There's a war on, you know," huffed the young man. He, too, had caught the sarcasm.

Emily flapped her free hand at him. "Oh, do tell! I may be old but I'm not deaf, Tom Green. I hears them devil's flies coming over during the night well enough, likely before anyone else, half the time. And not only am I not deaf, I'm not blind either. She's been up to no good, you'll see. Not to mention a great strapping girl like Issy can look after herself. What's the war got to do with a girl gone missing anyway?"

"Things happen during wars, Miss Miller," Green replied. "Unpredictable things. Bad things. Things that would be unthinkable during peacetime."

Edwin saw Green glance surreptitiously at Grace as he concluded his speech. He guessed the boy had never experienced anything more unthinkable than a hazing at a private school.

Grace ignored him. She was concerned for Emily. "You're pale. You know you shouldn't over-exert yourself. I wish you'd take more care."

"Nonsense, Grace! I can walk the legs off anybody you care to name. And since the constable insists, I shall carry on searching for that idiot girl. Come, Patch."

She hobbled off toward the opposite side of the clearing and her brown mongrel followed.

Edwin wondered if he should follow as well. He preferred to catch his breath. He couldn't say how many villagers Emily could walk the legs off, but she could certainly walk off his. "Miss Miller seemed to think it would be helpful to look around from up here. Take advantage of the height."

"Can't imagine why," said Green. "The whole place has already been searched. And it's too dark to see much down there. Blackout conditions have to be observed. She must be at least eighty. Dotty, you know."

"And liable to fall in the dark," Grace told him. "You'd better follow her, Constable Green." Her tone struck Edwin as unduly sharp.

Green's frown clearly indicated he would rather leave Emily to her own devices. Nevertheless, he left as asked, limping slightly. Green soon vanished through an opening in a welter of blackberry bushes that were fast becoming a featureless wall of darkness.

"Was he bothering you?" Edwin asked.

Grace studied him. "Ah, you heard us just before you arrived up here, then? You have sharp ears."

"Not at all. I simply…well…"

"Don't worry about Tom Green. He's our Special Constable. He was assigned here after our regular constable joined up. Still getting his feet under him."

"I see." Looking around, Edwin took in the ancient standing stones."So these are the famous Guardian Stones."

A rough circle of large lichen-covered stones stood in front of them, most half-hidden by encroaching blackberries and gorse. Foxgloves, a few in bloom, filled the center of the circle. A sapling leaned over one of the larger stones.

Another couple of decades and the Guardians would be completely overrun and hidden, unless someone took the trouble to clear away the brush.

"You'll be able to see them better in the light," Grace replied. "We need to be getting on. I wonder where the girl can be. I don't—"

She was interrupted by a burst of barking and a hoarse shout. "Quick! By the crater! We found her!"

"Crater?" Edwin managed to gasp as they scrambled down the path taken by Emily and Green moments before. "In this valley? Surely you're too far off the beaten track to attract the Luftwaffe?"

"It's the only bomb that's ever been dropped round here. The pilot likely got off course. We hear them going over occasionally on the way to Wales."

They came to the crater where searchers had begun to gather. Grace stood on the lip, staring downwards. The sides of the hole were still raw earth. Below, just visible in the fading light, a crumpled figure lay on its back, half in a pool of muddy water. Patch pranced back and forth, barking and flailing the air with his tail.

"But that's a boy!" Grace said. "Surely not two of them…?"

Green slid down into the crater to bend over the prone figure.

The boy leapt up with a shout and flung a handful of mud into the constable's face. "Fooled yer there, copper!"

"Mike Finch, you little bugger!" Green lunged clumsily toward the lad who scrambled out of his reach and up the opposite side of the depression.

"It's one of the evacuee children," Grace said. "Always causing trouble."

"Just like Issy Chapman," Emily Miller added.

Chapter Two

Constable Green returned to the hilltop and called off the search for the night. There was little chance of finding Isobel in the dark, he said, and moving lights might attract unwanted attention from the air.

Grace guided Edwin back down and through the forest by shaded torchlight. They emerged on a cart track at the edge of a field. The forest closed up behind them like magic, forming a seamless black barrier. Grace turned and headed toward the village, or so Edwin trusted. He could make out nothing in the darkness. Only after they had walked along the rutted path for five minutes did barns and houses begin to appear, dark shapes cut out of a starry sky. In the distance he heard Constable Green stridently arguing with someone about whether or not a light had been showing round their window.

"He's certainly keen, is Tom," Grace remarked as she let Edwin into her cottage. "Take the torch and shut the curtains, please. I'll light the lamp."

Edwin remembered that electricity had not yet reached this remote part of Shropshire. The warm light of an oil lamp sprang up, throwing shadows of well-worn furniture across whitewashed walls. The plain, polished pieces reminded him of his grandmother's neat parlor, where he had often spent evenings reading or playing with lead soldiers.

Now flesh and blood soldiers were fighting.

Grace carried the lamp into the kitchen and poked the wood fire in the stove into life.

"Isn't lamp oil hard to get these days?" Edwin asked.

"Depends who you know." Grace brought a covered pan out of the tiny scullery. "Now, here's a nice bit of rabbit stew. We'll heat it up and have it with bread and what passes for butter these days. You must be famished, rushing off into the forest practically before you unpacked."

Did he detect a note of approval in her voice, or was it just his imagination? An attractive woman, Grace was dark-haired and dark-eyed, with a broad rosy-cheeked face and wide hips. In a decade or so she would look like the typical farmer's wife, but for the moment she was aglow with youth. Whatever they were to become, at a certain age a person's overwhelming impression was simply one of youth. Or so Edwin had decided observing students during his years of teaching.

"I needed to stretch my legs anyway after that cart ride," he said. "I didn't expect a horse and cart."

"What? To get to Noddweir? Nobody has a car, even if you could find petrol." She brought a tablecloth and cutlery from an antique sideboard.

"Sorry there's no steaks! I hear Americans eat them every meal and twice on Sundays. You stir and I'll cut the bread."

Edwin shook his head as he stirred. "Never been big on steaks." He was still amazed at how people got along with wartime shortages. In London he'd been told that in some places you were lucky if you could get an egg a week! What if they dropped it on the way home? How would he eat his? Fried, perhaps. Scrambled was no good. Eggs shrank in a mysterious fashion when cooked that way. Boiled might be a possibility.

No, he decided while spooning stew into the bowls waiting on the table, I'll give it to Grace and maybe she can bake a cake with it.

Grace returned with a jug of cider. "Made in the village, this is. It packs quite a wallop, as you would doubtless say."

As they ate, Grace plied him with questions about his work. Did his studies of weird stones take him all over the country?

How difficult was it to travel these days? How long had he been retired? Did he like tripe?

Edwin fielded the questions but paused over the final query. "Tripe?"

"Sometimes it's possible to get some. Can't stand it myself, but Duncan—the fellow who runs the local pub—is quite fond of it. Of course he is Scottish."

"That explains it, then," Edwin replied. "No more cider, thank you." The cider—what he would have called hard cider—did indeed pack a wallop, particularly for a man used to nothing more than a sociable glass of wine.

"It's difficult to travel what with one thing and another," he told her, "so I thought I would try the more rural areas, and here I am."

"You can hardly get more rural than Noddweir."

"I understand the name is a corruption of the Welsh, nodd-wer. It means protector. Or so Mr. Wilson told me."

"Is it? Well, I guess the vicar would know but I can't imagine Noddweir being able to protect anything. How do you know the vicar?"

"We'd corresponded about the Guardians before the war. I expect to see a fair bit of him now. He has a very good library he thinks might be useful. I've found rural ministers are prime sources for information. When I'm unable to dig up something I want to know about a place, I look up a local minister and write to him."

Grace collected the crockery and took it away, returning with bowls of stewed apples. "I'm glad the vicar mentioned I had room for a lodger."

"He told me he regretted I could not stay at his house but he has a family of girls billeted on him. Not too much bother, he said, but noisy and always hungry. Not a good place to pursue studies."

"You'll have plenty of peace and quiet here," she reassured him as an elderly woman appeared in the kitchen doorway.

The woman arrived so silently she might have alighted there like the bird her fragile figure suggested. Unpinned white hair fell freely over her thin shoulders. "Entertaining your boyfriend, Grace?" She cackled.

"This is Martha Roper, my grandmother." Grace's cheeks flushed, more with irritation than embarrassment Edwin thought. "And no, Mr. Carpenter is not my boyfriend. He's the professor I told you about, who has come to lodge with us. I thought you were sleeping, Grandma. There's stew. I'm making tea and can probably squeeze another cup out the pot if you'd like one?"

Martha took an empty chair. "Got any sugar?"

"No. I told you this morning we were out."

"Don't bother with the tea, then. You always make it weak as maiden's water." Martha stared at Edwin. Her eyes were pale blue, her gaze sharp. "So you're the Yank with an interest in the old ways? I can tell you a fair bit about them. As for Isobel. She's been carried off by the devil because she ate blackberries last October. The devil, no doubt about it."

Edwin looked politely surprised.

Martha smiled. "Oh yes, Professor, I know about such things as anyone who lives round here will tell you. I've showed a few little spells—persuasions, I calls them—to Isobel. She took an interest in the old ways, unlike some in my family. Now mind, I told her never to try any of them. Too dangerous unless you know what you might be trying to persuade. They say that swine Hitler practices magic. Do you think he does?"

"I think it highly unlikely."

The old woman pondered for a moment. "It may be so. You never know, do you?"

"Oh, Grandmother, really. Are you sure you won't have some tea?"

"Didn't you say you got no sugar? No point asking, is there? Still, nice to meet our lodger. We'll talk when you have time, Professor. I can tell you about things you won't find in books. Now I'll leave you two to your privacy." She got up and went into the front room.

"Sugar, indeed!" Grace set the tea cups on the table hard enough to spill a few drops on the tablecloth. "She wanted to have a good look at you, more like. Couldn't wait until morning. She'll be wagging her tongue to anyone who'll listen. Our privacy, indeed!"

She must have seen Edwin's puzzled expression because she added, "Grandma's been failing the past few years. She doesn't always know what's...appropriate."

"Well, it's hardly a secret why I'm here. And it's not like I'm twenty-five, after all."

"Don't worry about Grandmother. She came to stay with Father and me a couple of years ago and we gave her the other downstairs room for a bedroom. She has trouble with the stairs."

"Your father enlisted?"

"Yes. That left the village without a policeman and that's how Special Constable Tom Green came into our lives. Not that there's much police work to do around Noddweir."

"Until now."

"Because of Issy, you mean? She's likely run off, is all. Her father's too fond of drink and it's well known he mistreats the girl." Grace took a sip of her tea. "Served in the first world war and never been the same since, especially after his wife died having Issy. I saw the girl earlier this week and there were bruises on her arms. I suspect she means to give her dad a good scare. Green will have been to talk to him about it, and Jack Chapman doesn't like the police, as Issy well knows."

"You're well acquainted with the girl?"

"Yes. She often has her dinner here, and she stays overnight when things get too bad at home. Normally I wouldn't want my grandmother filling up a child's head with nonsense but at least when Issy's here she's not within reach of her—" Her features hardened suddenly. She bit her lip. "Well, never mind that."

Edwin tried his own tea, finding it weaker than he would have liked. He suspected a second brewing from the same tea leaves. "Strange your grandmother would mention the girl eating blackberries in October. I know the belief, that the devil gets into blackberries that month. It's commonly held here too?"

"You might say so," Grace replied. "I don't care for them myself, although they do make good jam. If you can get the sugar. See, you haven't been here a day and already you're learning about the mysteries of Noddweir."

Edwin's suitcases sat on a chair at the foot of the metal-framed bed in his room, one of two bedrooms upstairs. Grace occupied the other across the hall.

His room's drawn blackout curtains clashed with the otherwise bucolic ambiance, the whitewashed plaster walls, the rustic dresser, and small table by the bed. Over the dresser hung a tinted Victorian print of *The Light of the World*.

He decided to put off unpacking until the morning. Springs squeaked and sagged when he sat on the bed to take off his shoes. Although it was a strange room in an unfamiliar place, Edwin did not feel any more or less out of place than he had for the past year. Since his wife's death his life had become a foreign country. After over thirty years of marriage he was ignorant of the customs of this place in which Elise no longer lived.

His life had lost all impetus. Before long he would simply roll to a complete stop.

He bent over and opened his briefcase filled with notebooks and research materials. He took out the framed photograph of his wife and sat it on the table.

They had joked that in all their years of marriage they had never spent a night apart because in those very rare instances when Edwin had traveled, usually to a academic conference, he had taken her picture with him. The thought ran through his mind as he positioned the photograph so he could see it when he awoke.

Chapter Three

Friday, June 13, 1941

The excited auburn-haired little girl in the doorway grabbed Grace's arm and tugged, trying to pull her across the step. "Come quick! Those bad children are being ever so bad! You must catch them!"

Edwin came downstairs blinking sleepily behind his eyeglasses. He felt embarrassed. After the train trip and the cart ride into Noddweir, followed by perambulations in the forest, he had slept until what he considered an unconscionable hour. "What is it? Have they found the girl?" He searched his memory, which was being sorely tested in his new surroundings. "Have they found Isobel?"

"No. This is Violet Gowdy. Her parents run the pub." Grace gently broke the girl's grip on her arm.

Violet, seeing Edwin, retired a few steps from the door, her arms clasped across a thin chest.

"All right, Violet, we'll go and deal with the bad children," Grace told her, adding for Edwin's benefit, "I always helped my father with these sorts of things."

Edwin tagged along, welcoming the opportunity to observe another slice of English country life.

Several children were running back and forth in front of the public house down the street.

"Eggs! They're throwing eggs!" Grace quickened her step.

"Bad children!" Violet kept saying, breaking into a skipping run to keep up with the two adults. "Bad!"

Though outraged she appeared to be enjoying the excitement.

Several miscreants scattered, disappearing quickly between the cottages and behind the hedges along the street.

"There go Betty's twins," Grace muttered. "I'll need to speak to her!"

A number of taller boys advanced. Edwin recognized the boy who had pretended to be a corpse the night before. He looked lively this morning, carrying a basket of ammunition. Although they were merely children, armed with nothing more dangerous than eggs, there was genuine menace in their defiance. Born predators.

The boys fired a salvo.

Edwin took an egg to the chest. Two others splattered against Violet's flowered dress. Her excitement vanished. She burst into tears and ran for the safety of her parents' pub.

Grace sprinted forward. Edwin noted with admiration that unlike Constable Green the night before, she caught Mike Finch. She wrenched the egg basket from his grasp."Where did you steal this from?"

"Dunno," came the surly reply in the flat accent of Birmingham. "Me brother gave it to me. Found it lying about, I suppose."

Grace gave the lad a rough shake he hadn't expected, judging from his ugly glare. "There's a farmer's wife somewhere wondering where these eggs went. It's not just theft, Mike. We can't afford to be wasting food, considering everything that's already being rationed. You should be locked up!"

"Gawn! You wouldn't bloody dare!" He twisted around, escaped her grasp, and raced down the street making a rude sign over his shoulder.

Grace made as if to follow. As she passed a hedge she leaned over it without warning and yanked into view a chubby boy whose eyeglasses were mended with sticking plaster.

"Bert Holloway! I might have guessed! How many times have I told you to keep away from the Finch brothers? You know they'll get you into trouble."

"Well, see, I—" the boy stammered. "I told 'em it was wicked. They'd be helping Mr. Hitler by wasting eggs, but...but...."

"Not another word. Do I have to write to your parents and tell them what you did? What do you think your mother would say if she knew?"

The boy hung his head, mortified. Finally dismissed, he nearly blundered blindly into Edwin before lumbering off.

Grace sighed as she watched him. "He's a nice kid but runs with a bad crowd. Or I should say waddles. Not too fast on his feet and they never let him forget it. Some of those boys will come to bad ends, I'm convinced of it. One of these days they'll go too far."

Edwin glanced down at the yolk on his shirt. People were lucky to get an egg a week. What kind of children would use someone's single weekly egg to ruin someone else's shirt?

A voice with a broad Scottish accent boomed out from the pub doorway. "Saw you coming down the street, Grace, so I left the majesty of the law to deal with those little swine. I was about ready to give them a thrashing myself."

The speaker was a short, chunky man with sandy hair. "What a waste of eggs," he continued as Grace and Edwin walked over the pub. "Not to mention someone's just lost a bit of income from black marketeering. Come in for a minute. The wife wants a word. Whose are the eggs, anyway?"

"Can't say, Duncan. My official investigation is not yet completed." She smiled.

"You'll have to give the evidence to that fool Green, then. I'm sure he'll ferret out the culprit in less than an hour, like he found out who stole my wife's best blouse off the washing line last month."

"The blouse has never been seen since," Grace told Edwin, before introducing the men. "Edwin, this is Duncan Gowdy. Duncan, this is Edwin Carpenter. He's here to study the Guardians. The stones, that is, not your pub."

"Oh, aye?" the publican replied, glancing up at his sign, which presumably depicted the stones in their heyday. Their size compared to the trees on the slopes below them seemed disproportionately large. The sign looked as if it had been copied from a postcard of Stonehenge.

Duncan led them down a stone-flagged corridor to living quarters at the rear of the building.

"That circle's an interesting bit of history, Mr. Carpenter," he said, "only nobody knows what it is, so everyone feels free to make up their own stories. Mind you don't take any notice of what Martha, for one, tells you, begging your pardon, Grace."

Violet was in the kitchen, having her dress scrubbed with a damp cloth by a plump redhead Edwin immediately recognized as the girl's mother. He was struck by how closely Violet mirrored the older woman's looks in miniature.

Meg Gowdy muttered a disinterested greeting when introduced to Edwin and continued fulminating about wild children who should be locked up. When she'd done the best she could to clean Violet's dress, she sent the red-faced and teary-eyed child up to her room to read.

"How many eggs you got left in that basket, Grace?" Meg asked.

"Half a dozen."

"What you going to do with them?"

"Duncan suggests I should give them to Tom Green. He can find out whose they are and return them."

The woman made a harrumphing noise. "Eat them himself, more like. I don't suppose you would consider selling them to—?"

"She's joking," Duncan cut in quickly when Grace looked uncomfortable.

His wife scowled and tossed the rag into a bucket by the back door. "Can't you and Green do something about these wretched kids, Grace? Nothing's safe. Mud thrown at washing, dogs tormented, knocking on windows at night scaring everyone."

"Boys will be boys," observed Duncan.

"You call those vicious animals boys? We should send them all back where they come from."

"I'm afraid we don't have much say over the evacuees we're sent, Meg," Grace replied. "Besides, the farmers are glad of the labor."

"Oh, I'm sure Harry Wainman is glad to have his little slaves. He can sit on his arse all day."

With that she grabbed her cigarette and stamped off.

Duncan shook his head. "We used to live in town. She misses the crowds and bustle and all that. Too quiet here. And Violet, playing with the village kids, she's picking up their ways, Meg says. Thank heavens she avoids these new city kids who've been forced on us. Some of the things they come out with! When I was their age, well...anyhow, thanks for sorting that lot out, Grace. I would offer you a drink but it's out of hours. What a life, eh?"

"And where was Green when the kids were fighting?" Grace asked.

"Long gone with another search party," came Duncan's reply. "Lucky you were still around or those kids would be smashing up someone's fence or worse." He hesitated. "You know Green's staying with us. Well, I noticed last night he had a drink or two with Joe Haywood."

"Oh?" Grace looked interested.

"Just thought I'd mention it. He'll have to be cleverer than he thinks he is to catch Joe out." He glanced at his watch. "The dinnertime news will be starting. Let's see if there's as much excitement in the rest of the world as there is here in Noddweir."

"I hope not," Grace said. "It's Friday the thirteenth, you know. Grandma already warned me not to spill the salt, or break a mirror, or walk under a ladder."

"And watch out for black cats crossing your path?" offered Edwin.

"Yes, we could use a black cat now."

"What do you mean?"

"For good luck," Grace replied. "Aren't black cats good luck in America, too?"

Chapter Four

Jack Chapman gazed longingly at the closed door of the Guardians pub as he trod gingerly past. A drink or two would calm the demons in his skull. Every time his foot hit the road it disturbed the demons and they tried to claw their way out. Nevertheless, he must look for Issy, not least because he wanted people to see him searching and say he was a good, concerned father to leave everything and go out looking for his daughter.

He stepped on something slippery, his feet came out from under him, and he sat down hard. The road tilted and houses whirled around in a crazy dance. He closed his eyes until the vertigo was gone.

There was egg yolk on the bottom of his shoe. Why were eggs lying about in the High Street?

He pushed himself up with difficulty. His massive arms felt strangely weak. He took a few deep breaths before continuing. When he reached the shade of the forest after he'd got his blood circulating, he was sure he'd feel better. He turned down the path running alongside Susannah Radbone's house. The former schoolteacher made her home into a stereotypical country cottage, perfectly whitewashed, with red shutters and a thatched roof. It stuck out like a sore thumb in Noddweir, he thought sourly.

Behind the fence at the end of Susannah's meticulously cultivated back garden the land fell away into a marshy depression partly filled by a pond.

Jack made his way through the vegetation as quickly as he could, taking a shortcut to the part of the forest he intended to search. He was going round a tall cluster of bushes when the screaming started.

The shrieks grew louder, coming from the direction of the pond. They were not playful. They were frantic. Terrified.

A girl's screams.

"Issy!" Jack yelled.

In the pond two figures held a third, their backs to him. Two boys and a girl, waist deep in the water. The boys pushed the girl's head down through pond scum into the water, held it there for a few seconds before letting her up, and then, just as another coughing, choking scream began, pushed it back under again.

Jack broke into a stumbling run. The demons in his skull joined in the screaming.

The boys yanked the girl up and shoved her back down. She flailed and thrashed, spraying water. The boys laughed.

Jack recognized the Finch brothers, raw-boned youths with wolfish faces. They were not yet adults but they had never truly been children.

"Issy!" Jack roared again as he reached the pond and flung himself into the water.

The boys whirled around, wearing identical sneers. In their frenzied state they would probably have challenged almost any other man in the village, but the sight of the bullish blacksmith wading inexorably toward them with fury in his eyes was more than they had bargained on. They released their captive and took flight like startled ducks. Jack fastened the iron tongs of his hand to Mike Finch's arm, lurched forward, grabbed the boy's shirt, and pulled him back into the pond.

"Let's see how you like it, you vicious little bugger!"

He jammed Mike's face into the shallows with such force it was covered with mud when he jerked him back up.

Len Finch danced back and forth at the edge of the pond. "What you doing, mister? You're crazy! You'll kill him!"

Jack ignored him. Inside his head the demons clawed and kicked. His skull felt ready to explode. He slapped mud off Mike's face and pushed him back down. He'd done something similar to kittens. The only difference was he felt a bit sorry for the kittens.

There was a searing pain in his shoulder. Bellowing curses, he reached around and grabbed Len, who stabbed at him again with a pocket knife. Jack grabbed at the knife, letting go of Len as he did so. Instantly both boys were racing away, faster than Jack could follow.

Only then did he remember the girl.

His fury had driven everything from his mind but his desire to take revenge on the boys.

He had nothing to see but the still surface of the water and broken reeds.

Now the demons laughed at him.

"Oh, God! Oh no! "

He splashed into the pond, desperately reaching under the water, grasping handfuls of mud, pulling up rocks and weeds.

Edwin and Grace followed Duncan along the corridor, this time going into the large public bar, dimly illuminated by small windows. Their footsteps sounded loud and hollow on the flagstones. A wide fireplace dominated one wall.

Behind the bar, Duncan turned on the wireless sitting on a shelf beside a couple of half-empty bottles. It was an ancient Philco, as elegant as a bread bin.

"I keep it in here for the customers," Duncan said over a sudden hiss of static. "Can't leave it on too long, though. Batteries are getting harder and harder to come by. I make a point to listen to the news. Buy a drink at the Guardians and you get your news free."

Music crackled around the empty room, fading in and out. Edwin didn't recognize the band. Elise would have. To the extent Edwin cared for English music, he preferred Elgar, whom Elise had considered rather dry.

Duncan fiddled with the dial and static receded as an announcer began speaking in tones sounding out of place in a country pub.

There wasn't much of interest. Listeners were assured Malta was in good heart, according to a senior staff officer who visited the besieged island. Edwin wondered if there was a dearth of positive news and perhaps too much bad news that the BBC might be reluctant to broadcast.

"Soviet officials continue to insist that there is no German threat to Russia," the announcer informed them.

When the newscast was over, Duncan clicked the wireless off. "So, is Hitler going to invade Russia? That's been a popular topic of debate the past couple of weeks. Opinion runs about two-to-one in favor."

"Noddweir knows something Stalin doesn't?" Edwin asked.

Duncan observed that Der Fuhrer would be mad to invade, but then he was mad anyway.

"Evil, is what he is," Grace said. "And evil doesn't recognize any limitations. Satan challenged God, after all."

A barrage of knocks rattled the pub door. "Open up!"

Duncan's jaw tightened as he strode over to a window and glared out. "I'll not be serving you before time, Jack! Get away now!"

The publican's refusal was met with more knocking. "I'm not here for drinks! I got something of yours to return."

When Duncan opened up, Edwin saw Violet standing in a doorway for the second time in less than two hours.

This time, rather than a neat, enraged little girl, the figure was soaking wet and crying, her face covered in scratches. Beside her, holding her hand, stood a muscular, middle-aged man with scanty brown hair, wet and plastered to his skull.

"They tried to drown me in the witch pond," Violet sniffed between choking sobs. "The Finch boys did. Those bad, bad boys. They said they'd kill me for telling about the egg fight." She began to wail.

"I was on my way to search for Issy when I heard her yelling," said the man. "The little buggers was dunking her in the pond.

And her thrashing and sputtering and screaming. For a moment I thought I'd lost her, but when I turned around, there she was sitting on the grass, crying her eyes out."

"Professor Carpenter, this is Jack Chapman, our blacksmith," Grace said. "Isobel's father."

Edwin added another name to memory. At the beginning of each school year he had a hard enough time recalling students' names with the benefit of a seating chart. Thrust straight into the life of Noddweir, meeting its inhabitants willy-nilly, he felt as if he'd been thrown into the middle of a Russian novel.

"Don't worry, Jack," Grace was saying. "We're still searching for your daughter."

"There's them thinks she's run off."

"We hope that's all it is."

"Hope! That's worth bugger all. I might as well have the vicar pray we find her."

"She'll be back soon. Remember Len Finch went missing for a day last month? Turned out he'd gone to Craven Arms."

"Everyone knows he was up to no good there for Joe Haywood," Jack said. "You're not accusing Issy of working for a black marketeer, are you?"

He turned and walked away before Grace could reply.

Edwin saw blood on the shoulder of Jack's shirt. Grace didn't remark on it. Either she hadn't noticed or didn't care. She was icy when she spoke to the blacksmith.

The commotion brought Meg back. "I told you to go upstairs and read, Violet!" Meg scolded as she entered the bar. Then she caught sight of the bedraggled child, standing in a puddle, sodden green hair ribbons along with strands of green pond scum dangling in front of her face.

She knelt down, put her arms around her daughter, and glared up at Duncan. "This is the last straw! You promised we'd buy a place in town! You promised when we married!"

Duncan raised his hands in a vague gesture meant to quiet her or perhaps to defend himself. "Meg, there are people—"

"You promised, Duncan! And where are we? And now, look, you've almost got our daughter killed. Next thing she'll be vanishing like Isobel."

The tenor of her voice was irritating enough to make Edwin wince.

"That isn't fair, Meg," put in Grace.

"You know I've done my best, Meg," said Duncan. "You can't blame me for the war. I've had to change my plans."

Meg stood up, arm around Violet's shoulders. She looked at Duncan with such transparent contempt Edwin was afraid she was about to spit. "A plan? You have another plan? Is it better than your first one, or your second?"

Violet stopped crying and looked from her mother to her father, eyes wide with alarm.

Meg's fingers tightened on the girl's shoulder, guiding her toward the door. "I hope to see the back of this god-forsaken place before too long. And when I'm gone the Boche can bomb it until there's nothing left but a hole in the ground for all I care!"

Chapter Five

Edwin decided it was time to visit the vicar whose letters had brought him to Noddweir. After the scene in the pub he wanted to settle his mind. He had always been a scholarly and somewhat solitary man. He was not comfortable learning that a couple's marriage was on the verge of breakup practically before he had memorized their names. He returned to his room, changed his egged shirt, and went looking for the vicarage.

The village Meg Gowdy would have been happy to see bombed into a hole in the ground nestled in a narrow fold between wooded mountains rising gradually north, west, and south. Cottages clung to the incongruously named High Street as if cowering away from the forest. A few branching roads doubled back or petered out in fields and meadows. The majority of the houses were small, built of brick or stone with slate roofs. The largest building, a sturdy church with its squat Norman tower, recalled a time when Noddweir had been more populous. The Guardians pub, the second-largest structure, sat beside the church. Beyond the village, where the land slanted upward, Edwin could see the knob-shaped hill of the Guardian Stones.

It was a short walk around the side of the church to the vicarage behind. The residence's stone walls were all but concealed by vines, matching the vines that crept up the back of the church. Rose bushes bloomed all around in profusion but no apparent order.

The rap of the knocker summoned a man in his fifties, with a drawn face whose pallor was accented by kindly, deep-set dark eyes.

"I've come to see Mr. Wilson."

"You must be Edwin. I'm Timothy Wilson, your faithful correspondent. Wonderful to meet you at last." He coughed and gave Edwin a surprisingly feeble handshake.

"Oh, indeed. I'm glad to meet you after all these years Mr.... Wilson. I...uh..."

"I see you're surprised. You expected me to be older."

"Well...actually..."

"The archetypical elderly country vicar dabbling in esoteric studies?"

"I have to admit...."

"Never mind. I rather like that image. Perhaps that's why I never bothered to mention I'd been gassed in the last war. The nice thing about correspondence is it doesn't matter what your respective ages may be. Or physical attributes. Unless, of course, we are speaking of *billets-doux*." He spoke in a raspy, gentle voice, little more than a whisper.

Edwin felt disoriented. He was used to a distant friend who was his senior. Once he had been shown to a Victorian loveseat by the window of a small parlor he tried to reorient himself.

Wilson served a pot of strong tea and slices of sponge cake, taking a seat opposite Edwin. Not only Wilson's age shocked Edwin, but his general appearance of ill health. "What were you doing in the war?" Edwin asked.

"Sky pilot. Afterward I was given this small parish. Nothing too strenuous, you see."

Edwin realized he was probably seated where a parade of troubled parishioners had sat—grieving a loved one, or a broken marriage, or regretting some destructive impulse too late. Hearing such stories was not what Edwin called a restful job.

He heard childish voices and the thud of running feet upstairs.

Wilson glanced up. "The pitter-patter of tiny elephants. My little visitors can be noisy but the oldest keeps her sisters fairly well behaved." He poured out tea. "I've got five billeted on me. The oldest also looks after our meals, though at times overcooks the vegetables. Still, these days we must be thankful for whatever we have. They've been here a few months and are quite settled in."

Taking his cup, Edwin leaned forward, to avoid spilling on the furniture. Elise had chided him about coffee stains on his sweaters. After a few years she gave up chiding and kidded him instead. "Not all the evacuees settled so well, unfortunately."

Wilson sighed. "Yes, young scamps, some of them. We must make allowances."

"That's what my wife always said. She taught grade school."

"I was sorry to hear about Elise's passing. I had looked forward to meeting her."

Edwin was thankful that Wilson did not mention God's will, or a better place, or any other platitudes that had come to enrage him more than the most cutting insults could have. On one hand it struck Edwin as odd, since Wilson was a minister, but on the other hand he had corresponded with Edwin for years and doubtless knew how he felt about such things.

"Elise would have loved it here, with all these troublesome children to take in hand," Edwin said. "She always saw good in the worst of the lot. Every year she would be trying to reform some little reprobate."

"A worthy occupation."

"Yes. I can't say her success rate seemed very high. Some people are just born bad, if you ask me. I had it easy. At college you get to teach the more civilized of the little monsters."

"Our own little monsters have certainly been stirring up trouble. And then there's Isobel. It's unfortunate you arrived at such a difficult time. No news, then?"

Edwin shook his head.

"We can only pray Isobel is simply stirring up trouble herself and will return safely. My sermon on Sunday will address the matter. Yet, I confess, while my flock can be difficult at times, I simply cannot see any of them harming a child."

Edwin took another sip of tea. "Excellent brew. I don't think I've had tea this strong since I arrived in England."

"But then it's folklore you're interested in, not tea! Do you know, some of the villagers I see at my services every week are among the most superstitious? When I came here I thought these old country beliefs would be a problem but with a bit of give and take on such matters as the proper form of harvest festival celebrations and blessing of cider presses it hasn't been too difficult. Of course, it probably helps that I always keep my sermons short. An instance of necessity being a virtue. Can't be long-winded when you're short of wind."

"You never mentioned—"

"We must not grumble about our own small crosses. My library is a great comfort." He waved a hand at a well-filled bookshelf against one wall. They were not new books. Some spines were torn, others displayed embossed titles and colored decorations faded by time. They were the sort of books Edwin preferred.

"The old books always are the most interesting," Edwin remarked.

"I have quite a few you'll find of interest. For instance—" Wilson stopped and coughed, taking time for his hacking to subside to a wheeze. "Excuse me. The dust produced by all those dear old vicars' compendiums may have done as much damage to my lungs as the mustard gas." He smiled but his eyes were watering. "I have a couple of notebooks my predecessors kept with fascinating details of Noddweir customs not totally unknown today. One I enjoyed was not throwing ashes out on Christmas Day because you would be throwing them in the Lord's face. Fascinating how these customs linger on in rural areas, isn't it?"

"I'd be most grateful if I could borrow the notebooks sometime."

Wilson rubbed his eyes wearily. "Of course. I'm making notes myself on all manner of things. My memory is not what it was. Did I show the two barrows near Noddweir on the maps I sent? I keep thinking I didn't. Some were copied from old ones I made after I arrived, but others I drew from memory. It's much harder for me to get around than it was."

"I had no idea how ill you were, Timothy."

"I didn't want you to have any idea, my friend. I hope you don't think the less of me that I'm not what you imagined. I never will become the eccentric old vicar you took me for."

"I wouldn't—"

"Oh, don't feel sorry for me. Millions of other men weren't spared. I still have my faith and my job and my studies. When I arrived here my predecessor advised me not to worry, I was perfectly fit to raise souls because souls weigh nothing. I would have liked to run outside to see what all the commotion was earlier but if I'd tried it would have been over before I got there."

"Some of those scamps you mentioned were having an egg fight."

"Let me guess. The Finch boys."

"That's right, and not long after that they dunked Violet in the witch pond."

Edwin noticed how Wilson's lips tightened into a narrow line. He added, hastily, "She's all right, just frightened."

Wilson forced a smile. "Yes. I suppose. I must tell you, though, that our so-called witch's pond is really the Witchford's pond. A family of that name owned all the land round it in the eighteenth century and as time passed the name was corrupted, as so often happens. But that's nothing to do with the Guardian Stones."

"Oh, I'm interested in anything you can tell me. Who can say what tales might lead back to the stones if we could trace the path?"

Wilson looked away, frowning. "Those boys have grown up surrounded by bad influences," he said. "Perhaps out here in the country, away from the city, they can be reached. I pray for all these unfortunate children."

Edwin wanted to say he would be very surprised if anyone or anything, including prayers, could reform the likes of the

Finch boys. Some people, as Violet had succinctly put it, were just bad. But he took a bite of sponge cake instead.

Once in the High Street, Edwin paused to contemplate the Guardians Hill. He thought of what had brought him here, the mystery of the stone circles scattered across England.

They were eerie reminders of a past shrouded in the mists of time, their builders leaving few clues as to why these circles had been erected, a purpose that at this remove could never be learned. They had been important to the culture of their time and they were scattered from Stonehenge—its huge stones supposedly transported from Ireland by the magician Merlin to windy Salisbury Plain in the south—to as far north as Stennes, where couples plighted their troth by holding hands through a hole piercing the Odin Stone. To pass an infant through the same hole was said to safeguard its health.

Many connected them with the Druids, a theory scholars had discarded but a great favourite of the general public. Some claimed the circles served as astronomical observatories, others that they were the grave sites of heroes, or marketplaces.

Their very mystery was a great attraction for Edwin, the feeling of being almost able to touch the ancient hands which had dragged boulders and stones, sometimes miles across difficult terrain and impossible hills, to erect in prominent places. Their brooding presence drew those who sought their secrets but revealed nothing.

Despite his familiarity with the circles—including those long since destroyed, but accounts of which could be read in older histories and documents—he always felt they were majestic and otherworldly.

To Edwin, entering what he regarded as their sacred space was akin to that strange hush the visitor to a church experiences, a sense of timelessness and sanctity heavy with the centuries. He had noticed in collecting information, no matter what outrageous legends he heard from local inhabitants, they tended to pay an instinctive respect to the ancient stones. Many were the stories he recorded of supernatural punishments meted out to those who dared attempt to destroy a circle or to take stones for constructing a farmhouse or cow barn. Perhaps that was why stories of witches were often connected with the circles or magical powers attributed to their stones.

As a Wiltshire resident had told him, "Them Stonehenge stones was here before the world and will see us out, you can be certain of that, sir." He then went on to relate how as a young man he had visited Avebury to see if a particular stone walked across the road at midnight, a story he had heard since childhood.

"And what happened?" Edwin had asked, pen poised over notebook.

"It were a foggy night, sir. I stood a bit away and watched that stone very close, you may be sure. All of a sudden there was a crash. I went all shivery-bivery, sir, and took to my heels."

Chapter Six

I'm dreaming, Emily Miller told herself as she stepped into the middle of the Guardian Stones.

A voice had called her name. Then she found herself leaving the forest to stand in the moonlit clearing. She didn't have her walking stick. How would she manage to get back down the hill?

And where was her dog Patch, who always accompanied her on walks?

Thunder rumbled and clouds swarmed past the moon. Foxgloves all around bobbed and weaved, brushing her nightgown. Their knowing touch repelled her and she flinched away. What foolishness brought her outside with a storm on the way? And not even properly dressed? What would people think, seeing her walking home in her nightgown?

She started back the way she'd come but a shadow crept out from the base of the stubby stone in her path. The shadow lengthened impossibly as it flowed away from the knee-high stone, resolving into the shape of a tall, hooded figure.

Emily whirled in the opposite direction. Grotesque shadows were crawling out from all the stones. Some might have been cast by men, others by creatures Emily could not imagine. Yet there was no man or creature to cast them, only the stones.

The thunder grew louder. Emily felt the ground vibrate. The air buzzed as if it were alive. Light drained out of the clearing. Looking up, Emily saw black clouds devour the moon. No, she realized, not a cloud. A buzzing, thickening swarm of enormous flies.

Thunder was incessant.

"Emily! Emily!"

She lay on her back in bed, the acrid smell of smoke stinging her nostrils. The thunderous banging continued.

Someone was hammering at her door.

"Emily! Get up! Fire!" came a shout, followed by more knocking.

Emily forced herself out of bed, threw on her dressing gown, and hobbled downstairs to the front door. She was slow, still feeling the effects of her exertions searching for Issy. Her heart was jumping from the terror of her nightmare. She opened the door to see Tom Green looming there.

"Your shed's on fire, Miss Miller. Get dressed and come outside, just in case. We're working on getting it out as fast as possible, but you never know."

Emily peered up at him. "Young man, I don't hear any devil's flies buzzing around at the moment so there's no fear of them seeing the fire, if that's what's worrying you." She used the same tone she might have if Green had been a naughty child stealing sweets from her shop. "I shall be out in a few moments."

It took more than a few moments to dress and make her way to the back of her house. Her heart kept leaping, pausing for too long then leaping again, like a nearly exhausted rabbit trying to escape a trap.

Shouts mixed with lurid language as villagers tackled the burning shed. Trembling firelight revealed a chain of men passing along buckets of water in a long line from the pond behind Susannah Radbone's house across the street.

Emily followed the swirl of sparks upward into the black sky until they vanished into the moon hanging there.

For a moment she lurched back into her nightmare. She clenched her hand around her walking stick and blinked to clear her head. In her dream she had not recalled her journey to the stones, so why should she recall returning to her bedroom?

"Don't worry," Green was saying beside her, "they've got a good grip on it."

"Aye," Duncan Gowdy paused for a moment, wiping his brow on the sleeve of his shirt. "Very suspicious, the whole thing, if you ask me."

Emily stared at the shed, still upright. There seemed to be more smoke than fire, but it was difficult to see the extent of the damage. She was having trouble breathing so she moved away until the air tasted fresher. Several women appeared, hair in curlers, nightgowns showing beneath hastily donned coats. Emily feared they would trample her vegetables, but nobody did. Every family cultivated and knew the importance of kitchen gardens.

"Ain't you going to help with the buckets, Constable?" came a woman's voice. One or two sniggers greeted the sally.

"Just stay well back now," Green replied. "We don't want no accidents."

The shed door fell forward, releasing a cloud of smoke.

A sudden silence fell.

A smoldering shape lay on the shed floor.

"It's Issy!" a woman shrieked. "My God!"

"Too small," Duncan muttered. "It's more the size of—"

"My dog! It's Patch!" Emily wanted to scream but couldn't. Her chest felt paralyzed.

She started toward the shed but hands grabbed her and held her back. She heard someone talking to her but the words were lost in a wave of dizziness and intermittent darkness. For an instant she heard the buzzing of the flies, saw the moon darkening.

Then she was sitting on the ground and saw Duncan and Green standing nearby. Duncan said, "That poor animal. To burn so much so quickly I wager he was soaked in lamp oil and—" He broke off. "Emily, are you all right?"

Emily nodded, felt a hand touch her shoulder.

"Come along, dear," said a familiar voice. Turning she saw a tall, thin woman with cropped gray hair. Her friend Susannah Radbone.

"I'm taking you to my house," Susannah told her.

Duncan helped her back to her feet and Emily allowed herself to be led across the street.

"I'm dreaming," Emily said in a dazed voice. "I was dreaming I was at the Guardian Stones and I'm still dreaming. It happens, sometimes, you dream you've woke up but you haven't. I dreamed about Patch. Is Patch…?"

"There now, Emily." Susannah settled her friend in the kitchen. "I'll make tea. We'll find out who's responsible for this outrage and make sure he's punished."

Even by lamplight Susannah's scrupulously neat little kitchen looked exactly as always. There was no dream-like quality to it at all.

Emily burst into sobs.

It took some time before she calmed down sufficiently for tea to be made and it had hardly been poured when a boy with tousled hair looked into the room.

"Miss Radbone, what is all the noise about? Are we being invaded?"

"No, Reggie. If we had been the church bells would be ringing. There was a fire at Emily's house."

"A fire!" His voice betrayed childish excitement and his gaze moved to the hall leading to the door.

"It'll be out by now," Susannah said sharply. "Go back to bed like a good boy."

Reggie's face clouded with disappointment. "Can I take the kitty with me?"

"Just for a little while."

The boy limped across the room, clinging to the backs of chairs and the windowsill to reach a black cat sleeping beside the stove. He scooped the animal up and with a sweet smile and quiet goodnight went back out.

Susannah sighed. "Such a shame. I've given him a ground floor room so he doesn't need to climb stairs. He will always need a leg brace and crutches. He's still upset about being sent away from home, and now there's this business with Issy and—" She broke off.

"Polio must have been sent by the devil," said Emily. "Like Hitler and whoever….did…did that to Patch."

Susannah made no reply, merely patted Emily's arm.

"Reggie's a good-hearted lad," Emily sniffed. "He always brought a scrap of something as a treat for Patch whenever he came to my shop, and now...."

She started to cry again.

Even though she was sure now she was no longer dreaming, the night had become a nightmare.

Chapter Seven

Saturday, June 14, 1941

Edwin felt uncomfortable as he stepped into the outhouse in Grace's back garden. His only previous experience of outhouses had been during visits to the family cottage many years before. As a child he had been self-conscious about performing his bodily functions outside, as it were, and he still was.

He pulled the door shut, fastened the flimsy latch, and gave the door handle a few tugs to make sure it would stay closed. Light shone through around the sides of the door, and from between the wall planks. A bird twittered nearby.

Edwin felt acutely exposed.

He had not expected to encounter such primitive sanitation arrangements again. During those family vacations, he and his playmates had been fascinated by the mysterious depths beneath the outhouse. They tossed pebbles down and listened to the hollow sound they made hitting whatever lurked below. Finally Edwin shone a flashlight in. It had not been a pleasant sight.

After he and Elise had begun courting he convinced her to visit the cottage. In those days, Edwin shared a tiny apartment with another assistant professor and though he and Elise had been furtively and hastily intimate before, this was the first time they had spent the night together and awakened pressed against each other.

It was a profound experience, Edwin told her as they lingered in the bed together.

He'd been hurt when she giggled.

"I'm not making fun of you." she said. "Who but you would say something like that? Now let's be profound again."

And why should a memory like that intrude while one was in an outhouse? Edwin wondered. It wasn't appropriate. Life, on the whole, was a messy and undignified affair. Men had philosophized on the meaning of existence for thousands of years, but it was arguable that the human brain was nothing more than a pot full of chemicals with delusions of grandeur.

Even before Edwin stepped into the kitchen he caught the delicious smell of vegetable soup simmering on the back of the stove. Unfortunately Special Constable Tom Green bulked large in front of the stove. His bland, pudgy face looked annoyed as he spoke to Grace.

"Bad news?" Edwin asked.

"Len and Mike Finch and Bert Holloway have gone missing from the Wainman farm," Grace told him.

Edwin tried to sort the names out and match them to what he had learned since his recent arrival in the village. The Finch boys were the pair involved in the pond incident, and hadn't Bert Holloway been the fat little egg-thrower Grace hauled out from behind a hedge?

"It's not unusual for them to go off for a day," Green said.

"They don't usually leave an obscene goodbye note," Grace snapped. "This time they won't be back."

Green winced and retreated. "Miss Miller has reported items stolen from her shop. They might have robbed the place and ran off. Yes, you might have something there, Grace."

"I know I'm right. The note, the robbery, killing Patch…it was all a gesture of contempt for us. I'm more worried about Bert than the Finch brothers. They're tougher than he is."

"They certainly sounded it yesterday," Edwin put in. He knew about the fire at Miss Miller's shop and how some fiend had burned her pet dog to death. Grace had told him when she came in the night before and found him up, awakened by the commotion. If the Finch boys could stoop to something like that it was just as well they were gone.

"Jack Chapman came round agitating about Issy," Green said. "He told me one of them Finches stabbed him yesterday when he pulled Violet out of the pond. I reckon that's why they've done a bunk. Unless it's because they had something to do with Issy's going missing. I didn't mention that to Chapman. Those boys think they're tough, but they'll learn better soon enough. When I catch up to them."

Observing Green's attempt to look savage, Edwin wondered what variety of petty clerk he'd been before the war handed him a plum role in law enforcement. Tom Green had better hope he didn't catch up with the Finch boys when he was alone.

Edwin inquired about Isobel.

"Nothing further to report," Green told him. "My theory is she ran off, to Craven Arms maybe, or Bishop's Castle. Bragged about her plans to the boys and now they've followed her. Or else they put her up to it, or frightened her away. They might have attacked her like they did Violet." He looked to Grace for agreement but she turned away, picked up a wooden spoon, and gave the soup a stir. Steam rose from the pot.

"Did they take their ration books?" Edwin asked. "Check the stores they're registered with. They have to eat."

"Oh, I'm sure they were careful to take their ration books!" Green gave a short, humorless laugh. "These are criminals, professor, not good law-abiding citizens. They'll just swipe what they need." The constable looked at Grace. "That soup smells better than what they serve at the pub. You're a woman of many talents."

"Martha keeps a pot of soup on the stove all the time," Grace said. "She throws everything in. Chicken bones, vegetable scraps. Makes good stock."

"I wouldn't mind sampling it sometime."

"I'll ask Martha to send the recipe over to Meg Gowdy at the pub." Her tone was curt and cold.

"Oh, well. I don't want to put anyone to any trouble." Downcast, Green lumbered off, limping noticeably.

Exaggerating lameness failed to elicit sympathy from Grace. She didn't turn from the stove until he was gone.

"That constable is certainly keeping you up to date," Edwin observed.

"He's appointed me his unofficial deputy, since I helped my father that way. It gives him an excuse to pester me."

Grace's color was high, as the Victorians might have said. Whether from anger or the steam from the soup, Edwin couldn't say. He realized he was staring at her. Embarrassed and hoping she hadn't noticed, he sat down at the kitchen table and studied the tablecloth as intently as if there were a chess problem marked out on its red-and-white-checkered pattern.

"Those kids would really run off without their ration books?" he asked. "Can they steal what they need?"

"They're cunning little beasts, trying to get home. Once back in Birmingham, dirty and tired and hungry, their parents will regret having had them evacuated. Well, in the case of the Finch boys, their mother will regret it. Their father ran off before the war."

"Do they supply you with their family histories when they arrive?"

"Hardly. Harry Wainman, who's been putting them up at his farm, got the story out of them and he's got a big mouth. Apparently the mother's quite respectable but what with her working in a factory all day they just ran wild. Never in school, already been prosecuted for petty thieving."

"Why would they tell things like that to Harry Wainman?"

"Bragging."

"Perhaps it's just as well a pair like has taken off. But then there's Bert Holloway and Isobel Chapman and it's two days since she went missing."

Grace shrugged. "We've covered every inch of forest near the village. She's run off and no one is surprised. That's what you'd expect of her."

"Well, you can never be sure. Children get a bad reputation and—"

"Sometimes they deserve the reputation." Grace scowled at him.

"I suppose you're right." Edwin recalled how many of Elise's reclamation projects hadn't worked out. She forget those immediately and remembered the successes. "It's just troubling to imagine kids out there, in some sort of trouble."

Grace's expression softened. "You have children then?"

"No. Actually. We wanted children, but…" Edwin trailed off, feeling he'd said too much.

Chapter Eight

Edwin had always been a reticent and private man, more comfortable with books than people. Since his wife's death, however, he found he was prone to talk too much, to develop too much intimacy too quickly. A vital part of him had been torn away leaving him open and exposed, functioning strangely, dangling wires making unwanted contact with the world. He supposed it was grief but he had not yet managed to regain control of himself.

Yet he had to keep moving.

Runaway children were certainly not going to stop him.

He needed to begin investigating Noddweir's stone circle, starting with the barrows the vicar had described in their correspondence. They may have been built by the same people who erected the standing stones. He could have begun with the stones themselves, but he was still exhausted from the trip and interrupted sleep. He was never comfortable confronting the most difficult part of a job unless he felt he was functioning at one hundred percent. He was meticulous about arranging his work to insure maximum efficiency.

Besides, his initial glimpse of the stones, as dusk was falling during the search for Isobel, was unsettling. He was reluctant to plunge straight into the forest again after the unnerving search for the missing child. It was better to familiarize himself with the terrain first.

According to Mr. Wilson's hand-drawn map, the barrows were located in a field to the southwest of the village.

As soon as he stepped outside, the peculiar clarity of the morning air, so unlike city air, struck him. It might have been scrubbed clean while he slept.

Edwin went down the High Street and then took the path that curved around the back of Emily Miller's shop. Trying to interpret the spidery lines on his map he almost ran into Jack Chapman coming through the gate in Emily's fence, a hammer in one massive hand and two horseshoes in the other.

"Morning," the blacksmith grunted.

Edwin saw the door of Emily's burnt shed had already been replaced and boards were nailed up over some of the charred spots. A horseshoe now hung over the door.

"I nailed one up for all the good it'll do anyone," Jack told him. "My smithy's covered with horseshoes. There's so many on my roof, a gale wouldn't budge it. Issy throws them up there. For luck, she says. More like she just loves heaving them up there. What luck have I had?"

Isobel's father had not shaved and looked very much the worse for wear. He scowled at Edwin. "What are you staring at? Come to ask more questions? Nosing about, are you? I won't have it!"

"I assure you, Mr. Chapman, that—"

Jack threw his hammer down, barely missing Edwin's foot. "Oh, you talk pretty but that Grace Baxter's a worse gossip than Emily Miller. Loves to talk, yak yak yak. I'm sure you've heard all the scandal about my family."

"No, I—"

"That's bad enough, my character blackened and no defense possible being as I wasn't there, but now I'm suspected of causing me own child to run away."

Edwin began to reply but Jack cut in. "That fool Green's just been grilling me. Thinks I mistreated her and that's why she ran off. Why isn't he getting help from town? Craven Arms has real police. Now I suppose Grace's sent you to see what you can find out. I saw Green coming out of her house on the way over. He didn't see me. Thinks I don't know what's what, I'll be bound.

She knows I wouldn't give her the time of day, so she sent you instead. Go on, admit it."

Jack moved close enough that Edwin could smell the alcohol on his breath.

"I'm actually on my way to look over some barrows," Edwin told him, taking a step backwards.

"Why would you be interested in some piles of dirt? You professors are a funny lot, you are!"

Jack shook the horseshoes he was holding. Edwin sensed they could mean very bad luck for him. "Grace has no say in what Constable Green does. She doesn't necessarily approve of his methods." True or not, Edwin needed to cool the brawny blacksmith down.

Jack drew back and stooped to pick up his hammer. "I'm feeling poorly this morning. Haven't slept since Issy vanished."

"Grace says Isobel is sure to be picked up soon, most likely walking down the railroad tracks or at a station."

Suddenly Jack was crying, wiping his eyes with the back of a grimy hand.

"She might have got a lift into town," Edwin said, uneasily. Who was he to give reassurances? What did he know about life in this tiny, out-of-the-way village? How had he become an unofficial assistant to the village's unofficial deputy?

"She couldn't stay in Craven Arms this long. She ain't got no money." Jack snuffled. "Last time I saw her was around midday. She'd just burnt the dinner again. Useless lump, she is." Maudlin tears streamed down his stubbly face. "I shouldn't have spoke to her so harsh. Where can she be?"

"I'm sure—"

Jack's eyes narrowed. "You think it was because I beat her? Isn't that it? You think I done it on account of the burnt dinner so she ran away!"

"No, not at—"

"Let me tell you, Professor. Issy is a bad girl. Bound to be, being as she was born when the moon was waning. And having her, it killed my wife. Them born under the horns of the moon always comes to a bad end." He waved his hammer. "Don't believe everything you hear. I never touched my daughter. Maybe if I had she'd still be here. I should have taken me belt and beaten the badness out of her."

Noddweir turns away from the forest.

Perhaps it is afraid to meet the gaze directed upon it from behind the trees. It prefers to pretend it is not being observed.

From behind, the village takes on a different aspect. Instead of neat housefronts, well-tended hedges, and painted fences, the ends of the gardens show rotted, crooked palings, crumbling walls largely concealed by crawling vines. Black, twisted trees, revenants of long-lost orchards, reach arthritic limbs toward the cultivated beds on the other side of the half-ruined barriers. Bushes escape from cultivation to grow rank and noxious, scrape at the walls and fences.

Homeowners do not see the ghastly trees or the rampant brush. Their worlds end at the back of their gardens. The wild vegetation beyond is a backdrop signifying nothing.

There is much to be seen in the back of Noddweir at night. A girl pushes quietly through a rear gate and creeps along beside the fences to where a boy is scrambling over another. Then both vanish together into the darkness. A young lad stands behind a shed, smoke from a stolen cigarette a pale phantom rising into the sky.

One shed shows evidence of scorching.

Now, in the day, through black crisscrossed limbs and a welter of leaves, some dark, others translucent, a pond and surrounding field look like a green and blue stained-glass window. At one place near the edge of the water, grass, and mud is churned up. Footprints are visible. Reeds are broken. A few still float on the still surface of the water. Aside from that there is no motion except for darting dragonflies, no sound but humming of insects.

Noddweir cannot guess what happens beyond its garden walls.

First there was the girl, but now the girl is gone.

The girl was not what she could be.

She was not enough.

Not nearly enough.

Chapter Nine

Edwin consulted the vicar's hand-drawn map again. The barrows should be on the right hand side of the road.

They weren't there.

He saw nothing except a flat expanse of tall grass. It was discomfiting.

He walked further, feeling the hot sunlight on the back of his neck, stopped to scan the field once more, then moved the map closer to his face and peered at Wilson's maddening squiggles.

Neither the map nor the landscape had changed.

The air hung utterly still. Unseen insects clicked and burred and chattered. Edwin could smell the dry dust of the road and a faint perfume. Wild roses?

Had he taken a wrong turn? The fact that signposts had been removed to thwart German invaders rendered some of the map's notations useless.

Jack Chapman upset him. He didn't like confrontations. He hurried away from Isobel's overwrought father. Had he gone left when he should have veered right? Did he stray off the roads shown by the map onto one that the vicar hadn't drawn?

What had looked like an easy walk in two-dimensional pen and ink felt totally different in three-dimensional reality.

How had the philosopher Alfred Korzybski put it? The map is not the territory.

Edwin kept walking. At this rate, he thought, I shall end up in Wales. Not that I'll know where I am with all the signposts taken down.

The road he was on dwindled to a narrow track flanked by fields behind hedges.

He found himself at the corner of a field demarcated by a line of fence posts, all leaning at crazy angles, and apparently held up by the barbed wire strung between them. A couple of horses gazed over the ruined fence. A heavyset, balding man with a bright red face knelt beside a horse-drawn mower that might have been used by Queen Victoria, in the unlikely event the diminutive queen had ever mowed hay. The rusty metal contraption consisted of a excruciatingly uncomfortable looking seat perched high behind two wheels and a cutting bar with blades the size of fossilized dinosaur teeth. The fact that the bar stood in the safe upright position rather than being lowered for cutting made it look even more menacing.

The red-faced man, who pushed up and glared at Edwin, was not welcoming. He wore grubby corduroy trousers and a sweat-soaked collarless shirt. Edwin's shirt was neater but just as damp.

"You're here to tell me Jack Chapman's too drunk to work today," the man growled.

"No. Actually, I spoke with him earlier. He didn't seem drunk to me."

"He said he'd be here an hour ago to look my equipment over for me. I'll need to be cutting early this year, what with all this heat."

The man turned back to the machine.

"I seem to have got lost," Edwin displayed his map.

"Got a map, I see," came the suspicious reply. "We don't see many strangers around here. Where are you going?"

Edwin told him.

"Barrows, eh? I can show you a couple of wheel-barrows if you like!" The man laughed and thrust out a calloused hand. "You're the Yank staying with Grace, studying our quaint ways and such, so I hear. Name's Harry Wainman."

"Edwin Carpenter." They shook hands. Wainman had a strong grip but he made no effort to grind Edwin's bones, as some of the most bookish of his academic colleagues had a habit of doing. "The boys who ran away were staying with you, weren't they?"

"That's right." Harry hitched up his trousers and scratched his chin. "Since you just come from the village, any news of them?"

"I'm afraid not."

"Damn! Just when we need the extra help! Not but what they had to be watched every minute or they'd help themselves to anything left lying about." Harry shrugged. "But what can you expect? Them Finch boys are nothing but budding criminals. The wife's convinced they killed Emily's dog as a two-fingered farewell. She's still angry about her eggs. Sooner they're old enough to be called up the better. If the war lasts long enough, we can loose them against the Germans."

"You may be right," Edwin replied. "But about these barrows..."

"Oh, them. Damn things get in the way of plowing. You need to go back the way you come. Turn right at the next road. Then keep on for a couple of miles."

A couple of miles? Edwin gazed disconsolately at his map. Obviously not drawn to scale. He folded it up. "Thanks. I'm particularly interested in those barrows as well as the Guardians."

"Nothing but trouble, them stones. You hear about the midsummer celebrations up there years ago?"

Edwin shook his head.

"Used to dance around naked, so the old folk say." Harry winked. "That wasn't all neither. A lot of kids them days was born in the spring. And sometimes there were strange noises in the forest at night. You could hear them clearly if you was anywhere nearby."

"You've heard them yourself?"

"No, but I've heard about them from my father and grandfather. Lot of rubbish, if you ask me. Nothing but owls or a rabbit caught in a snare. Waste of breath even talking about it. What use is all this ancient stuff anyhow? I'll tell you what'd be useful. Some of you Yanks could come over and give us a hand against them Jerries."

"It well may come to it," Edwin replied.

Harry scratched his chin again. "I wonder. Let everyone else bleed and keep out of it yourselves, that seems to be the way you Yanks think. Never mind sending soldiers, we'll send some old geezers to take in the sights."

"I appreciate the directions," Edwin said. "I'd better start back now."

"You planning to write a book?"

"I may."

"God help us! Then those damn stones will have us overrun with tourists. Talk about a curse. 'Course, by then they might be German tourists. I'd charge them twice the going rate, the swine." Wainman spat and knelt back down beside the mower.

"Hell," he muttered, as much to himself as Edwin. "Maybe I ought to tell old Radbone to send that cripple of hers to help me. He'd be better than no help at all."

Chapter Ten

Reggie Cox lay on his stomach on the bank of the pond behind his lodgings at Susannah Radbone's house.

His inconvenient leg with its metal brace stretched straight out behind him. He stayed still as death, barely breathing heavy air that smelled of stagnant water and decayed vegetation. Clumps of coarse grass with blades sharp enough to cut the skin hid him. Delicate, straggling plants covered with tiny blue flowers spilled out over the bank. Reggie had never seen such flowers in Birmingham and they did not interest him.

What interested him was catching a frog.

His gaze was fixed on the water, or rather the lumpy green mat covering the pond near its banks. Reeds thrust up from the scum and, in places around the edges of lily pads, water caught sparkles of sunlight.

Catching frogs was one of the few things he liked about the countryside. It was something a boy with a bad leg could do, unlike roughhousing with his playmates or kicking a ball around, or much of anything else children did for amusement in city streets, a great deal of which required very fast running afterward. All frog-catching required was patience, a quick hand, and the proper technique.

Frogs were a revelation to Reggie. There weren't any in Birmingham in the area where he had lived before being evacuated. In fact, there wasn't much of anything in that rough part of the city as unobservant, soft, and defenseless as a frog.

From the cracked front window of his family's flat he could see the bombed-out ruin that had once been the building where his best friend lived. Not far away was an anti-aircraft gun which kept him awake most of the night. He spent time waiting anxiously in the dank, foul-smelling air raid shelter underneath the nearby school. Because of his weak leg it was difficult for him to rush to safety when the sirens started to wail. Usually he had to be helped, and that was difficult to endure as well.

He never saw the monsters that terrorized him and the rest of the city, only their planes, as far overhead and unreachable as the moon. Nazis, Germans, the Boche, Hitler, Himmler, the Luftwaffe, were all names for a formless evil that lurked everywhere. Polio was another name for the evil. An even worse name, a grownup word he heard his parents use only when they didn't know he was listening. He knew now that it was a disease, but when he had first heard it, at a younger age, he had the impression it was the sort of thing you feared might be waiting for you under your bed when the lights went out.

A hideous dragonfly swooped at his face, buzzing and whirring. He managed not to flinch.

Reggie scanned the scum in front of him, searching for the green turret of a frog's head. The frogs blended in, unlike Reggie. And unlike him they were sleek and fast. That was part of the reason he enjoyed catching them.

In Birmingham the day had come when he joined a group of children who were being evacuated. His mother cried at the station while his father looked somber, reminding Reggie to carry his gas mask at all times. Reggie suspected they were both happy to see the back of their defective offspring. Each child was given a brown paper bag holding tins of sardines and Spam. It was raining, and the train journeyed through an endless, dismal countryside. Occasionally Reggie would glance out the window but he would always see the same barn, or the same field, or the same trees he had already seen five times before.

He was dozing when a faint clanking brought him awake with a start. His seatmate, a gangly boy with a face not unlike a grinning skull, was tapping the cage around Reggie's leg with the flat of his knife blade.

"Can you swing this thing?"

"Swing…?

"Swing yer leg. Be like having brass knuckles but on yer leg, see?" He grinned his horrible grin.

"I suppose I could swing it, if I got mad enough." Reggie tried to look fierce and failed utterly. "I never thought about it."

"No? Soon as I saw it, I thought about it. I'm a thinker. I think of all kinds of things. Stick with me and you'll see." He clicked his knife shut and stuck it back in his pocket.

"Sure," Reggie said. "I'd like to stick with you, er…"

"Len Finch," the boy answered Reggie's questioning look. "I'm here with my brother Mike, only he's chatting up some girl."

"I'm Reggie Cox."

"No, yer called Gimpy. Got it? Gimpy. Every gang needs a cripple. No one suspects a cripple, see?"

With that Len Finch settled back in his seat, closed his eyes, and said nothing more.

What felt like a long time later, when they must have reached the end of the world, the train pulled into a station and children were bundled into wagons and hauled, like so many sheep, into Noddweir.

Assembled in the church, they were given biscuits to eat while their escort lectured them on rural life and proper behavior. Reggie paid no attention. He sat with the Finch brothers. The three whispered and snickered as they tried to decide what animal was ugly enough to resemble the lecturer, a middle-aged woman dressed as if for a funeral.

A crow," suggested Reggie.

"Naw," Mike said. "Crows is all shiny black, not dull like her. A vulture maybe."

"You ain't never seen a vulture," snorted Len. "I know what she looks like. I seen some kid get hold of a cat once and beat it with a board and burn it. That's what she looks like, an old, beat-up, burnt cat!"

Reggie wanted to stay with the Finch brothers, but before long the evacuees were ushered into the street and lined up as if they'd joined the army.

A handful of men—farmers, Reggie understood later—had come into the village for the first pick. Farming was important to the war effort and manpower in short supply. Len and Mike went off with a fat man with hardly any hair. When the farmers were done, Reggie was the only boy left behind older than a toddler. Even the lump of blubber with sticking plaster on his glasses had been chosen. Bert someone had called him, went with the Finch brothers.

Then the Burnt Cat, as Reggie now thought of her, humiliated as he was, led the girls and young kids and Reggie, all carrying their suitcases and gas masks, from house to house. A woman would emerge from each and walk up and down the line, peering and ruffling hair and turning heads this way and that. Reggie felt like a vegetable at the market. And who would want a tomato with a worm hole? As soon as anyone saw Reggie's leg brace they immediately looked away and didn't glance in his direction again.

Most of the older, stronger girls were chosen before the pretty ones.

Finally even the crying toddler in threadbare, stained shorts was taken.

Limping painfully by now, Reggie followed the Burnt Cat from door to door, meeting with one refusal after another. "Why would you billet children like this on us?" one woman scolded. "What do you expect of us? There's a war on, you know."

They arrived at a single-story cottage that looked like a picture in the book of fairy tales Reggie had stolen from the library. He recalled the boy who had gone into that house had been baked into a pie or suffered some equally horrible fate. As the door swung open, Reggie hung back but the Cat got her claws into his shoulder and dragged him around in front of her.

The woman who appeared in the doorway towered over the Cat. She was scrawny, with a mean face and wore her hair cut as short as a man's.

"I am sorry to have to ask—" the Cat began.

"Polio," the homely woman said, interrupting her. "Poor child."

"Do you suppose you—?"

"I have retired from teaching, madam, but I will never retire from looking after the welfare of children. Come in, young man."

Reggie supposed he should have felt more grateful to Miss Radbone, as her name was. Perhaps he was an ungrateful little bugger like his old man always said. Not that he wasn't grateful at all. Still, it would have been better if Miss Radbone hadn't immediately shaved his head and burned his clothes. "We don't want lice or fleas, do we?"

Now, as he lay on the bank of the pond, the sun was beginning to burn Reggie's bare scalp. Where had the frogs gone? He surely couldn't have caught them all. Perhaps they weren't as dull-witted as he supposed.

As usual, as soon as he was sure the hunt would be futile, he spotted the green periscope of a head push up a scrap of pond scum. Two bulging eyes, half submerged, goggled at him.

Reggie's hand shot out into the water. The frog instantly vanished. He didn't aim for where he saw the frog, but where he guessed it would be in a second or two, as it thrust its powerful legs to propel itself away. You couldn't hold onto a slippery frog, Reggie had learned, unless you got hold of its extended legs. That was the frog's vulnerability. You clamped your fist tight around those long, bony legs.

And he would have done so, except for a rustling in the brush behind him. A shadow fell across the scummy water, reaching to the widening hole opened in the green algae where Reggie's hand had plunged through.

In the rippling water Reggie saw a reflection.

A face.

Grotesquely distorted.

Almost the face of a huge, nightmarish frog.

Chapter Eleven

The face staring back at Edwin startled him. It looked old and haunted. How could that be his own reflection in the dark windowpane? Only yesterday he'd been a schoolboy, savoring the long summer of freedom still ahead. He told himself he was just tired from hiking around without enough sleep.

He closed the blackout curtains in the living room, noticing a framed photograph sitting on the side table by the window. Grace. No, he realized, turning the photo to catch the lamplight. It was an older picture of another young, broad-faced woman with dark eyes and hair.

"My daughter, Mae. Grace's mother." Martha came into the room.

Edwin moved his hand away from the photo, feeling like a guilty child caught in the act of…what? Looking more closely at a photograph? But hadn't he heard a note of disapproval in Martha's tone?

Martha dropped into the chair closest to the cold fireplace. She let out a grunt and pulled a potato out of a pocket in her baggy, mud-colored cardigan.

"Guards against the rheumatics," Martha explained to him, shoving the potato into a more comfortable pocket. "Grace refuses to carry one with her when it's chilly. She'll be sorry. Stubborn girl. Takes after her mother. I tried to teach her all my secrets but she never wanted to know."

"Where is Grace?" Edwin had abandoned his quest for the barrows after his run-ins with Jack Chapman and Harry Wainman. He returned to find an apparently empty house, until Martha emerged from her room.

Martha buttoned her cardigan. "Must be out on patrol. That's where she usually is, when she isn't home. Unless she's got a boyfriend."

Edwin ignored the last remark. Hadn't Grace said that Martha's mental facilities were not what they once were? "It's very late," he said. The country was on war time and darkness came at a totally unreasonable hour.

Martha stared at Edwin so intently he wondered whether her eyesight was failing, though the pale blue eyes looked clear enough. "You're here to study the Guardians, aren't you?"

"That's right. You offered tell me about local folklore."

Martha looked flattered. "Get your notebook, then."

Soon Edwin was scribbling snippets of herbal lore and Noddweir superstitions, hardly able to keep up with Martha's torrent of words.

"Lavender, now," she said. "A few drops of lavender oil in a bowl of hot water is what you want. Stick your feet in, it'll perk you up when you're tired. It were an evil day when we heard we were supposed to dig up flowers to plant vegetables. Dig for victory, you know. But we managed to keep lavender."

She rubbed arthritic hands together. "Horehound tea, that's the stuff for coughs. Ragwort will rid you of sciatica."

She ruminated for a moment. "'Course, you can't get lemons these days. The juice did miracles in stopping hiccups. Did you ever have raspberry tea? Good for gargling, that is. My preparations are better than that rubbish they sell at chemists, but people don't believe. The old ways are dying. I done my best to pass along knowledge to Issy. I wish there was news of her."

For a moment she fell silent. Her small hands stopped darting around to punctuate her words. The wild hair falling in disarray over her shoulders glowed preternaturally white in the lamplight. She shivered. "A curse on that devil Hitler. Someone should poison his dinner and give him a nasty death."

"Something in the herbal line?" Edwin suggested, surprised at her sudden change of mood.

Martha smiled grimly. "I could give his cook a few suggestions. And speaking of devils, about the Guardians..."

Edwin adjusted his glasses. "Yes?"

"Well, now." Her momentary gloom lifted immediately. "T'is said a wise woman who lived in the forest went to the top of Guardians Hill every time there was a horned moon and there she worked persuasions."

Edwin noted her choice of words—persuasions and wise woman rather than spells and witch. "What do you mean by horned moon?"

"What you'd call a crescent moon. It exerts a malign influence. Them as is born under the horned moon is born close to the devil."

"Cursed, you mean?"

"Depends on how one looks at it. Close to the devil's a powerful place to be." A shadow passed over her face. "But we was talking about persuasions, not curses."

"Going to the hilltop, wouldn't that mean working these, er, persuasions in full view of the village?"

"Why not? The villagers consulted her for help."

"And these persuasions were for good?"

A sly smile quirked Martha's lips. "Some say so, some say not. But as time passed, whenever things went wrong, when a cow lost a calf or a wife strayed or a family member fell down the stairs and broke a leg, she got the blame. Soon it was said she danced with the devil, and meant to kill everyone in Noddweir one way or another. A dozen men from the village decided to do something, went up one moonlit night, and never came back. In the morning there were thirteen stones standing up there. All the men and the wise woman, who had turned them and herself into stone. And there they remain."

"But why are they called the Guardians?"

"Because the men are guarding the wise woman, making sure she can't do harm or get away."

Edwin had not yet counted the stones in the overgrown weeds but he guessed there were more than thirteen. Then too, they were not nearly man-sized. And wasn't it strange that the wise woman had apparently also turned herself into stone? He kept his doubts to himself. Folklore was not necessarily rational. Instead he asked about the barrows which eluded him earlier.

"Oh, them moundy little hills in the middle of fields, you mean? What we call tumps. Nobody knows anything about them. Not worth bothering with if you ask me, but if you want to poke about one, you don't have to go that far. There's one closer in the forest. Just follow the path coming out on the other side of the pond behind Susannah Radbone's house. It's the house with the red shutters."

Martha continued to ramble, telling stories about the village. Edwin learned of a quarrel about a horse that resulted in one family not speaking to another for several years and that the election of Meg Gowdy as head of the local Women's Institute caused lingering ill-feelings, certain villagers objecting on the grounds of "her being an outsider and all." And this despite the fact that she and her husband had run the Guardians pub for years.

Noddweir was one of those places where one who wasn't a native remained eternally an outsider. Edwin hated to imagine what sort of alien creature the villagers considered him to be, a man from another country altogether.

The lecture went on. When Martha began to repeat something she'd just told Edwin five minutes earlier, he gently reminded her.

"Ah, well. If you say so," she said, resignedly. "It's old age, you know."

Aside from that her mind seemed clear. Edwin learned that it was unlucky to kill a bat and that local farm laborers, on hearing the first cuckoo of spring, celebrated by taking the day off and still tried to do so, even in wartime.

He also recorded more tales about the Guardians, including the belief that on certain midnights they danced in a circle, but since the dates appeared to be unknown, nobody had actually seen this happen. Village children were warned, however, never to be within the circle after sunset. There was, to his delight, a children's rhyme, or so Martha said.

Time stands still
On Guardians Hill
Circle round
Unholy ground
The Guardians dwell
In deepest hell
Don't go alone
Inside the stones
That surmount still
Guardians Hill

Despite being fascinated, Edwin glanced frequently at his watch. It was now well toward midnight and he was worried about Grace.

Finally Edwin looked up from his notebook to see that Martha had fallen asleep, her head against the back of the chair, halo of white hair spread out over the antimacassar, sparrow's beak of a nose pointed toward the ceiling.

His gaze fell on the photograph of Grace's mother, so like her daughter. Taken around the same age, he guessed. Early twenties. Why was she absent? Had she died? Asking Grace would be rude. It was none of his business. He didn't see any photo of Grace's father.

The front door opened and Grace stepped into the room.

She looked haggard and distressed.

"What is it?" Edwin asked.

"We've been out searching again. It's Reggie Cox this time. The crippled boy who's staying with Susannah Radbone. Now he's vanished, too."

Chapter Twelve

Sunday June 15, 1941

If Reggie Cox was limping along a road or railway line on his way back to Birmingham, he would be very damp and cold on this Sunday morning, thought Reverend Timothy Wilson. Grace had arrived early, while Wilson was lighting the lamps, to tell him about the crippled boy's disappearance.

A heavy fog clung to Noddweir, swirling against windows and concealing the forest. His parishioners shook moisture off their hats as they entered the Church of Saint Winnoc. If Reggie had any sense he would have taken refuge in a barn until the sun came out. Then again, if he had any sense he wouldn't have even thought about fleeing on foot with one leg in a metal brace.

Wilson brought out extra lamps. Their flickering light animated the stained glass window behind the altar—Saint Winnoc grinding corn in a hand mill. Grey daylight struggled in through the remaining windows. The altar flowers he had hurriedly arranged without Issy's assistance this week looked washed out in the dull light, but their scent was strong. The stone-flagged floor chilled the air. Despite the miserable weather, the church was unusually full.

Under the circumstances, was it surprising?

He surveyed his congregation.

Susannah Radbone sat with a pale and dazed Emily Miller near the front. He guessed Susannah, a notorious skeptic, was present as a kind gesture to Emily. She had once told him bluntly that she did not expect to see the inside of his church until her funeral, and only then in a metaphorical sense. Wilson could not imagine she had come to seek divine aid on behalf of Emily or her own vanished evacuee lodger, let alone to seek solace for herself.

Then again, he had observed soldiers who, after an artillery barrage, found God amid the scattered remains of their colleagues.

And there was Joe Haywood, a broad-shouldered presence huddled in a great-coat, who had not set foot in church either. He sat alone at the far end of a back pew. No one wanted to be seen with him, at least not in church. Who could he be here for, except himself?

The Wainmans, also largely absent from services, sat in front of Haywood. Louisa's plain, weathered face wore an angry expression and rubicund Harry looked apprehensive. Marriage trouble, or losing three young farm laborers they counted on for help with haying? Wilson would have expected Harry to be the angry one, since the surly farmer was angry as often as not. Harry turned toward his wife, who immediately opened a hymn book and stared at it fixedly, as if she were memorizing a verse or two.

Louisa might be visiting the vicarage before long, Wilson thought. What would he say to her if she asked his advice? Marriage was a sacred bond, but from what he knew of Harry Wainman, he didn't like the man. However, it wasn't his job to represent his own viewpoint on such matters.

Muffled laughter rose from the back pew across the aisle from Joe Haywood. A gaggle of boys—all evacuees—had congregated as far from their families as possible. They were freshly scrubbed, but the hair once plastered to their heads was stirring, stray strands swinging down across their foreheads as they pushed and punched one another.

A movement caught out of the corner of his eye pulled his gaze to the front pew, where Grace Baxter sat with Wilson's thin, solemn-faced friend who was lodging with her. Edwin looked uncomfortable. He had never mentioned attending church in their correspondence. But those two had not drawn his attention. Rather it was Martha Roper, sitting between them.

Her presence was more than remarkable. It was tantamount to a miracle.

A miracle Wilson preferred to do without.

Martha's ancient brown hat, perched on her mist of white hair, was in danger of falling off. She scowled at Wilson with a malignant expression. He couldn't help thinking of old wives' tales about the evil eye.

Seeing him look in her direction, Martha smiled.

He looked away quickly, scanning the church. Was it his imagination or were the families huddled away from their neighbors, casting tense, suspicious looks at each other? Were they wondering if a person sharing their pew knew more than they were telling about the missing children?

Did Martha's malevolent stare put the idea in his mind? His nerves were bad enough as it was.

Wilson cleared his throat and began his sermon in the soft, hoarse tone that was as strong as he could manage to project.

"We all follow the war in Europe, yet it is also right here in our own hearts and homes. Our cities are nightly infernos and we have taken in children who need shelter, to keep them safe. But now another trial has beset Noddweir. The children we seek to protect flee as if being lured away by a malignant heart."

He stopped for a moment to study the tense, exhausted faces before him. "We are tired," he continued. "Tired unto death. When will it end? Where do we find the strength to carry on?"

He saw Louisa Wainman bite her lower lip.

A boy in the back pew stuck out his tongue.

Wilson half turned and gestured at the stained glass behind him. "Every Sunday you see here our saint, even in his old age, even though it is the Sabbath, grinding corn, laboring while I stand here and talk and you sit and listen. Of course, Saint Winnoc was not able to do it by himself. He prayed for divine aid and the Lord caused his mill to grind corn without assistance. If only we could pray and the Lord would return our children to us, would cut our hay for us, would endure this time of fear and deprivation for us."

Harry Wainman gave an audible snort.

Wilson coughed as discreetly as possible into his handkerchief and paused, less for effect than to catch his breath, before continuing.

"But the Lord does not do our work for us. The miracle of Saint Winnoc's corn mill does not teach us that the Lord will do what we should be doing for ourselves. Remember that Saint Winnoc was born to a noble family. Not far from here, just over the border. Yet when he joined a monastery he did so humbly. He spent his life performing the most disagreeable manual tasks. Even when he was enfeebled with old age he wished to continue working. So he prayed to the Lord and the Lord enabled him to continue."

Wilson's voice had already begun to lose what little strength it possessed. The parishioners, mindful of his weakness, made not the slightest sound, not even shifting uncomfortably in the hard pews.

"That is the message Saint Winnoc has for us," Wilson resumed. "If we are truly determined to endure, we need only turn to the Lord and He will grant us the strength to do so. As is said in Hebrews '...let us run with patience the race that is set before us, looking unto Jesus...' What better advice can we find for this long race we are even now engaged in, this race of good against evil?"

The fog was lifting as the congregation emerged from the church. However, the still clammy air sent everyone hurrying away without exchanging greetings and gossip.

Louisa Wainman waited until she and Harry had turned off the High Street onto the road to their farmhouse before she spoke.

"Well, Harry, what did you think of them flowers on the altar?"

"Flowers?"

"You heard me. Didn't get an early look at them this week, did you?"

"What?"

Wisps of fog rose from the fields beside the road and huddled in the shadows of distant trees. Louisa stopped walking and caught his arm. "Don't pretend you don't know what I'm talking about, Harry." Her voice was venomous. "The entire village knows you met Issy there on Saturdays, when the girl arranged flowers for the vicar. I can barely hold me head up whenever I meet one of those old gossips."

"But—"

His wife sneered. "No point in denying it. Nosy parkers made sure I know you've been seen leaving the church then, when you'd supposedly gone off to market."

"But I did go to the market! Remember, I got hold of that tea you wanted last week."

"Bought it off Joe Haywood, more like. But you don't have to stay long to finish your business with that little tart. I should know. Then you can shove off to what you're supposed to be doing."

"Louisa, do we have to go through this again? I told you before there was nothing to the talk. I even promised I'd go nowhere near the church, even though I hadn't been there to begin with."

"With you, promises are made to be broken."

"What do you think I am? How could you suspect me of.... of...?" Harry's yanked his arm out of his wife's grasp. His fists clenched and unclenched. "Isobel Chapman was nothing but a child."

"Was?"

"What are you thinking? Is. Was. She's gone. Missing."

"Do you know something?"

"Louisa!"

"You just better hope nobody else thinks about that as well. Particularly that fool Tom Green."

Before Harry could reply, Duncan Gowdy hailed them from behind. "It's Bert Holloway," he shouted, running. "He's back!"

Chapter Thirteen

"One down and four to go." Grace unpinned the hat decorated with an artificial spray of flowers she'd worn to church. She tossed it on the chair by the fireplace.

"Do you really think it will be that easy?" Edwin laced up his boots. No church-goer, he'd attended because Grace took it for granted that he would and he hadn't wanted to offend her. When in Noddweir...By rushing home to change his suit for more casual clothing, he had missed Bert Holloway's homecoming.

"Bert said the Finch brothers persuaded him to come with them. They finally said he was holding them back and left him behind."

"Where were the boys headed?"

"Home, he said. To Birmingham. So they're accounted for at least."

"Still, there's Isobel...."

Grace dropped onto the other end of the settee occupied by Edwin. "Bert says she ran away too. The Finch boys told him. They decided if a girl dared to run away, why shouldn't they?"

"Which is not to say she hasn't run into trouble."

"My guess is that Issy, Mike, and Len are practically to Birmingham by now. It's too much of a coincidence, them all vanishing at practically the same time."

"And Reggie?"

"Copycat. He gets around better with that leg than you might think. You look doubtful, Edwin."

"The fact that one child is accounted for—"

"Three. Bert confirmed the Finch boys ran off, remember."

"All right. Three accounted for doesn't necessarily mean that the same explanation holds for Isobel and Reggie."

"What other explanation is there? Someone lurking in the forest? Who just happens to start preying on village children at the same time other children start running away?"

"When you put it that way, it seems unlikely."

"I should say so." Grace had dressed for church in a plain navy blue dress with gold buttons and slightly padded shoulders. Her red lipstick matched the flowers in her hat. "It's not polite to stare," she said with a smile.

"Oh...was I....?" Edwin felt his face flush and he concentrated on tying his boot laces with fumbling fingers.

While seeking the barrow Martha had described, Edwin thought about the plight of the missing children. Children he didn't know, most of whom by all accounts he was fortunate not to know.

Foolish of him. Had he picked up some of Elise's indiscriminate compassion for every black sheep she found in her classroom? He had been pleased to educate his more mature and marginally civilized college-aged charges, not save them from themselves. He often pointed out to Elise the irony of their teaching positions—she filled kids with hope for the future and then Edwin taught them history, a long, bloody parade of hopeful futures gone bad.

He squelched through the marshy depression behind the house with the red shutters. Whose house was it? Susannah someone-or-other. He couldn't recall what surname Martha had mentioned. As he passed the pond he heard the plop, plop, plop of frogs hitting the water just ahead. He wasn't quick enough to catch a glimpse of them.

The great tragedy of Elise's life, apart from the ending of it, had been their—his—inability to have children. Usually Edwin appreciated irony, but in this case it was simply cruel. That a person who cared so much about children and was so good with them could not have and raise her own, that perfectly normal human function, yet so much abused if the truth were known.

If Edwin believed in the supernatural, he would be convinced there was a malevolent force abroad in the world which eventually stole from every person exactly what they most cherished. He often thought so, sitting alone in his hotel room in London. Luckily, though, he was not a religious man. It was, he knew, only his own bleak nature speaking.

He made his way to the far side of the pond. Martha claimed that the barrow in the forest wasn't far and, better yet, sat within sight of a path, so Edwin had decided to seek that one first, before the elusive barrows mapped by Reverend Wilson. And before returning to the stones.

The air warmed, filled by the hum of bees feeding on the clover and flowering weeds in the boggy clearing. Laurel and tall, thick bushes replete with thorns sealed the edge of the forest.

Edwin walked back and forth before he spotted the narrow rut of the path. Pushing aside leafy branches, he stepped into cool but humid shadows. His eyes dazzled by the sun, he might have been passing from day into night. Beyond the tightly woven barrier the forest opened up. After his eyes adjusted, Edwin saw that the rocky track wound off into oaks and beech.

His new boots were already pinching his feet. He detested shopping. He always rushed to finish, arriving home with a shirt of some ghastly cut he'd snatched up on account of its pleasing color, a beautifully patterned tie that didn't match anything he owned, or a pair of expensive boots that weren't quite the right size.

He'd tried the boots out back in Rochester, in Durand-Eastman Park by Lake Ontario. He'd told himself they were tight but just needed breaking in. The path he was on now, narrow, rutted, studded with rocks, and crossed by treacherous roots, reminded him of those he and Elise had often walked.

She used to jokingly tell him to keep his eyes out for the local ghost, the White Lady, knowing very well that her husband, for all his scholarly interest in folklore, prided himself on being the least superstitious man alive.

The White Lady, reputed to haunt the park, was said to be the spirit of a mother whose young daughter was raped and murdered there. Some claimed to have seen her rising in a silver mist from the lake or appearing as a hazy glow at the bottom of a ravine, as she wandered the park endlessly seeking her daughter's murderer. Edwin regarded the White Lady as a common tale of the sort popular all over the world.

The legend reminded Edwin of the missing Isobel. He hoped she had merely run away as Grace insisted and had not met the fate of the White Lady's daughter.

In spots the path passed through thick stands of rhododendron so that he walked as if through a narrow dark green canyon, able to see only the canopy of leaves overhead, coruscating with brilliant sunlight when a breeze agitated the leaves. In open places he walked through pools of light. He was glad the sun was shining brightly. These wild places, these gloomy woods could almost make an intelligent man like Edwin expect to see apparitions.

He walked for longer than he expected, feet increasingly sore, without seeing anything resembling a barrow. Had he passed it? He couldn't have taken a wrong turn, because he hadn't turned off the path, as far as he could tell.

Maybe the countryside simply didn't like foreigners and intentionally hid its secrets from him.

Finally he saw a knoll off in the trees to his right. Could that be the barrow?

The path was barely visible. Pushing through thick bushes he noticed the barrow was covered by saplings. He climbed gingerly over rotted trunks that blocked his way.

Then he saw the shape lying at the base of the barrow.

"No!" he said. "No!"

He told himself to calm down. He could barely see through the intervening thicket and its welter of leaves fluttering in the wind.

Wait. The shape moved. Hadn't it?

Edwin remembered the trick Mike Finch had played on Constable Green, leaping out of the bomb crater after feigning death.

"Don't think you're going to surprise me," he called, striding forward. "You stay right where you are!"

Chapter Fourteen

Violet underhanded pebbles into the water at the bottom of the bomb crater while she waited for Bert Holloway to catch up. Each pebble vanished with a hollow glug that sounded loud in the quiet of the forest.

Bert had spotted Violet going into the forest and tagged along. She didn't mind. He might be chubby and slow, but he wasn't loud and nasty and crude, and he made her daisy chains even though the other boys poked fun at him for it.

Bert told her that after the Wainmans picked him up following his return they had argued all the way back to the farmhouse, and once they got inside they started yelling at each other. It frightened him, so he crept out. He didn't know what he was going to do. He couldn't run away properly but he couldn't bear staying there either.

"Things will look better in the morning," Violet advised him, because that was what her mother always said, although not as much lately. "It's such a nice day. Maybe later we'll look for daisies."

When Bert caught up with her, Violet led the way up Guardians Hill. She had grown up playing in the forest and was in no danger of getting lost.

They came to a flat terrace, an indentation in the side of the hill filled with saplings and weeds.

Bert's eyes widened. "This is one of them places evil fairies make burnt sacrifices when the moon is full," he whispered.

"Len Finch told me so. He said they like to sacrifice fat boys because they burn for a long time, and because they can catch them, seeing as how fairies have short legs."

Violet giggled. "Oh, Bert, you shouldn't let Len scare you."

Bert broke a limb from a sapling and poked around in the weeds, uncovering several lumps of charcoal. "See." He picked a lump up and held it out to Violet, who put her hands behind her and stepped back in horror.

"You're scared too," he said.

"I just don't want that nasty dirt all over me."

Bert turned the charcoal around in his hand. "Doesn't it look like part of a bone? Maybe a finger bone." He dropped the lump and wiped his hands on his shirt.

"You'll catch it for that!" Violet scolded. Then she added, "It's charcoal. They used to make it here by burning piles of wood."

Bert looked dubious.

"You'd rather believe in evil fairies?" Violet asked. "There was a man who came every summer to make it. He lived in the forest while he did. To keep an eye on the fire, you know."

"Do you think it's him…?" Bert blurted out.

"What do you mean?"

"Do you think he's the one who killed Issy?"

"Who says anyone killed Issy? I think she ran off, like those bad boys."

"Well, I suppose she did."

"Anyway, the charcoal man hasn't been back for ages."

Bert looked around, anxious, and suggested they go somewhere else.

"Now what are you looking like a scaredy cat about, Bert?"

"When you said charcoal man I thought of a man all burned up into charcoal, roaming the forest in the dark so you couldn't hardly see him until he grabbed you."

"So what if he did grab you? If he was made of charcoal he'd just fall right apart, wouldn't he?"

They left the terrace and climbed to the top of the hill. Violet wanted to sit on one of the stones but Bert looked scared again.

"Don't go alone, inside the stones. Isn't that what you say around here?"

"Oh, silly, we're not alone, are we?"

Instead of going into the stone circle, they sat on a fallen tree trunk cushioned with moss with their backs to it. A breeze cooled them after their climb up the steep path. Fleecy clouds grazed across the sky, aerial sheep promising more hot weather to come.

After a few moments of silence, Bert spoke round the stalk of grass he was chewing. "Won't you cop it from your mum for coming out on your own?"

"She won't miss me. She's at that meeting they're having. There's more people at the pub than there was in church this morning. I don't know what it's about. Anyhow, I'm sick of being sent up to my room to read."

Bert grunted. "At least you don't have to listen to your parents shouting and carrying on half the night. You should hear the Wainmans going at it hammer and tongs! That's why I like the forest. It's quiet. You can sit and think."

"Where do you think those bad Finch boys are?"

"They told me they was going back home."

"Were they telling the truth?"

"I hope so. What if they come back?" Bert looked as if he would burst into tears.

"Did they kill poor Patch?"

Bert nodded. "Do it soon as look at you, they would. They are just horrible. They'd trip me up and call me names and make me give them all my sweets."

"You poor thing! You should have told the Wainmans."

"Len said if I did they'd drown me in the witch's pond," came the gloomy reply.

Violet shuddered. "They would, too. But then why did you run away with them?"

"They didn't give me much choice, did they? It was that or the pond."

"Look!" Violet pulled a small, sticky paper bag from her pocket. "Bull's-eyes. Have one."

The pair sat for a while, sucking on the sweets.

"Where do you think Issy has gone?" Bert eventually asked.

"Then you don't really think she joined up with the Finches?"

Bert did not reply, so Violet continued, "Do you think the monsters got her?"

"Monsters?"

"Yes," Violet nodded. "I heard mum talking about monsters last night. She reckons there's monsters in the village. Well, I looked all over today for signs of them but I haven't seen any at all."

"She might have meant them rotten brothers," Bert suggested.

"Maybe the monsters got them?"

Bert giggled. "Hope so."

"But....but what if the monsters live in the forest?" Violet whispered.

The children looked around uneasily.

"I'm sure there's something bad in the forest." Bert whispered back. "Let's go back."

The children jump up from the log. For a moment it appears as if the girl will turn around to look directly at the stubby stone surrounded by tall grass and overgrown by a bramble bush which has left a space near the base of the stone, forming a thorny tent. But she is only smoothing wrinkles in her dress. She says something, but a breeze rustling the grass obscures her words, except for one. "...monsters.."

It is not clear whether she is afraid or is advising her companion not to be afraid. She does not move as if she is in any hurry to run away.

The two go down the slight incline at the edge of the clearing. As they descend, the tall grass gradually obscures them, first their legs vanish from view, then the torsos, finally a windblown wisp of auburn hair sinks beneath the grass.

There remain only the tops of the trees at the forest edge and the fleecy clouds drifting in the blue, eluding the thorns that reach out for them.

Chapter Fifteen

By the time Edwin and Grace arrived for the meeting at the pub there was nowhere left to sit. Normally Edwin would not allow himself to be late but on leaving the house he noticed a smudge of dried blood on his shirt cuff and felt compelled to change. It took him a while to button up his fresh shirt because the sight of blood started his hands shaking again. They had shaken as he'd made his way back through the forest and during his talk with Constable Green, even after he'd been relieved of his burden.

Chairs had been pulled around to face Green, who stood in front of the bar. Most of Noddweir's adults were present, their grim faces reflected in the long mirror behind the bar.

Edwin and Grace stood beside the fireplace.

Green was speaking as they arrived. He gave Grace a slight nod which she ignored. "Evacuees running off is one thing," he was saying. "We can all understand them wanting to get back home, dangerous as home might be these days. Bert Holloway is one example and I'm sure the Finch brothers will be found soon and brought back."

Edwin thought Green looked as if he were enjoying himself. His newly slicked-back hair glistened and his usual lazy slouch was gone. Edwin was beginning to dislike the man. What kind of person would take pleasure in such a meeting? Then again, he was only a callow youth struggling awkwardly to project an air of authority.

"Be a pity if them troublemakers come back," someone in the audience remarked loudly. "Why can't we have a whip-round for their tickets if they're desperate to go home?"

Several men nodded and one asked whether Meg Gowdy's blouse had been found yet since it couldn't have run away. The speaker smirked in the direction of Meg Gowdy who was standing with her husband at the end of the bar, but she ignored the remark.

Green's bland, round face flushed. "This is more serious than a missing blouse. But as a matter of fact we have found some clothing. That is to say, Professor Carpenter did, while walking in the forest."

He reached behind the bar and pulled out a bundle of pale blue cloth displaying large patches of dark red.

"Oh, have some decency for God's sake!" Grace muttered as Green brandished the blood-stained garment.

Edwin decided he did dislike Green. The display went far beyond any clumsy attempt to look like a real constable exhibiting evidence.

Grace's words were extinguished by the uproar from the crowd.

"This is the dress Isobel Chapman was wearing the night she vanished," Green said when the noise had died down. "Her father has identified it. Isn't that right, Mr. Chapman?"

Jack Chapman, sitting in a corner as far from the bar as possible, acknowledged Green's statement by letting out a dull grunt and lowering his face into his enormous hands.

"Professor Carpenter said he found it in the forest. Would you like to repeat your story for everyone's benefit, Professor?"

"Certainly." Did Green suspect him of lying? Was he testing to see if Edwin had got his story straight and would not contradict himself in the second telling? Was he trying to impress Grace with his cleverness and command of the situation?

Edwin described looking for the barrow Martha had mentioned to him, and how he'd spotted a crumpled shape. "For a moment it moved. I thought it was one of the children playing a trick again, but it was only a bit of the skirt waving in the breeze."

"This discovery naturally puts quite a different light on Isobel's disappearance." Green lifted his bundle higher. Edwin noticed Grace glare at the constable, her gaze smoldering with a disapproval to which Green appeared oblivious.

"You're thinking Issy didn't just run off?" The hoarse voice belonged to Timothy Wilson.

"We can't be certain." Green dropped the clothing behind the bar. "But judging from the evidence, I'd have to say she's come to harm."

"Killed you mean! Murdered!" Meg Gowdy screeched. She'd been angry when Edwin first met her and she was still angry. Duncan Gowdy put a cautioning hand on her arm. She shrugged it off, shook her hair, and strode over to Green. "Raped and murdered you mean! By some pervert!" She pointed her cigarette in the constable's face. "Some degenerate lurking out here in this god-forsaken back of beyond!"

"I can assure you there is more crime in your average city than—"

"What do you know about crime in the city?" someone shouted. "You weren't no constable 'till you come here!"

"No constable now neither," added another voice.

"Tell Issy how safe this place is!" Meg's voice trembled. "Tell that to the poor child! And whose child is next?" Meg stuck her cigarette firmly between her lips and stalked away, though not to her husband's side.

"She has a good point." Timothy Wilson spoke again. "When children start to disappear, you can't help but think of predators."

Green frowned. "We have no indications any of the others haven't simply run away. Bert Holloway told us he ran off with the Finch boys."

A severe-looking woman, sitting ramrod straight directly in front of Green, spoke. "Come now, Mr. Green, what about Reggie Cox? Do you really think he could have run away with that leg of his?" She pursed her lips and frowned.

Grace identified her for Edwin as Susannah Radbone, who had taught school in a city before retiring to Noddweir. He had already met Emily Miller, seated beside her, while searching for the missing girl upon his arrival in Noddweir.

"I think maybe he weren't so crippled up as he let on."

Edwin recognized the big man with the loud voice as the farmer he'd met during his initial foray seeking barrows. Harry Wainman.

"Good excuse for him to avoid doing any farm work," Wainman continued. "You'd be surprised the places I seen him wandering around, but all of a sudden helpless if he realized someone was watching. Either he run away or got grabbed by this pervert. And if he could wander far enough for the swine to get him, he could've wandered far enough to run away."

"A most comforting thought, Harry," Susannah sniffed.

"I'm just a realist, Miss Radbone. Just a realist." Harry was mopping his big red face with a matching bandana. With so many people packed into the bar, the place was stifling. There was a faint aroma of perfume the women present had worn to church earlier, but the smell of sweat was beginning to overpower it.

Edwin scanned the assembly the same way he scanned the room on the first day of classes, matching faces to names, taking a measure of next semester's group. He wouldn't find the likes of most villagers in the pub in his history class at the University of Rochester. Timothy Wilson would have fit in, and Susannah Radbone, the former teacher.

Susannah put her hand on top of Emily Miller's. "Have you considered, Constable Green, that those hooligans, the Finches, are responsible? Boys who would burn a pet dog are capable of any sort of atrocity."

"Dammit, she's right!" shouted Jack Chapman. "Why talk about strangers lurking in the forest when you've seen them buggers in action? They tried to drown Violet, and when I rescued her they took a knife after me. Knives is just the thing to draw blood. Why do you think they run off? Because of what they done to Issy. Those monsters come back here, I'll break their necks."

"Why not? You about broke Issy's neck more than once, Jack. Or maybe you finally managed it, by accident. Maybe you got carried away. She could be a handful, couldn't she?"

Jack leapt up, looking around furiously for the speaker. He found a plain woman with a weathered face.

Now why'd you say that, Louisa Wainman? After all the work I done for you and Harry on the farm? Don't you know me better'n that?"

"I know you, Jack. Everyone knows you. They know you're rough with your daughter." Lousia's voice quavered and she bit her lip. "Everyone knows—"

"That's enough," Harry Wainman snapped. His face had gone white with anger. "That's more than enough." He grabbed his wife's arm and pulled her toward the door. "I think we'd better be going."

Green didn't ask them to stay. Edwin detected anxiety in the young man's eyes. Clearly if the burly farmer and the even bigger blacksmith got into a fight, Green wouldn't know how to stop it.

"You have to remember there's a war on." Green's voice sounded a note higher than before. "There's a lot of odd characters loose right now, what with everyone moving about the country. Troops and such, strangers in Craven Arms, and for all we know one might be queer in the head. Some came back from the Great War like—" He broke off. Jack Chapman was giving him a look of hatred.

"Could be a plot by German saboteurs," Duncan Gowdy suggested quickly.

Someone asked him to explain what he meant.

"It's obvious, innit? They can't bomb every village but they can spread fear by showing nobody, not even children, are safe anywhere. You can't trust a German. Swinish lot, they are. I know, I fought them last time."

"For that matter, it could be deserters," said someone else.

Tinkers and tramps then came under suspicion, as they always did.

Green broke into the conversation as it wandered off the path into the forest. "I have in mind the sort of strangers who aren't usually seen in Shropshire."

Edwin wasn't certain if Green was looking at Grace again or at him. "You surely don't consider me a dangerous stranger, do you, Constable?"

"You claim to be here studying folklore—"

Grace's eyes narrowed. "And he is, Tom. What's the matter with you?"

Green paused and licked his lips. "What I was saying, Grace, is that he claims to be here studying the stones despite the fact there's a war on."

"I know you need to consider every possibility," Edwin said, trying to damp down flaring tempers. "I can easily prove I'm a former professor of history from the University of Rochester. I'm afraid I can't prove I am not a pervert. Perhaps you can prove that you are one, but it is exceedingly difficult to prove a negative."

Green stared at him but said nothing.

"You've made some good points." Edwin feared he'd gone too far. "We can't be certain who's wandering around the countryside right now and there's plenty of monsters in the world. I'm sure you've heard of Albert Fish. Who can say how many children he killed? He claimed it was a hundred. And though it was twenty years ago, some of you must recall the Abertillery murders. Two young girls killed by a madman."

"I'm surprised you heard of that in America," Green replied. "But then, you are a professor."

Edwin ignored the sarcasm. "My wife and I were Anglophiles. We planned to move over here after my retirement."

"I hope you bloody well like it," snapped Meg Gowdy. "And the murderer of those girls lived in the town, didn't he? He was well liked. They brought him up for one murder, acquitted him, and right away he killed again. Why, our pervert might very well be sitting here in this room, a well-respected resident of Noddweir." She snickered and blew out a plume of smoke.

Duncan Gowdy stared daggers at his wife from across the room.

"We don't need to start suspecting our neighbors, Meg," Reverend Wilson said quietly.

"Of course a man of your profession might naturally be inclined to think the best of people," Green replied. "Those of us on the front lines need to be suspicious of everyone."

"The Abertillery madman wasn't even a man," Emily Miller blurted. "He was only sixteen. A child. Just like them Finch boys. Whoever's responsible for whatever happened to Issy doesn't have to be a man. Evil grows up fast." Her eyes were red and watery and her voice trembled.

"Evil's what it is," piped up a husky, middle-aged woman Edwin didn't recognize. Her hair was wrapped up turban-fashion in a faded scarf. "Evil has come upon us!"

"Hush, Polly" said Susannah Radbone, swiveling in her chair to face the speaker.

"Don't be telling me what to do, Susannah Radbone. All yer learning's not left room for a lick of common sense in that stubbly gray head of yours!" the other retorted.

Grace, who had remained silent, turned to the woman. "You've been talking to Martha too much, Polly. My grandma's a dear but she don't always know what she's saying." She whispered to Edwin. "She's a little slow, is our Polly."

Edwin felt her lips brush his earlobe. As she looked away he could swear she gave Constable Green a mocking smile.

"You need to listen to yer grandma, young lady," Polly shot back. "She'll tell you straight. It's them stones. They're evil. They're casting their evil over Noddweir. Their curse. There's things in the forest as well. The stones is reaching out, using evil hands."

"Yes, thank you." Green spoke loudly. "Your theory has been noted." He looked directly at Grace. "And how about you, Grace? What does my deputy think about all this?"

Grace flushed, then inhaled and very slowly exhaled. "I will be of assistance if I can, Constable Green, but I am not your deputy."

Chapter Sixteen

"The nerve of the man," fumed Grace. "His deputy, indeed!"

"Maybe you're overreacting," Edwin followed Grace out onto the High Street. The residents of Noddweir had spilled into the twilight and were on their way home. Grace hung behind to talk with the publican, mostly, Edwin suspected, to make sure Green was well away on his blackout patrol. "He probably didn't mean anything more than he sees you as his unofficial deputy, just like you were when your father was constable."

He was trying to convince himself as much as Grace. Constable Green's attitude irritated him intensely.

"You can see the way he looks at me." Grace screwed her face up in disgust. "Ugh!"

As they walked slowly up the street Edwin said, "You can't blame a young man for looking. If I were younger…well, I'm not, of course." He stopped himself. What a stupid thing to say. What was the matter with him lately?

Grace's expression was unreadable in the growing darkness.

When they reached the house, Grace cried out in dismay. The door was ajar.

The front room was dark but the door to Martha's room was wide open.

Grace stuck her head through the doorway. "Grandma's not here. Damn! She's taken to wandering at night. Green had to bring her home the night before you arrived."

"Maybe she's visiting a friend?"

"Perhaps." Grace sounded dubious. "She just gets it in her mind to wander."

They went out to look for her. It was dark. Houses, blackout curtains drawn, were masses of black. There was no sound except for the atonal music of summer insects. A door slammed somewhere.

Their search dragged on, Edwin now wondering if adults would start disappearing.

A dim flash of light drew their attention as they came back up the High Street. Susannah Radbone gestured from her open front door to the kitchen where Martha sat at the table, a black cat on her lap.

"When I pulled the curtains I saw her walking in the street, talking to herself," Susannah whispered. "I persuaded her to come in for a visit. I was about to fetch you."

Grace shook her head wearily. "Thanks, Susannah."

Susannah gave a wave of her hand that meant never mind. "No one should be out walking by themselves after dark with what's been going on, let alone Martha. Whatever it is that's going on."

Martha frowned as Grace came into the kitchen.

"You have to stop going about at night, Grandma," Grace scolded.

"So now my little granddaughter is ordering me around?"

"You had us worried. What were you doing?"

"Just gathering plants for my persuasions." She tapped at a bunch of greenery on the table in front of her. Edwin could only recognize foxgloves. "And visiting."

"With Susannah?"

Martha smiled. "Oh, and others. And others. They was calling me, you see."

Grace closed her eyes for an instant. "All right, Grandma, but we need to be getting home now."

"I only just got here! I was explaining about my persuasions to Susannah."

"And a lot of old rubbish it was too, Martha!" Susannah said.

Martha scratched the cat's ears. "You may think so, but you don't know country ways. I could tell you a few things that would surprise you. I've got my suspicions about what's happening here in Noddweir."

"I'm sure you do, Grandma." Grace sounded tired. "Come along, it's getting late."

"Her suspicions are probably as good as any Tom Green has," Susannah put in. "I've never seen anyone so hopeless at their job, unless it's the vicar."

"The vicar does the best he can," Grace pointed out, "Consider how ill he is. He's never recovered his full strength."

"At least he has some excuse," Susannah admitted. "What's Tom Green's? Why is he bumbling around Noddweir rather than shooting at Germans? Not that he'd hit any."

"He hasn't confided in me, I'm pleased to say."

Susannah's narrow lips threatened to smile.

"Neither of them's worse than Issy's father," Martha growled. "A Johnny-knock-softly, he is."

"He may be a bit idle but at least he doesn't spout supernatural nonsense," Susannah responded.

"I hope you don't think that of me and the vicar," Martha retorted.

"If the hat fits, wear it," Susannah replied.

Edwin kept quiet, feeling abashed, as if he were listening in on a domestic conversation that was none of his business. Which, in fact, was the case.

"Oh, I'm sorry," Grace said. "Have you met Professor Carpenter? I almost forgot to introduce you. It seems like he's a villager already. He's here to study our local customs. His wife taught school too."

Edwin and Susannah made the usual polite acknowledgements. Standing straight as a soldier at attention, with her cropped battleship gray hair, a cigarette between her thin lips, Susannah looked formidable. She must have kept her students in a perpetual state of terror, the opposite to Elise's approach.

Martha stood reluctantly. The cat, dislodged from her lap, hit the floor with a loud thump and cast a malevolent gaze around the kitchen.

While Martha gathered up her plants, Susannah spoke quietly to Grace. "I saw Martha at church this morning. She looked pretty sprightly. Are you sure she's in as poor health as she lets on?"

"She has good days and bad, like all of us. Her mind's less reliable than her legs."

Susannah studied the end of her cigarette. "Is she taking advantage of your good nature, Grace, letting you wait on her hand and foot? She's family, I know."

Grace shrugged. "You heard her, saying someone was calling her. You said she was talking to herself in the street. What can I do? She isn't fit to live by herself."

"No, I suppose not."

Martha finally joined them, moving unsteadily. "Are you sure I didn't bring my hat?"

"Yes, Grandma."

When they went out the door Susannah followed. "I told Emily I'd check up on her." She dropped her cigarette butt on the garden path. "Emily keeps telling me I ought to give up the habit. That's what I told my students when I caught them at it. They didn't listen to me, and I don't listen to Emily. Anyway, the shape the world's in these days, we may as well enjoy ourselves as much as we can." Her gaze moved to Edwin. "Nice to meet you, Professor. I'm sorry you had to find Issy's dress. Not a very pleasant introduction to our little village. Be careful."

Edwin opened his eyes in the dark, disoriented. He lay on his back, seeing only blackness. Once he was awake, it took him several seconds to remember he was in a strange room in an English village and not in his own bedroom in Rochester.

A throbbing noise made the air vibrate. He could almost feel it inside his head.

Is that what had awakened him?

"Edwin, are you awake?" Grace rapped at his door "There are planes coming."

He muttered an acknowledgement.

He should have recognized the sound immediately, the distinctive throbbing of the engines of German bombers. He'd heard it often enough in London.

He fumbled to light the lamp, illuminating the photograph of Elise on the bedside table, smiling unconcernedly. On the wall the Victorian Jesus held his own lantern.

Edwin grabbed his clothes and dressed quickly as possible, straightening his collar as he hurried down the stairs.

The throbbing was louder. An insistent, senseless, repetitive noise. He heard voices outside.

It looked as if most of Noddweir had gathered in the street to stare into a starry sky, faintly lit by a half moon. No one sought shelter or wore gas masks. Adults kept a hand on their children.

"Ain't coming for us."

"Headed for Swansea, likely."

He found Grace and Martha and stood silently beside them. Planes took shape against the dark sky. Stars blinked as planes occluded them.

They wouldn't bother with Noddweir. The village was in no danger. Unless some German got nervous and ditched his bombs prematurely.

A few villagers hurled ripe curses upwards.

The deep throbbing continued. Edwin had heard the Germans deliberately de-synchronized their engines to create the nerve-wracking fearsome sound when bombers flew in formation. Whether that was true or not, he couldn't say. In his imagination, a monstrous subterranean gate had been thrown open to the distant engines of Hell.

He listened for the familiar eerie whistling of falling bombs. It was a sound you didn't want to hear because it meant the bombs were nearby. In fact, it might be the last sound you heard.

Edwin remembered the M.R. James ghost story, "Oh, Whistle, and I'll Come to You, My Lad." It wasn't the same sort of whistling, but the terror it engendered was the same.

After a long time he heard only summer insects chirping and smelled grass and earth wet with night dew. The planes were gone. Somewhere else innocent people might already be dying.

The crowd dispersed.

The red end of a cigarette flared.

He felt a light touch on his arm.

"It must have been worse in London," Grace said.

"Yes."

Back in his room undressing, he discovered he'd had his shirt wrongly buttoned.

He couldn't sleep. He was the only patron in a darkened movie theater watching *The Perfect Life of Edwin Carpenter*.

He knew the last reel was missing.

He watched the film anyway, over and over.

Chapter Seventeen

Monday, June 16, 1941

Edwin slept late.

When he opened the blackout curtains he blinked in bright mid-morning sunlight. Never one to sleep in, he did not intend to start in his retirement.

Elise's photograph smiled good morning.

Edwin dressed and went downstairs. The house was quiet. Martha's door was closed. Where had Grace gone? He reminded himself he was a lodger, not a family member. It was none of his business.

The sun felt hot against Edwin's shoulders. People passed by. A woman hung out her washing. From somewhere came the sound of hammering. The world was up and about while he slept.

The pub was all but deserted, a contrast to the crowd it had held the day before. Joe Haywood sat at a table near the end of the bar. Meg Gowdy put a plate down in front of him. He said something and Meg laughed. Duncan Gowdy slowly and meticulously wiped the top of the bar, its length already shining in the morning light.

Edwin said he hoped he could get something to eat.

"How about eggs and bacon?" Duncan suggested.

"If you have them."

Haywood laughed loudly.

"Meg," Duncan raised his voice, "cook up some more eggs and bacon for our customer here."

She frowned at Duncan over her shoulder, said a few more words to Haywood, then went out to the kitchen.

Edwin leaned against the bar and watched Haywood methodically devour his breakfast. He was a broad-shouldered young man, with a Roman nose and dark hair, slicked back and glistening.

Duncan gave Edwin an uneasy look. "We've all got ration books, of course, but things out here in the countryside's a little different than in cities. We might not have electricity yet, but what with one thing and another we have a decent amount of food."

Edwin nodded, not knowing what to say. He hadn't been thinking about rationing until Duncan mentioned it.

"Grace must be out searching for Issy again," said Duncan.

"I suppose so," Edwin replied.

"Looking for her body. Or more likely where Jack buried her body," Haywood observed. His knife clicked against his plate and he forked more bacon into his mouth.

"Just because a man drinks doesn't mean he'd kill his own daughter," Duncan said.

"You would stand up for him, seeing what a good customer he is." Haywood chuckled.

Duncan threw his cloth down angrily. "How long have you lived in Noddweir, Joe? You don't know nothing about us."

"Oh, I know what I need to, Duncan."

"You don't know Jack Chapman took to drink after what he saw in the war. I can't blame a man for that, I was there and I saw some things. Turning to booze isn't so bad. There were young men, all their lives before them, who purposely slept with tarts until they caught the pox just to get out of the trenches for a while."

Haywood smiled. "Women, pox, and getting out the trenches, eh? Two out of three isn't bad, Duncan."

Meg set a plate of fried eggs and bacon in front of Edwin. Her lips were painted a bright red to match her hair. His bacon was limp and his eggs runny.

"I wouldn't have thought you were old enough to be in the war," Edwin said to Duncan.

"I lied about my age. Even then it was almost over by the time I got there." Perhaps he saw Edwin's gaze following Meg as she walked over to Haywood's table to retrieve his empty plate. "I'm a bit older than my wife. Robbed the cradle."

Edwin could not see Meg's face but guessed she wasn't smiling at Duncan's joke. "Oh, I wasn't thinking about that. My wife was somewhat younger than me."

"Oh, aye? She was, you say?"

"She passed away last year."

"I'm sorry."

Edwin looked down at his plate and cut his egg. He had never quite got the knack of expressing sympathy, let alone accepting it. "Never imagined she'd go before me."

Meg came past with Haywood's empty plate. "You'd be surprised how many wives go first."

Haywood stood and hitched up his trousers, freshly pressed with a crisp crease. "Back to work. I'll be in again tonight, Duncan."

Duncan grunted a vague assent.

"And we'll have to get together some evening, Professor Carpenter. I'd like to hear about your studies," Haywood continued. "Those stones, now, queer things they are. I'll buy you a drink. It'll pay for a lecture on the mysteries of Noddweir." His smile showed big, white, even teeth.

"Certainly. It would be my pleasure."

Haywood left, whistling.

"What does he do?" Edwin asked Duncan.

The publican looked uneasy. "Oh, well, everyone knows he works for the Wainmans. Rents a rundown farmhouse owned by Harry Wainman. Louisa Wainman's father lived in it for years before he died. With so many people off to war, the Wainmans were happy to find a tenant."

"What is he, early thirties?"

"He's a conchie, if you're wondering why he isn't fighting. Here to do farm work."

"He looks well-turned out for that sort of job." Edwin cut another piece off his runny egg, put it into his mouth, and swallowed without chewing. He was particular about having his eggs well done.

"Mind, I'm not saying he does much farm work or that he might not do a bit of other business on the side," Duncan admitted.

Edwin smeared the remaining yolk around his plate rather than forcing it down, feeling like a wasteful child for doing so. "Surely Constable Green must know what Haywood's up to?"

"Knowing and proving is two different things, particularly when no one but Green wants it proved."

Edwin recalled the vicar's exceptionally strong tea. Did Emily, with her shop, deal with Haywood too, or was he a competitor? Though the black market was contrary to the war effort he found it difficult to be too enraged. He suspected most people felt the same way, especially when they were the beneficiaries of the bit of sugar needed for a cake or extra ounces of tea to brew a decent pot.

"Sorry if Meg was rude," Duncan changed the subject. "She gets in these moods. It's hard on her, living out here in the country. She longs for the bright lights."

"She might not enjoy the bright lights right now with the Germans dropping bombs on them."

"If there was a cinema closer...but the nearest one is too far these days."

"My wife—Elise—loved the theater. On our honeymoon we went to the London Palladium. It hadn't been opened long, back in 1912."

"I was still in short trousers then. Five years later I was in France."

Edwin searched his memory, as if reconstructing those days might bring back Elise. "We saw Ruth Vincent, the singer."

"Oh, aye, that'd suit Meg a treat. Before the war we'd go to see all the musical films. Fred Astaire is the one she likes. Fred Astaire." He let out an unhappy laugh. "Can you imagine me doing the Continental?"

The short, chunky publican spread his thick arms, hands palms up, and shrugged. A hint of belly was visible where the lower buttons of his rumpled shirt had come undone.

"You have more hair than Fred," Edwin told him. "I'm not keen on musicals myself. Elise was. I only watched them for her sake." He stopped abruptly, put the brakes to his thoughts, trying to avoid the memory—that memory.

"Fancy restaurants too," Duncan continued. "She'd sooner be dining on something or other I can't pronounce than serving up bacon and eggs. But then wouldn't we all?"

Edwin finished the under-cooked bacon and put his knife and fork on the plate. "Fancy restaurants make me uncomfortable." He immediately regretted it for fear Duncan would think he was an ascetic.

"If you don't like fancy eating establishments, you're in luck here. Come over later today. I'll have the wireless on. Mr. Churchill is giving an address."

"What is it? Have the Germans attacked Russia after all?"

"Nothing like that. Some American university is giving him a degree. He'll be talking to the Americans. I'm hoping he'll give them what for, hanging back like they are. No offense to you, Professor."

Edwin asked if Duncan knew what university was involved.

Duncan narrowed his eyes and scratched the sandy hair at the back of his head, which may have triggered his memory. "English name. Rochester. that's it. Never heard of a Rochester except the one in Kent. Have you?"

"Yes. Rochester in New York State is where I taught."

Duncan looked bemused. "Well, there's a coincidence for you. You're from the same university that's giving a degree to the prime minister. And here you are in Noddweir! You're not a spy, are you?"

Chapter Eighteen

"Why do I want to listen to old Winnie?" Emily Miller asked. "If fancy words could kill Germans we could've shouted them devil's flies out of the sky last night."

Susannah Radbone tut-tutted. "Devil's flies indeed! You sound like Martha Roper. It's our duty to listen to what the prime minister says. Besides, he's a wonderful speaker. He inspires the nation to keep persevering."

"People hardly need to be inspired to keep going. What else are they going to do, die?"

Susannah smiled to herself. Emily's spirits must be improving if she felt up to being irascible. "You will come along to the pub to keep me company even so?"

"Are you afraid Joe Haywood might press his attentions on an unaccompanied lady?"

Susannah tut-tutted again.

Several jars of gooseberry jam sat cooling on her kitchen table. A second batch bubbled gently on the stove while she and Emily topped and tailed berries for a third batch.

"Why didn't you wait until they were riper? Wouldn't need so much sugar then," Emily said, as her knife seemed to work automatically, clicking rhythmically against the chopping board.

"What, and let the birds get half my crop?" Susannah winced in mock horror. "Besides, since I don't take sugar in my tea I had enough saved up for the job."

"You'd better not let Green hear that. He'd call it hoarding."

"That young fool better not cross swords with me."

They worked on in companionable silence for a while, a mismatched pair—the tall, angular former schoolteacher now standing watch over the stove, and the short, round shopkeeper sitting and chopping. Finally Susannah wiped her hands on her apron and lifted the simmering pan off the heat.

"I must say gooseberries aren't my favorite fruit." Emily laid down her knife.

"Nor mine, but jam's jam," Susannah replied. "Take a couple of jars when you go. You can probably swap for something you prefer. I had a good crop this year. Last year half the berries disappeared in one afternoon. Wasn't birds, though. One or two of our reluctant young visitors looked green about the gills next day. But then boys will be boys."

"Unfortunately."

"I taught for years and found most children good-hearted. Not all of them, it's true." Susannah paused, thinking about Emily's dog, Patch. "It's life as much as anything that eventually hardens them. Of course, sometimes the parents—"

"When I was young, children were seen and not heard," Emily interrupted. "But with the war splitting up families, children with no supervision, fathers gone, mothers away all day working at this or that, is it any wonder kids go wild, the little beasts? If they'd tried to billet them on me, I'd have refused."

Emily sounded fierce. Perhaps it was a result of a lifetime spent guarding her counter against nefarious little sweets predators. So much sneakier than adults, she'd once confided. But Susannah knew very well that her friend always had spare sweets set aside for children whose families were going through hard times.

Susannah had been judged as an authoritarian during her teaching days. In her opinion, when children came from homes with no supervision at all, discipline at school was necessary. Better a ruler across the knuckles now than a police officer's truncheon on the head later, she explained to her students on the first day of school.

"Children without supervision often come to no good. That's true. They tend to revert to a state of nature. But they aren't all bad. When I was still teaching—this was in Newcastle—one of my pupils brought a kitten to me. It had a broken leg. She found it lying in a back lane. And who do you think was responsible for the broken leg? Some lout of a boy having what he called fun. The kind of boy who would grow up to enjoy dropping bombs on innocent people. Including girls who rescue cats." Susannah sighed. "When this war ends things will get back to normal and life will be better for all of us."

"I doubt it. There'll just be more little savages running about, causing trouble."

"I daresay. Poor Reggie Cox won't be running about, wherever he's got to." Susannah paused. Thinking of the vanished Reggie brought tears to her eyes. She was used to having temporary custody of children who disappeared into an unknown future at the end of their final school term.. But those departures took place in an orderly fashion on a predictable schedule. Reggie was like one of those students who simply, unexpectedly, stopped coming to class. Usually Susannah never found out why, and if she did find out, the reasons were often unpleasant—accident, illness, a father losing his job, an impoverished family doing a moonlight flit, leaving their lodgings secretly in the middle of the night.

Susannah turned away from Emily long enough to blink the moisture from her eyes. "Reggie is a good boy, basically. Even if I did have to give him a scrubbing when he arrived. His family is respectable enough. His father's a porter. But they're poor. The poor don't always have time to train their children properly. All he needs is guidance, a firm hand."

"Well, being crippled don't make you a saint," grumbled Emily. "Look at Long John Silver."

"Oh, Emily! Really! Is that what you're reading in the shop now, Robert Louis Stevenson?"

"I've have a lot of time to read, considering how few customers I've had lately. Do you think I should read something more educational? I want to see how the story comes out."

Susannah's black cat trotted into the room, sniffed, shook its tail disdainfully at the scent of gooseberries, and stalked under the table.

"Remember how fond Reggie was of—" Susannah broke off. She didn't want to remind Emily about the death of her pet.

"Blind Pew frightens me," Emily admitted. "Yet why should I be frightened by a book when there are worse things lurking everywhere these days?"

"Is it easier to believe the frightening things in books?" Susannah suggested. "We try not to believe in things that happen in real life."

"Like what happened to Issy?"

"All that's been found so far are some clothes."

"Blood-stained clothes," Emily pointed out.

"We can still hope."

"And Reggie? Do you think the same thing happened to him?"

"Surely the Finch boys had been bragging to him about how they were going to run off? Maybe he decided to follow them."

"Maybe." Emily sounded doubtful.

"I warned Reggie those boys were trouble, but he's an innocent. There are all sorts of possible explanations for these children vanishing, and there's no reason to imagine all the disappearances are related. Coincidences happen. People are too quick to find relationships between things. That's where your superstitions start, isn't it? Somebody opens an umbrella in their house and next day they trip on the stairs and break a leg. Suddenly the umbrella's the cause of bad luck. But the umbrella didn't trip them."

"Try opening one on my narrow stairs and you'll fall down them, sure as eggs is eggs."

Susannah gave a sour laugh. "You and Martha Roper would get along. She's as superstitious as the vicar. She's sure the Guardian Stones are responsible for all our problems. How, I'm not certain, and I don't think she is either."

"Martha isn't certain of anything these days," Emily said. "Sharp as a tack at one time she was, too. It's a shame. You have to admit, though, that Issy has come to harm. And someone's responsible."

Susannah felt angry, not at Emily so much as at the whole confounding situation, and at herself not being able to form a coherent opinion. Susannah did not tolerate sloppy thinking, least of all in herself. "Maybe Issy is responsible. Maybe she brought it on herself. She hasn't had proper guidance from that father of hers."

Emily nodded. "Girls today have no morals. What about that one who came round last month knocking on doors looking for a fellow name of MacDonagh who supposedly lived in Noddweir, wanting him to marry her and soon? Of course the man gave a false name. If the description of the culprit fitted Duncan, what with the name and his accent and all, that wife of his would have had plenty to say."

"Be almost comical, wouldn't it, if it had been him? Meg with her stuck up ways! But it's a shame for the baby." Susannah skimmed surface scum from the waiting batch of jam.

"That baby'll be like his father," Emily predicted. "No sense of responsibility, breaking windows and stealing gooseberries and blouses for a start. Not to mention worse. Who was it set fire to the Bertram's hen house last summer? That evacuee from Manchester. Only six, mark you, and already—" Emily stopped abruptly. A shadow of pain fell across her face.

She's reminded herself of Patch, Susannah realized. Seeking to change the subject she glanced out the window over the sink. "Who do you think is just coming out the vicarage?"

Emily pushed herself up with difficulty and grabbed the back of the chair as a cat went flying out from under the table.

"Blackie just tried to trip me, Susannah!" She stepped over to the window and looked out. "Why, it's Joe Haywood. I doubt he'd be visiting the vicar for spiritual comfort. Wonder why he was there?"

Susannah shrugged. "What does Haywood do anywhere? I'm sure the vicar feels the pinch of rationing like everyone else. It's one thing to preach about the spiritual benefits of poverty, and quite another to actually live with them. Or even to be without sufficient tea."

"You're being nasty, Susannah. So what if the vicar has an extra pot of tea? Poor man. Look at what the Germans did to him. He'll be lucky to see peace again, the way he wheezes and coughs."

"You don't do business with Haywood?"

"We all have to make our own choices."

Chapter Nineteen

From his lumpy bed in the attic, Bert Holloway could hear the Wainmans arguing downstairs. They had not stopped shouting at each other since coming back from church the day before. During the night he woke to hear unintelligible but unmistakably angry words, vibrating up through the bare floorboards. Planes droned overhead while the Wainmans fought below. Planes didn't frighten Bert as much as angry words. He had heard planes too often in Birmingham—and anti-aircraft guns and bombs as well.

Afraid to go downstairs to breakfast when no one called him, he ate some stolen sweets he had hidden from the Finch boys. He felt queasy. The attic was already stifling as the sun rose higher. The sunny, peaceful fields visible through the tiny window in the end wall called to him. A wasp buzzed in the dim, hot space. He would be better off billeted in the barn. The smell of dry hay was better than the dusty smell of the attic.

He heard crockery shattering below. Mrs. Wainman liked to throw cups.

Mr. Wainman's booming voice rattled.

Bert decided he better know what the argument was about. He pulled up the trapdoor and eased down the ladder into the upstairs hallway.

Suddenly their voices were much louder. He could smell bacon frying.

"How many times do I have to tell you…?"

"You're not telling me everything, Harry!"

Bert tiptoed to the stairs and crept down, although with the racket the Wainmans were making he could probably have run downstairs ringing a rusty cow bell from the barn and they wouldn't have noticed.

They were in the kitchen.

Which meant he could escape out the front door.

"…killed her…." he heard.

Killed her? What could they be talking about?

Instead of bolting for the outside he took a deep breath and inched along the corridor until he stood beside the kitchen doorway. From here he couldn't see the Wainmans any more than they could see him, but he knew the hulking farmer would be pacing around threatening while his wife stood her ground.

"So that's it. You finally come out with it. How can you think I killed her?" Harry shouted. "Why would I kill her?"

"You've got a violent streak in you, Harry."

"I have a violent streak? You should talk."

With a clatter, fragments of a cup skittered out into the hall, as if Wainman had kicked them. A small piece, decorated with a blue flower, spun around and came to rest against Bert's shoe.

"If she was murdered can't you find a better suspect than your own husband?" yelled Harry. "A tramp, a deserter, some pervert. But no, you point to me. What about that so-called professor? Who knows anything about him? Claims to be from America, studying those stones, in the middle of a war. Studying stones."

"Don't change the subject, Harry."

"You're looking for a murderer. Look at this stranger poking around stones with a war on. I caught him sneaking by with a map. A map! Think about that. Who is he? Might be a German spy, a trained killer. He found Issy's blood-stained dress. By chance, he claims. Why not suspect him? You know me, Louisa."

"Only too well. How about that pregnant girl who came knocking at the door last year? Looking for some man who gave her a false name."

"She visited every house in the village!"

"Did she? Maybe. With what's happened since…"

"Nothing's happened! I keep…"

"Don't deny you were seeing the little tart Issy Chapman! God, you make me sick…."

A second of silence before Bert heard her spit. He could smell bacon burning.

"There's no reasoning with you, is there? You've always been jealous, Louisa, busy imagining things. How many times do I have to repeat myself? You're soft in the head."

"You wish."

"If you think I could kill that girl because she threatened to tell about what you imagine was going on…if I could do that, why accuse me? I'd kill you too, wouldn't I?"

"Would you have the guts?"

"Damn you, Louisa! Am I a monster?"

"Maybe you didn't have the guts to kill the little slut. Maybe you meant to scare her into keeping her mouth shut and that temper of yours got the better of you."

Bert edged away from the door. A scuffling noise. Wainman bellowed a scream that froze Bert where he stood.

"Christ! You bitch! You bitch! That's hot grease….what are you doing? Christ, look at what you've done!"

"Don't ever touch me again, Harry Wainman."

"Damn you, I'll—"

"What? You'll what? Kill me? Like you killed the tart? Did she have a bread knife like this in her hand, Harry? You want to try and kill me?"

Was a chair knocked over? Thrown?

Bert tried to run but couldn't.

Harry Wainman, half his face fiery red, stomped into the hall and saw him.

Chapter Twenty

No one suspects you of Isobel's murder, Edwin assured himself. Except for Special Constable Green. And why not? Wasn't the person who reported a murder always a prime suspect?

He laid his notebook at the foot of the nearest Guardian Stone and took a tape measure from his trouser pocket. He sharpened his pencil and then paused, looking at his penknife as if it had magically appeared in his hand.

Good job Green only wanted to examine my passport and not my pockets, he thought, remembering the amount of blood on the clothing he had found in the forest.

"You shouldn't have touched that clothing," Green had told him. "Why did you do that?"

"At first I wasn't sure it was clothes." Clearly Green suspected Edwin had placed the bundle in the spot he claimed to have found it.

He had met Edwin in the High Street and asked for his passport.

Fortunately Edwin made a habit of carrying that document and produced it immediately.

"I see you traveled from Portugal earlier this year," Green said. He compared the photo of Edwin with the man standing beside him, a man who was grayer, whose face appeared far more gaunt. The passport photo might well have been taken in another life.

"A strange place by all accounts, Portugal," Green went on. "Neutral. Crawling with spies and Nazi agents."

"That may be so, but as far as I know I never met any," Edwin replied. "Coming by way of Portugal is the obvious way to get from America to England these days."

"Spies are a clever lot," Green persisted. "Disguise themselves as all sorts of people. Even Americans. A spy never looks like a spy."

Edwin a spy? The lifelong academic skulking about on some cloak and dagger mission? He would have laughed were the charge not so serious. He wasn't back home among friends.

He bit his lip. He had work to do and he would do it and leave as soon as possible, though he would be sorry to say goodbye to Grace and the vicar. He was sure Green was enjoying this confrontation. The youngster was smirking, although he probably didn't realize it. He wouldn't have looked out of place in an SS uniform.

"Since you insist on interrogating me, I retired several years back and I've come to England as a neutral Anglophile to offer my services in any way they would be useful. Right now I'm preparing a series of talks about ancient British monuments I've been asked to give by the BBC. I'm visiting the more remote rural areas first, and here I am."

"A plausible explanation, I suppose. But there's been talk in the village. Some go so far as to say there's no proof you are who you say you are. And you did show up the day after Isobel Chapman disappeared."

"Who exactly has been talking?"

Green handed the passport back without answering. "That seems authentic enough to me. Of course, they are superb forgers, the Nazis."

"Should I return to my lodgings and show you my nun's habit and parachute?" Edwin snapped. "Isn't that how all of us spies enter the country? Did you catch Mother Superior? His real name's Heinrich."

For a few seconds Green gaped at him and then laughed. "Pulling my leg, Professor?"

Edwin grinned. It was not a nice grin. "I'm going up to the Guardians now, Green. You can send the firing squad up there when it arrives."

Remembering the scene, he was sorry for displaying anger. Grace had mentioned her worry that villagers were drawing apart and keeping to themselves. Fingers were pointed, old scores aired. Edwin, an unknown quantity, was at the mercy of a woefully inexperienced special constable with a swollen ego.

Now, as he stooped over the ancient stones which had surely seen many strange events during the thousands of years they had occupied this place, Edwin's anger was soothed by the sun's warmth, birds calling to each other, a squirrel chattering not far off. There were tales that the stones were cursed, but he could not feel any evil presence in this sunny clearing, where foxgloves were blooming amidst scattered gorse. A light breeze cooled his face as he measured the height and girth of the lichened rocks, recording the results in his notebook. When people thought of standing stones, they pictured the enormous monoliths at Stonehenge. Most were much less impressive, more like the knee-high Guardians.

As he worked he recalled Martha's legend about the wise woman who tried to do good and was accused of evil. There was also the witch said to be responsible for the Rollright Stones story, according to that local legend. One day she'd seen an army camped out, led by a man seeking to depose the king, and predicted that if the treasonous leader saw Long Compton he would indeed ascend the throne. Fortunately for the royal head and British history, the witch, being loyal, turned the traitor and his men to stone. Their leader stood to that day only a few paces from the brow of the hill above the village mentioned in the prophecy, and his men still sat in a circle close to him.

An interesting feature of this particular legend was a nearby cluster of five stones dubbed the Whispering Knights, supposedly standing with their heads together, plotting against their leader and turned to stone with the rest.

Edwin didn't know if there were any other groupings of stones outside the circle here in Noddweir but he would look.

It was said that nobody could count the true number of the Rollright Stones, though many had tried, employing exotic methods when pointing and counting failed to work. A baker put a loaf on each and could never get the same total, another man marked each stone with colored chalk and found a different color when he went round again. Nor could he get the same total twice running.

The Guardian Stones here might also be difficult to count, but only because many of them had fallen over or were hidden by brambles. Edwin began to sketch the stone he had just measured. If he were spotted, his sketching would add fuel to the blaze of speculation, although what military secrets might be hiding in this narrow, isolated valley he had no notion.

Well, he had discovered a secret. The shape of a heart was cut into the stone, so weathered as to be all but invisible. He could see a *J* and an *O*. John? Joe? The other name he couldn't make out at all. Just some grooves where letters had once been. He rubbed at the lichen partly covering the inscription. The stone had already absorbed hours of sunlight and felt warmer than the air. Some of the lichen powdered off, revealing no more detail.

Who had made that carving and when? It might have been centuries earlier. At any rate Joe or John and his unknown love were long parted by death. Had it been a childish romance? Most likely. Then again the two might have married, lived, and died in Noddweir. Their descendants might still be living here.

It might have been Grace's great-great—who knows how many greats?—grandparents professing their love. How long had her family lived in Noddweir?

Then again, the carving could have been much more recent, shallow and so quickly eroded. Perhaps the missing name was "Martha."

Edwin moved on to the next stone in the circle. Those who hated history mistakenly thought it was about dates. Dates of battles and treaties and endless other scratches by which people marked time. But, really, history was about people.

Measuring the height of the stone he crouched over, he noted crude scratches near its apex. Even after a close examination he was not certain what they were. Initials? Another pair of lovers? A mark left by a passing tramp?

Perhaps not.

The scratches looked new but dirty, where no dirt could have reached them, blending in with the pitted surface of the ancient rock.

Had someone sought to leave a message that would only be noticed by one who knew where to look?

"What do you think you're doing, Tom? Get your paws off me!"

Opening the front door Edwin was greeted by the sight of Grace shoving away the ham-like hand of Tom Green. The constable was bent slightly forward, about to bestow a squeeze and a peck on the cheek. When Grace pushed, he lost his balance and grabbed the arm of the settee for support.

"I only meant to—"

"I don't care what you meant. Keep your hands to yourself."

"Come on, Grace. We should get along, working as close as we do."

"I'll help you carry out your duties. God knows you need the help. But that's all."

Green stared at Grace like a loyal dog that can't believe it's been chided by its master. Grace kept her furious gaze on the constable, daring him to try anything. It was several seconds before they noticed Edwin observing them in embarrassed silence.

"Professor!" Grace said, startled.

Green glared at Edwin and squared his shoulders before striding out. Edwin moved quickly to one side to allow him to pass.

"You've come to my rescue again."

"I hope he wasn't getting too impertinent." Edwin closed the door.

"Nothing I couldn't handle, if necessary."

Her normally rosy cheeks bright red. To avoid staring at her as fixedly as Green had been, Edwin looked away.

Martha appeared from her room and gave a cackling laugh. "What's this Grace, kicking out one boyfriend for another?"

"Oh, Grandma! I'm not in any mood for your silly jokes! Did we interrupt your nap?"

"No. Not unless you were calling my name. Someone was calling me."

"You were dreaming."

Martha shuffled to the settee and plopped down. "Maybe I was dreaming. Doesn't mean someone wasn't calling me in my dream." She laid her head back against the crocheted antimacassar and closed her eyes.

Edwin followed Grace into the kitchen and set his notebook on the table beside a lined sheet of paper, torn from a school exercise book. Writing covered part of it.

"The constable and I started setting down what we'd learned so far about the missing children," Grace explained.

"What have you learned?"

"We didn't get far. He was more interested in investigating me than the disappearances."

Edwin pulled the paper over to see a list of names.

"That young constable is rapidly outgrowing his britches." He told Grace how Green had stopped him in the street, wanting identification.

"The nerve!"

"It wouldn't be so bad if he knew what he was doing, but I get the feeling he's in over his head, playacting for effect, and doing a poor job of it. It's too bad your father isn't here."

"Some might say so."

"He was experienced in law enforcement, unlike Green."

"We never had anything like these disappearances before. Oh, country kids run off to the city all the time, but not so many at once."

"I'm sure your father would have been in touch with the authorities in Craven Arms by now."

Grace took a loaf from the bread bin. "Try some bread and gooseberry jam. Emily brought it over. It's barely cool."

"That was thoughtful of her," Edwin remarked as Grace sliced the bread and put it on plates.

"It was an excuse to badger me about how I ought to be doing more to find those beasts who killed her dog." Grace's knife rattled around the rim of the jar and she slapped jam onto the bread as if the slices offended her. She brought the plates to the table and sat opposite Edwin.

Edwin nibbled the bread and jam and his lips puckered. "Rather tart."

"Susannah made it. What would you expect?"

Edwin chuckled. "I'll bet she was a tartar in the classroom."

Grace allowed herself a tight-lipped smile. The bread vanished into her generous mouth in four or five huge bites. She wiped her lips with the back of her hand, leaving a crumb at the corner of her mouth.

"It's none of my business," Edwin went on, "but don't you think it's time outside authorities were brought in?"

"Well, at least you know it's none of your business, Professor Carpenter."

"Sorry."

Grace put her elbows on the table and leaned forward. Edwin had a sudden urge to wipe the crumb from her lip but refrained. Was he staring again? Her tongue flicked out and removed the crumb.

"Maybe you don't understand how country people are," she said. "We take care of our own. We don't like outsiders meddling. People like Tom Green."

"Or myself?"

"You're not meddling though, are you?"

"Hardly."

"I'm glad to hear it. Now look, Professor. Country kids get bored and leave the villages where they were born, even in peacetime. How many of these evacuees scattered all over England must be running away from unfamiliar places they don't much care for? We don't have enough police as it is and have to depend on the likes of Tom Green. There are more runaways than police. Besides, what could the authorities do that we can't? They don't know the forest around here like we do. What kind of a search could they make, even if they were willing?"

"If it were only a matter of runaways..."

"It is right now."

"But Isobel's blood-stained clothes..."

"Prove nothing. Where's the body? How did the clothes get there? Why would the culprit leave them where they were sure to be found? In fact, we don't even know they belong to the girl."

Edwin finished his bread, looked for a napkin, and seeing none licked his lips. "But surely...."

"Surely nothing! We asked that fool of a father to identify the clothes. He said they were Issy's but what else would he say, the state he's in? Do you think he ever noticed what she wore? I went through what few clothes were in her room to check their sizes to see if they matched, but they were all different sizes." Grace shook her head crossly and continued. "The war again. We all wear clothes that are threadbare or second-hand, whatever we can manage. You can darn a lot of socks with an unraveled sweater, or even knit a sort-of new one. It's hard to get by, but that's what we do. In fact, part of the work I'm doing with the WVS—that's the Women's Voluntary Service—is running clothing exchanges in town." Grace swept their empty plates off the table and dumped them into the sink.

"But who else could those clothes I found belong to?" Edwin asked.

"That's not our problem, is it? I'm sure none of the boys that vanished were wearing them."

"You're right," Edwin conceded. "I'm sorry, Grace, you know your job better than I do."

He felt her hand briefly on his shoulder, her touch as light as one of the birds he'd heard singing in the forest.

"Never mind, Edwin. I know you mean well. It's almost time for Churchill's speech. Come over to the pub with me. I want to hear Churchill but I don't want more trouble from Tom Green."

Chapter Twenty-one

The prime minister might have been standing behind the bar of the Guardians pub so strongly did his voice ring out from the battery-powered Philco. His words echoed around a room that was only sparsely occupied. Susannah and Emily were there, as well as a group of farmers. Green lounged at a table in the back, scowling in Grace's direction. It was just as well Edwin accompanied her. He had served as chaperone during innumerable university field trips

He caught Green peering at Grace again and gave him his best "I've got my eye on you so don't try anything" look. Green dropped his gaze. Susannah and Emily, although seated side by side, might each have been alone, staring straight ahead. The farmers all craned their heads in the same direction. Everyone peered so raptly at the boxy wireless, it might have been a religious icon. Were they looking to Churchill to save them from the evil of Nazi Germany? Edwin couldn't grasp an evil that large. Yet, he clearly felt evil that was small in the scheme of things—the sort that cut a loved one down prematurely or stalked a child.

Polly, the woman Grace had described as a little slow, sat huddled in a corner muttering about evil forces and "Oh, there are malign powers abroad all right! Evil forces and the evil power of the Guardian Stones!"

"Quiet, Polly," Duncan said firmly. "Let's hear what Mr. Churchill has to say."

"Piffle," added Susannah. "The woman's touched in the head."

Grace rolled her eyes at Edwin, but Edwin wasn't so sure that what Polly said was a matter for eye-rolling. Standing stones were strange things. Older than history. No one knew why they had been placed here and there, but intelligent human beings had done so for what they considered good reasons.

Edwin heard whispering from the farmers. Were they sneaking glances at him or was he imagining things? He looked at Grace but she was staring past Duncan at the radio. Duncan, an elbow on the bar, was half-turned away from the room. Neither appeared to be paying any attention to the farmers. Emily and Susannah did not turn to look behind them.

When Churchill finished and the BBC announcer came on, Duncan turned the wireless off. The farmers got up and walked over to Edwin and Grace. He didn't take them in as individuals. There was no time. They were like the students rushing into his classroom on the first day. But rather than an undifferentiated group of callow youths these were big, weathered, rawboned men. A huge hand grabbed the front of Edwin's sweater and yanked him to his feet. "Harry Wainman said we ought to welcome you to Noddweir," the farmer told him. Grace jumped up but another farmer had already put himself between her and Edwin.

"What do you think you're doing?" Grace demanded.

They ignored her.

"Harry says you claim to be studying them rocks on the hill. In the middle of a war," said the man gripping Edwin's sweater. "He said we might want to show our appreciation for Americans who come over here to live in our houses and eat our food and draw pictures of rocks while this country's on its knees. You think we haven't been watching you?"

"You've been spying on me!" Edwin's outrage overrode his physical fear.

"Spying," one said. "Now there's a word for you!"

"Stop this immediately," Grace said.

Revolted, Edwin grabbed the stranger's hand grasping his sweater and tried to pry it off. The fist might as well have been made of stone.

The farmer laughed. "Uncomfortable, Mr. Big Professor? Imagine how we feel over here, left to fight Hitler by ourselves."

Edwin hadn't been in a physical fight since he was a child. If he had, he might have been more keenly aware he was no match for any of these men, let alone four of them. But his anger and humiliation overwhelmed his sense of self-preservation. He swung at the mocking face.

Blood exploded from his assailant's nose. Obviously, the fellow had been totally unprepared for a counterattack.

"Oh, you silly bugger," he heard Grace murmur as the farmers raised their fists. Suddenly they stopped and retreated, cursing, before vanishing out the door.

Duncan stood behind the bar with a rifle. "I wish you hadn't hit him, Professor." He lowered the weapon. "They knew very well I was going to bring this out before they had a chance to lay a finger on you. It was just for show."

Grace wiped fretfully at the blood spots spattered on her blouse. "You were a little slow stepping in, Duncan."

Edwin suddenly felt shaky, dropping into his chair. "Sorry. I haven't had time to catch on to all your local customs."

Grace looked around the room.

Edwin realized what she was seeing. Or not seeing. "I wondered why Constable Green didn't help. He must have left early."

Chapter Twenty-two

Special Constable Tom Green ambled down the path between the sides of the ugly old church with its vicarage and Susannah Radbone's cottage. The church was darker than the graveyard. The fading light of dusk glimmered on headstones above former residents of the village. Every one of them had probably been christened and married in the church and made a final visit to that same chilly building before having dirt piled on them.

Strange that most of Noddweir's residents had probably never set foot outside their own county, except for a prewar holiday in Blackpool. Tom reckoned if he'd been born here he would have run off the first chance he got.

Now of course the handful of the village's young men not in reserved occupations were serving overseas, in places unrevealed in brief letters home so no clues would be provided to the enemy if they captured a bag or two of letters. On the whole Green was happy enough to be in Noddweir, given the circumstances.

Thinking of the enemy reminded him of the American professor. A quick wash of anger heated his face as he paused halfway down the path, noting the Radbone cottage was already blacked out, its thatched roof stenciled against the remnants of the day.

Pity. He would have enjoyed bawling the old girl out. He'd already corrected a couple of villagers who were careless with their blackout curtains, despite it not being totally dark yet.

No good leaving important things to the last moment, was there?

Next time they'd be lucky to get off without a fine.

His thoughts returned to Edwin Carpenter. What right did a foreigner have to come over here and interfere in a bit of harmless flirting? So what if there was a wife and child waiting for Green to visit them in Liverpool?

Now he thought about it, Hilda was not particularly worried when he was appointed as a special constable. Where he was to serve annoyed her.

"Some poky little place where nothing happens except the cows get out and trample someone's cabbages," she had sniffed. "Forget that. I'm staying here with Mother. Besides, I've got real war work to do."

And welcome to it, Green thought. Thank God for the withered foot keeping him out of the forces. Though he walked with little trace of a limp, running was awkward and marching long distances well nigh impossible. Now the defect he hated had come to his rescue, taking him away from Hilda and his in-laws, not to mention the fretful baby.

He'd have gone daft if he'd had to listen much longer to it squawking all night.

Not to mention his in-laws quarreling with Hilda. Fact was, if they had not been bombed out they would not have moved in with her parents.

As for Hilda's war work, she liked driving ambulances. Gave her an excuse to get out the house.

Was she as glad to be shot of him as he was of her?

His thoughts returned to the professor. If only he hadn't shown up when he was attempting to cuddle Grace, she would have been obliging. Of course, she'd pretended to be offended, just like all of them, but really she was interested in him. Overdid the dislike act, in his opinion. These country girls were not as subtle in their ways as those in town, going by experience.

Besides, the blackout offered new opportunities in that line.

He paused beside the churchyard to rest his foot.

The evening air carried the grating sound of children's voices quarrelling. From the vicarage, no doubt. The vicar had allowed himself to be burdened with a whole gang of brats.

He shuddered.

Nasty things to have underfoot, children.

Green turned away to retrace his steps when a loud shout from the darkening forest attracted his attention.

Jack Chapman appeared from its depths, coming toward him, unfortunately.

"Constable!" Chapman shouted.

"What's the matter?" Even in the dim light he could see the man was terrified. He must have been, if he would accost Green for help.

"Seen it…up there by the stones…horrible, it were….not natural…" Chapman gasped.

"You saw something?"

"Said so, didn't I? Weren't human…a white thing…"

"Calm down and tell me what happened," Green ordered.

"You stupid bugger! I'm trying to tell you! Stop interrupting!"

Green clamped his hand on Chapman's arm and shook it. "Get on with it then, you fool!"

Chapman recovered his breath. "It were like this, Tom. I been working on one of Wainman's machines and since it's getting dark I took a shortcut back through the forest—"

"Yes?"

"Just listen, will you?" Chapman said. "I was going along the path past the Guardians when I heard what sounded like singing."

"Singing?"

"Just said so, didn't I?"

"What kind of singing?"

"Can't say. Strange singing. Like church hymns, but it wasn't. Point is, I looked up and I seen a figure that weren't…well, it weren't quite right, you know? A white figure. Like a ghost."

"Is that why you carry that rifle, to protect yourself from ghosts?"

Chapman glanced down at the weapon. "Oh, no, not ghosts. You never know who you'll meet."

"Poaching, was it?"

"No," Chapman snapped. "You have to be prepared for anything these days! Spies, for instance."

"Well, you better get home then and meet your dinner, hadn't you? I'll go up and look around."

Night had already claimed the forest as Green climbed up the path from the village.

Chapman was an idiot. He'd obviously been poaching. Next time he'd not let him off. Still, Chapman owed him a favor now, which would likely be useful.

Rustlings in the undergrowth sounded strangely loud under the vast bowl of a starry sky glimpsed here and there through the overreaching limbs.

Green was uneasy. This wasn't Liverpool where the night was never as quiet as it was out here in the back of beyond. After a while the sound of traffic and the noise from docks and factories, all hard at work in the war effort, blended into the background, hardly to be noticed.

Here the quiet kept him awake.

He did not like the forest—too wild, too mysterious. Give him paved streets and raucous singing as the pubs turned out, foghorns hooting mournfully in the mist, hammering and crashing and shouts of men at work on the river, even air raid sirens. Not the smothered rustling of this mysterious dark place.

Walking along the narrow path, hemmed in by solid walls of shadowy vegetation, felt like walking into a dark alley.

And walking into dark alleys was dangerous.

Now stop that, he chastised himself as he stepped with relief into the open space surrounded by the Guardians. You're as big a fool as Chapman, listening to the ravings of a drunk like him.

Nothing different here, is there?

No?

Right.

Back to blackout patrol.

Green escaped thankfully down the path to the village.

Chapter Twenty-three

The sound of a door closing woke Edwin. Or so he decided when he tried to pinpoint what had interrupted his sleep. It was the middle of the night. His bedroom was pitch black. His heart pounded as if he'd had a nightmare.

Had someone gone out or come in? Front door or back? Was it someone who had a right to be in the house?

Or had he only dreamt the sound?

No, he was sure he had heard something. He sat up in bed and listened for noises from downstairs—footsteps, voices. He heard only the ringing in his ears.

There was nothing suspicious about a door closing at night, he told himself. Besides, this wasn't his house. Grace, or Martha for that matter, could come or go as they pleased. Still, with everything that had been happening…

He'd best go and see.

He wished he had a proper weapon, although the bedroom fireplace poker would do. He'd never had any use for guns. In Rochester he kept a baseball bat under the bed. Where the bat had come from, he couldn't remember. He'd had about as much interest in baseball as in firearms.

Unfortunately, the bat was still in upstate New York.

Groping in the dark, he found his dressing gown at the foot of the bed, pulled it on, padded to the bedroom door, and quietly opened it a crack.

A pale glow from downstairs partially illuminated the hallway. It was unlikely an intruder would have lit a lamp.

Edwin went slowly downstairs, holding his breath. Grace, fully dressed, sat in the armchair by the fireplace. The clock on the mantelpiece showed ten minutes to midnight. Not as late as he'd imagined.

Edwin drew his dressing gown closer around him.

"Oh, Edwin there you are. Can't sleep?"

"No, I…er…was on the way out back…" Edwin lied.

"Hold on a moment." Grace blew out the lamp. "We don't want Green coming round telling us to put that light out at this time of night, do we?"

Edwin gave a feeble smile, unseen in the darkness, and fumbled down the hallway to the back door, returning a few moments later having indeed found need to use the facilities.

"You can put the light on again." He popped his head into the room where Grace sat.

"Yes. Come in a moment, would you?"

Edwin fumbled his way to a chair and sat down.

Grace made no move to re-light the lamp. "I've been sitting here for a while. I keep thinking about those missing kids," she said. "Where in God's name could they be? I've prayed for them. I suppose we all have."

Edwin hadn't, but he didn't say so. He couldn't see Grace in the darkness, yet she was more than a disembodied voice. He could feel her presence, could hear the faint creak of the armchair as she moved, could smell a hint of…what? Perfume, powder?

"You might as well pray as depend on Green," he said. "He's a fool. A dangerous fool. I wouldn't be surprised to be arrested one of these days."

"You don't believe in prayer then?"

"Well…I have nothing against it."

"I like to think that there is a reason for everything that happens. That, however terrible, in some mysterious way, everything is God's will. It makes things more bearable, don't you think?"

"What does it mean? Bearable? I suppose we have no choice but to bear things, bearable or not." It hadn't occurred to Edwin that Grace might be a religious person, but then why not? And what possible difference could it make to him?

She must have sensed his nervousness. "Don't worry, Professor. I wouldn't have taken you for a religious man. People who think with their heads rather than their hearts don't tend to be religious."

"I always thought of you as a hard-headed young lady."

"Always? You've been here less than a week."

"Oh…well…it seems longer, what with everything…"

"You should talk to your friend the vicar. He's an intellectual himself, but it doesn't stop him from praying for the children."

The subject of religion had never come in Edwin's correspondence with Wilson. "I would like to believe there is something… more…something beyond all this…something better than this world," Edwin offered.

"It can be hard to accept that what goes on here is part of God's plan. The wars, the horrible things that happen to ordinary people for no reason we can understand."

"Yes, that's true."

He felt a touch, light as fluttering wing, as Grace bent forward and patted his knee. "I'm sorry. I made you think of your wife, didn't I?"

"Don't worry about it. I think of Elise all the time."

"I hope she wasn't ill for long."

"No. It wasn't illness. It was one of those stupid things." He nervously pushed his glasses up his nose even though the room was dark. The intimacy he felt from their sitting alone in the darkness and quiet had loosened his tongue. "It could have been prevented so easily," he went on. "We'd gone to New York to see a new musical. Elise loved musicals." He did not mention he did not particularly like them and had been reluctant to take the journey from Rochester to New York.

"We saw *Cabin in the Sky.* We'd come out of the theater and I heard someone shouting. Looked back to see what was happening and just at that instant Elise walked out into the street between two cars. It was a taxicab. Killed her instantly."

"How terrible, Edwin."

"It could have been avoided so easily. If I'd kept my hand on her arm, or walked in front of her. If I hadn't looked round. If I'd reacted more quickly, I could have saved her."

"All ifs are followed by buts. It was an accident. There was nothing you could have done about it."

"But that's not true."

"You mustn't blame yourself. I'm sure Elise wouldn't want you to do that." After a pause during which the ticking of the clock sounded louder than usual, she continued, "I'm going for a walk. It may help me sleep."

Edwin offered to accompany her if she would wait a few moments while he dressed.

"I'll be safe enough," came the reply. "I'm not going far and I've got a police whistle if I need help. You sound tired. Don't wait up for me."

Chapter Twenty-four

The village pub was dark inside by the time Tom Green finished his patrol.

He let himself in the back door and, flicking on his torch, went up the steep stairs to the room he was renting. The treads squeaked in the oppressive silence. He could hear his own labored breathing. He noted with some satisfaction that his foot ached. No, it would be impossible for him to serve in the forces, despite what anyone might say.

He could see a thin line of light beneath Violet's door. Was she afraid to sleep in the dark? He couldn't blame her. It wasn't safe for little girls right now in Noddweir.

Staccato snores emanated from the Gowdys' bedroom. Lying in his room at night, Green speculated on whether it was Duncan or Meg who snored. It sounded coarse, more like a man than a woman, but could he really tell a man's snores from a woman's?

Redheads attracted Green. Was it Meg who snored? Unfortunately her affections were accounted for and he knew enough not to play with women someone else had already bagged. Especially when he wanted to stay on the good side of that someone else.

As he stepped into his room he saw a pale rectangle lying on the floor by the door.

A piece of writing paper. When he picked it up he smelled faint perfume.

He shone his light on the paper. The handwriting on it looked feminine, every letter sprouting exotic blooms of loops.

"Meet me at the Guardian Stones after midnight," the note said.

There was no signature.

Green's mouth curved into a wide, smug smile. "Ha!" he said to himself. "Ha! You can't fool Tom Green. I knew you fancied me."

He closed his eyes, put the note to his nose, and inhaled the perfume.

Then he went back out. He had forgotten all about red hair. Grace's glossy, thick dark hair struck him as infinitely more desirable. He imagined himself pressing his lips to her rosy cheeks, running a hand along her wide hips.

He sensed she was about to admit her attraction to him when that ancient, meddling lodger of hers had interfered. He should have given the old man a thrashing. What business was it of his what Tom and Grace did?

The path through the forest to the stone circle did not feel as foreboding as it had when he'd reluctantly taken it earlier to check Jack Chapman's incoherent report. Nevertheless he purposely tramped along, snapped off twigs that got in his way, muttered to himself, creating a tiny pocket of comforting noise in the enormous silence.

Just as he reached the place where the path began to climb steeply enough for him to feel it in his withered foot a weird sound stopped him cold.

He wasn't sure what it was, but the sound had penetrated through the noise he was making.

He stood frozen. His stomach seemed to turn inside out.

The sound came again. A sobbing, almost human but not quite, hollow as an echo.

"Bloody hell!"

Again the eerie call filled the dark forest. There was nothing to see except amorphous black shapes of vegetation against the slightly lighter sky that showed through in isolated spots.

"Whooo...whoooo..."

An owl, he realized.

Owls were creatures that for him existed only in books, like elves and fairies. Of course, he knew owls were real enough but he had never expected to hear one.

He took a deep breath, belched—which seemed to put his stomach right side out again—and continued on.

He concentrated on what awaited him at the top of the hill. Grace. And how much of Grace? A girl didn't invite a man to meet her in the middle of a forest in the middle of the night for a peck on the cheek, did she?

The path bent around a limestone outcrop, pale in the blackness. For a moment, from the angle of the turn, he could see a flickering light at the top of the hill.

"Already there and waiting for me, are you? Done playing hard to get, then, and as ready as I am!"

He pushed upwards more rapidly, even though it made his foot tingle as if it were going to sleep. But when he emerged from the wall of vegetation surrounding the crown of the hill, the light had vanished.

A low hanging moon spilled an icy radiance across the stones. Had it been moonlight he'd seen?

No, the light he glimpsed had been warmer, more orange.

He straightened his shoulders and strode across the clearing to the stone circle, taking care not to stumble.

He didn't see her.

Was she hiding behind one of the stones?

Not likely unless she had decided to lie down for him already.

None of the stubby rocks looked big enough to hide a fully grown woman. He'd seen more impressive rubble in bomb craters.

Stupid superstitious country bumpkins. What did they find frightening about a bunch of little rocks? They ought to see some of the sights he had in Liverpool. And who said anyone had put them there? Some professor somewhere. Was it so surprising rocks had ended up in a circle by chance? That was the trouble with them who were overeducated. They thought too much about the wrong things.

Look at the geezer staying with Grace, he told himself. Twisting his brain in knots fretting about stones in the forest. If I was living under the same roof with Grace, rocks would be the last thing I'd be thinking about. Not that Grace wouldn't laugh in the old man's face if he were to have a go at her, but if it were me, I'd chance it.

Green walked into the circle and felt foxgloves nudging his legs.

He didn't see Grace, but the light had told him she was nearby.

"Come on out, Grace," he called. "Don't be playing silly buggers with me."

There was no reply.

Silence closed in around him.

Glancing around, he saw scratches on the stone nearest him. Clearly illuminated by the moonlight, what the strange symbols meant he couldn't say. He ran his fingers over them. They weren't deep and looked fresh. Were they some of those signs left by tramps that only they could read? A message saying something like "easy pickings in the village"? More likely it was the work of an idle kid messing about up here.

Green stood up. "I know you're having me on, Grace. Come on out!"

He heard a soft rustle behind him. His lips curved into a wide smile as he turned.

"Grace?"

The circled stones stand stark and silent in the dead white moonlight. Like the moon they are only partly illuminated, their shadowed sides, where the light does not reach, sketched in by the eye, but actually invisible, merely imagined.

It is possible to imagine taller stones, more upright, less weathered.

Someone or something leaves the stones. From a distance it is only a moving shadow, flickering into and out of existence, as it is obscured and then reappears in ragged gaps in the black tangled brambles.

Something has happened here.

Something abhorrent?

Or something perfectly right?
It might well be Grace leaving the circle.
Or anyone.
Its passage is indicated merely by a shadow.

Chapter Twenty-five

Tuesday, June 17, 1941

Grace was making fried bread when Edwin came down to breakfast. He looked dubiously at the slices sizzling in the grease when she asked him if he would like an egg with them.

When in Noddweir, he thought, and accepted both.

To his surprise he enjoyed the crisp browned bread.

"You're not having any, Grace?"

"Not too hungry."

"You look tired." In fact, she looked as if she'd been up all night. Purple smudges underlined her eyes. She looked ten years older, but, even so, more than young enough to be his daughter.

Edwin hadn't slept. He had been forced against his will to relive the moment of Elise's death outside the theater. Or so it had seemed as he tried vainly to suppress the memory that replayed in his mind again and again. But what would force him to view that scene that he wished never to recall? His conscience? A malign power that stalked the world? No, it was nothing more than the result of stirring up memories by confiding in Grace.

He would have welcomed a visitation from Elise's ghost. Of course he didn't believe ghosts any more than he believed in God, but then ghosts were not God. They did not require one to believe in them, did they? Her ghost could have reassured him. Would have reassured him by its very presence. If only he might have heard her voice, or deluded himself that he had heard her. Instead he realized that their happiness had not simply been cut short in that instant, but that every minute of their happiness had been stolen because now each bit of recalled joy led to the same horrific ending.

The hellish night was his deserved punishment for blurting out his innermost thoughts to a near-stranger. Be honest, Edwin chided himself, wasn't it because Grace was an attractive young woman? He had always admired British reserve. They weren't as eager as Americans to serve up steaming platters of their private angst for anyone who cared to partake. What had she made of his babbling?

He felt uneasy, almost shy, around Grace this morning. They had, in a way, been too intimate the night before.

"You haven't heard a word I've said, have you?" he heard Grace say.

She carefully poured fat from the frying pan into a blue-and-white striped bowl. "I must look a fright," she continued. "I'm worn out because I walked too far, thinking about what might have happened to the children, and what might happen next."

"Was that wise?"

"I walked miles but I didn't go far away. I just went up and down the streets."

"It's as well no one spotted you. They might have been suspicious."

Grace suppressed a yawn and Edwin had to suppress a yawn in return.

"It's cloudy now, but it'll warm up later," Grace said. "Are you off to the stones again?"

"Yes. I've been doing some sketching and measuring."

"What do you hope to find out?"

"I have no idea. Which is part of what makes the work so interesting. Maybe I'll end up learning nothing. If not, I will have at least documented the Noddweir stones. There isn't much information available about them."

"They aren't exactly as well-known as Stonehenge."

"No. In fact Reverend Wilson told me they were more or less ignored until recently, buried in brambles. He thinks the crown of the hill might only have been cleared during the last century."

"Grandma wouldn't agree with that. She insists they've lorded it over Noddweir for eons so could hardly have been ignored. She'll say don't bother taking notes, go and wait in the middle of the circle for long enough and they'll start to talk to you."

"Do you think so?"

"That's what she told me when I was younger, and it's what she told Isobel when she used to visit, as well as Polly. Poor Polly took it all to heart. "

"What about Isobel?"

"She was fascinated because she liked to hear stories she could use to scare the other kids."

Edwin smiled. The night horrors receded. "Aleister Crowley would certainly be proud to hear about esoteric knowledge employed in the creation of mischief."

"Aleister who?"

Edwin waved his hand. "Never mind. Not someone you'd care to know. I'll fetch my notebook and be off. I hope I don't find our special constable bothering you when I get back this time."

Grace narrowed her eyes. "I'm happy to say Green's not shown up this morning. His absence is always a good start to the day."

Edwin mopped up his yolk with the last of his fried bread. The action reminded him of seeing Joe Haywood being served egg and bacon by Meg Gowdy at the pub.

Recalling that, he mentioned not seeing Haywood since.

"He's not gone missing, more's the pity." Grace took Edwin's plate to the sink. "He's not from Noddweir. Deals on the black market and there's talk some of the kids help him. The Finch brothers, for example. You know, delivering stuff here and there to Haywood's customers."

"Does Green know?" Edwin asked.

"Of course he does. But he has to catch him at it, doesn't he? If he wants to, that is. If he did catch him, he wouldn't be very popular, seeing as quite a few round here deal with Haywood.

A bit of extra tea or half a pound of sugar. Supposing Haywood was arrested? Then where would they get their little luxuries?"

"I suppose he's under suspicion like me?" Edwin asked. "Not being a native and all."

"Well…" Grace paused, tea towel in hand. "Nobody knows much about him or his comings and goings, or if they do they stay quiet. But that doesn't make him a murderer."

"Then again, these disappearances might be the work of someone who visits the area to deal with him. Criminals associate with other criminals, and if it were one of Haywood's associates that might make him an accessory."

Grace looked pensive. "Yes, it would. But would even a black marketeer keep silent where children in danger are involved?"

It was strange how the mind worked. All night long Edwin had been tormented by the memory of Elise's death. Had wished, irrationally, that she would speak to him, and now in the day-lit kitchen, she did speak. He knew it was merely a memory. But he heard her distinctly, as she railed against the parents who should never have had children, parents to whom a night out or the next bottle of liquor was more important than their own offspring. Parents who couldn't care less whether their children lived or died.

He could not associate the tirade with any particular child she had brought home for a clean-up, a lecture, and a new pair of shoes. They all blurred together, dirty unformed little faces, wild hair, deplorable clothing. How would Elise feel about what was going on in Noddweir?

Or what was not going on so far as getting to the bottom of things?

"Do you think Green and Haywood might be working together?"

"What would make you think that?"

"You're not sure our intrepid young constable really wants to catch himself a black marketeer, are you?"

Grace wiped her hands on the tea towel "Who knows what Green wants? Except…well…"

"Is it possible Green might not have made any effort to check up on Haywood?"

"Possibly. I simply assumed he had."

"I understand Haywood rents a house from the Wainmans." Edwin hesitated for a moment before continuing. "Do you think it would be useful if we took a look at the place?"

Chapter Twenty-six

Joe Haywood did not answer Grace's knock.

The front door was locked. The back door, sagging on its hinges, its lock long gone, was secured from the inside by a chain.

Grace stepped back and scanned the house. "I remember when old Jasper lived here," she told Edwin. "Louisa Wainman's father. Even then he'd been too old to work the farm for years. He left all that to Harry Wainman."

The crumbling walls might have been held together by the ivy growing on them. The roof, sunken in spots, was green with moss. To Edwin, the structure looked as if it might have been only slightly predated by the Guardian Stones. "His name was Jasper?"

"Oh, that's what we called him because he yelled at anyone who came within sight of the place. One of us kids read about a villain named Jasper and the name stuck."

"There are a lot of Jaspers in the world." Edwin wondered who Grace's childhood friends had been. He hadn't seen many women her age in Noddweir. Most of the men were off to war. A lot of young people, both women and men, didn't wait for a war to leave an isolated village.

Grace went to the nearest window and pressed her face to the glass. Edwin waited, standing thigh-deep in the weeds that ran right up to the house. Unseen insects whirred and ratcheted. Pieces of abandoned, rusted farm equipment stuck up from the weeds, the bones of mechanical dinosaurs. Where the tall grass ended, impassable brambles began. Behind the brambles lay the forest, a painted backdrop, without shadow or depth on this humid, cloudy day.

"The glass is filthy," Grace said. "I don't think it's been cleaned since he lived here."

Edwin forded the grass to the window next to the one where Grace stood. He gingerly cleared away a gray lace of decayed spider webs and bent his head forward until his thick eyeglasses clicked against the window pane.

This window was not entirely opaqued by dirt. In the muted light of the interior he saw a room half-filled with crates and cardboard boxes. A tarpaulin was thrown over something in one corner and several canvases were wrapped around mysterious bundles.

Grace's hair brushed his cheek and he felt her face beside his as she moved over to peer inside.

"The Wainmans might be using the place for storage," she offered.

"I don't see any dust on those boxes."

"You're right."

"Do you think there might be a cellar door we could try?"

"Maybe. I don't know." She clapped her hand to Edwin's shoulder. "Let's get back to the village. It's ridiculous, but I feel like Jasper is going to burst out of the house and start shouting at us."

She must have been subconsciously aware of footsteps behind them, Edwin later realized, because when they turned from the window, Joe Haywood stood twenty feet away, pointing a service revolver at them. "What do you two think you're doing?"

Edwin thought it odd a conscientious objector would be armed, but if Haywood intended to frighten Grace he hadn't succeeded. "In case you haven't been paying attention, there are very troubling things happening around Noddweir lately," she snapped. "We're checking all the houses. Now, if you will kindly let us in so—"

"You aren't anything to do with the police. Not officially. If you have suspicions, go tell Constable Green." He wagged the revolver theatrically and gave Grace a wide, toothy, and thoroughly unpleasant smile. "Now clear off my property."

"I'm sure your landlord would be happy to let us in," Grace told him.

"Fine. Go ask Wainman's permission, then, and see where it gets you."

Grace walked away around the side of the house and Edwin went after her, reluctantly exposing his back to Haywood's gun. He wasn't happy with the way weapons were suddenly popping into sight in Noddweir.

They went along a wide dirt track between a hedgerow and a fenced field.

Grace scowled down at the dusty path. "Maybe you're right, Edwin. Haywood may be storing merchandise. A lorry could probably navigate the edges of the fields, coming in from the road down further, without alerting anyone by driving through the village."

"A military vehicle would have no problem," Edwin said. Then added, "He can't be doing that much business in Noddweir. Maybe the house is his central storage point. It's isolated enough. The whole place could be filled with black market goods."

"You'd think the Wainmans would know what was going on. I'm going to take up his invitation to talk to them."

Indeed, Edwin thought. They should have some idea what their property was being used for, even if it was well hidden from their farmhouse by fields and hedgerows. They walked through a yard littered with pieces of machinery. A tractor missing a wheel sat beside a ramshackle barn.

Grace rapped at the Wainmans' door for so long Edwin was sure that it wouldn't be answered. Finally a latch clicked and there stood the plain woman Edwin recalled from the meeting at the pub. She'd been vociferously accusing Jack Chapman of maltreating his daughter, Issy. Today, Louisa Wainman was subdued, pale as a ghost, except for bloodshot eyes.

"Yes? What do you want?" Her voice cracked. She sounded on the verge of hysteria.

Grace said, "We only want to talk to you and Harry for a minute, Louisa. Is something the matter?"

She shook her head too vehemently. "No. No. I'm just a bit poorly today. Come in, please."

Harry Wainman sat at the kitchen table. He nodded silently at Grace. His glare was not welcoming. The left side of his face looked as red as if it had been grilled.

"Harry," Louisa said, "Grace wants to talk to us."

"About what?" Harry growled. He made no effort to get up but rather set his elbow on the table and propped his head up in his palm, a maneuver that failed to cover the reddened area completely.

"Your tenant," Grace said.

"What tenant?" Wainman replied.

"Joe Haywood. He's renting old…that is…Louisa's father's old place."

"He ain't."

"But I understood—"

"He ain't," Harry repeated.

"He bought it off us," Louisa put in. Harry shot her a furious look. "Well, he did."

No wonder Haywood had so blithely invited them to talk to Wainman, Edwin thought.

"I'm surprised," Grace said. "Mr. Haywood must be well off. I wonder where he came by—"

"Ain't none of my business," said Harry. "Nor any of yours."

"Sorry we bothered you," Grace told him. "We've been checking houses, looking into the children who've gone missing."

"Looking 'into' or 'for'?" Harry's eyes narrowed. "Are you thinking them Finch boys run off no further than somewhere on the edge of one of my fields? Are you're looking for bodies?"

"Oh, Harry…" Louisa groaned.

"Maybe you expected to find a corpse in that rundown ruin of Haywood's?" Harry continued, ignoring her.

"I didn't expect anything in particular," Grace replied.

"I'm just happy to have it off my hands before it fell down."

"You would be," Louisa said coldly.

Harry turned his gaze toward her. "If your old man's shack has so much sentimental value to you, go and move in with Joe Haywood. He's a real toff, ain't he? Just the type women go for."

"At least he's an adult," Louisa replied.

Grace quickly broke in. "Louisa, how's Bert doing now he's back safe and sound with you?"

"Oh, he's—"

"Bert's fine," snarled Harry. "He's just fine. Now you can see my dear wife is under the weather, so if I could ask you to go and mind your own business and do it elsewhere while you're at it...."

Grace gave him a piercing look. "What happened to your face, Harry?"

"Like I said, mind your own business."

Edwin felt his face flush with anger but he bit his tongue. He didn't know these people and he didn't want to interfere with Grace's investigation, unofficial though it might be. He remained silent until he and Grace were on the road back the village, then he speculated about what was going on between the Wainmans.

"Harry Wainman's always been a surly sort, Edwin."

"Uncouth, I'd call it."

"He's a farmer. I don't suppose you see many farmers at your university."

"As a matter of fact, I've taught quite a few sons and daughters of farmers. Granted, the ones who go to college probably don't intend to return to the farm."

"Well, Harry Wainman is known as a man who isn't averse to bettering himself. People claim he only married Louisa to get at her father's land. They have a son, you know. Nobody mentions him. Particularly the Wainmans." Grace stopped and sat on a stone wall at the roadside, where the last living limbs of a wretched apple tree formed a patch of sparse shade.

"Overseas, is he?" Edwin sat beside her. He patted the sweat off his forehead. Despite clouds the thick air felt uncomfortably hot.

"He's been missing in action a while. Neither of them want to be reminded. Last person who brought it up, Harry went berserk and broke the fellow's arm."

That was a way to deal with grief that wouldn't have occurred to Edwin.

"All the talk about missing children must be difficult for them to hear."

Before Grace could respond there was the ching, ching of a bicycle bell and down the road came Duncan Gowdy pedaling steadily. As he rode past, he raised a hand in greeting.

Edwin saw a box tied to the back of the publican's bicycle.

It was resembled the boxes he and Grace had seen in the back of Joe Haywood's house.

Chapter Twenty-seven

Back on the High Street, Grace told Edwin she needed to sleep in before her evening patrol. Having been up most of the night, she was exhausted. Edwin felt restless. Rather than accompanying her back to the house, retrieving his notebook, and heading for the Guardian Stones, he strolled around the village. Walking always calmed him. He'd shed a lot of nervous anxiety on the paths of Rochester parks.

The day grew hotter. He felt he was being watched, even though no one else was abroad in the dusty street. He took refuge in Emily's shop. The shop's sign had been whitewashed, presumably to avoid giving away the village name to passing enemies. Even this small cluster of houses in the Shropshire countryside was suffering from distant events.

The door was open for ventilation. Emily sat behind the narrow counter in her front room, busily knitting something in khaki wool. Edwin was reminded of Madame Defarge who sat at the foot of the guillotine, knitting while heads rolled. It was an unkind thought, he realized.

"Ah, Professor. Come to pass the time of day or to buy something?"

Edwin glanced at the shelving on the wall behind her, which displayed more bare wood than goods and a couple of glass jars half-filled with sweets. One or two tins stood sentinel on each side of obviously handmade pull-along toys. The sight touched Edwin. Despite the state of the world, children still could have toys.

He thought of buying a small gift for Grace. "I don't suppose you have any chocolate?" he asked hopefully.

"No. It was taken the other night."

Two women outside the open door raised their voices.

"You left your kids at home alone? You should be arrested!" one said, folding her arms across an aproned chest. "'Course, with so many you probably lose count of them! However do you feed and watch over them with your man away?"

Angry at the insinuation the other retorted "If it weren't for that old witch's help, you'd have ten of your own to worry about. And as for feeding 'em, don't tell me you weren't making sheep's eyes at the butcher in Craven Arms last week! I was in the queue and we all saw how 'e gave you an extra bit of bacon!"

Eavesdropping made Edwin uncomfortable. The quarreling pair's shrill voices did not bother Emily, who kept knitting even as the women resorted to foul language. From sheer habit formed by decades of keeping discipline in the classroom, Edwin stepped into the doorway and admonished them. "Ladies....are you coming in? Please don't mind me."

"Oh, it's 'im," the woman in the apron sniffed. "No, I'm not coming in. As for 'er—" with a nod of a head covered in curlers "watch out she don't pinch anything, Emily."

She stalked off up the street. Emily looked up from counting stitches. "Want something?"

"Er, no, I was just passing by." The other walked quickly away.

"On the way to visit Haywood," Emily observed. "See that purse in her hand? There's nowhere else to spend money in the village except the pub, and it's not in that direction. Mind, she does tipple a fair bit. All them kids would drive anyone to drink."

Especially with the way children were vanishing, Edwin thought. Out loud he observed he had always imagined villages to be peaceful places.

"Everyone's nerves is on edge," came the reply. "What war hasn't done, these disappearances has. People are getting suspicious, falling out. You wouldn't believe it, but them two women have been friends since childhood. Look at the way they went on just now." Emily shook her head over busily clicking needles.

"I saw Haywood this morning," Edwin remarked. "Bit of a mystery, I gather?"

"I can't say, since I always avoid him. You might want to ask Meg Gowdy." The suggestion was offered with a slight, grim smile.

Never one for gossip, Edwin tried to make a graceful exit when she continued with an abrupt change of subject. "Susannah is awfully upset about Reggie going missing. Keeps asking Green what he's doing to find those kids. She'd been thinking about trying to adopt Reggie if his parents was willing. Wouldn't think of it to look at her, but she has a kind heart and the poor lad needs affection and a bit of care."

"Some teachers look on all children as their own."

"It just seems as if troubles never end. Speaking of which, got my own ideas on who burgled my shop. Green's useless! No idea where to even begin to look. I'm going to sleep downstairs for a while in case they try again. God knows there's little enough to steal, but some folk'll take anything not nailed down. I caught Issy at it a couple of times."

"Oh?" Edwin had tried to help find the girl, but unlike everyone else in the village, he didn't even know what she looked like.

"She wasn't what you'd call a beauty," Emily said in response to his query. "She's big for her age, rough in her ways. Not surprising given she was raised with no mother. Clever in a cunning way, always had a good story to tell when caught out. Bit of a tomboy, Issy was."

"Was?"

"Is, then. Slip of the tongue." More clicking of needles. Edwin waited patiently for further information.

"If she'd been mine, I'd have kept a closer eye on her," Emily went on. "Wouldn't have allowed her to spend so much time with Martha. Filled her up with rubbish about spells and herbal potions and such like. Mind, Martha makes a good cough mixture and gives it free to them as needs it, which is more than you can say for the stuff you get at the chemist."

"A wise woman, then," Edwin said.

"You might say that. But a nasty tongue. If you think that pair just now was bad, you should hear her when someone crosses her! I don't know how Grace puts up with it, even if she is her grandmother."

"Her mother's mother."

"That's right."

"And Grace's mother? Is she…um…?"

Emily gave a wave of her hand. "Mae? Went off long ago. Her and George Baxter never got on. No surprise. Married when they were practically kids and George is no prize. Martha was very angry. By running off Mae broke the chain of what you called wise women."

It struck Edwin that a mother who ran off and left her daughter with a father who was no good wasn't much of a prize either. Apparently Grace had not had the easiest childhood. No wonder she had little time for Martha's so-called persuasions.

Edwin bought a couple of postage stamps before leaving. Emily apologized for not having postcards of either the village or the stone circle. She thought that all American visitors wished to send dozens back home from every place they set foot. Edwin assured her that there was no one to whom he particularly wished to send a postcard.

Chapter Twenty-eight

Edwin hoped Emily didn't wonder why he was looking for chocolate. What had he been thinking? What would Grace have thought if he'd presented her with chocolate, like a schoolboy with a crush?

As he passed Jack Chapman's house he abruptly decided to speak to the man, notwithstanding his earlier unpleasant encounter. Isobel's father could tell him more about her than Emily could, if Jack could be persuaded to talk. The house fronted the High Street. The smithy sat behind. He went down the alley leading to the smithy. Yokes, rusted wheels, and axles littered the hard dirt yard. All the scene lacked to resemble the site of a multiple wagon collision was a dead horse or two lying against the smithy's brick wall.

The disarray inside the building was worse. A welter of work benches and crude wooden boxes overflowing with inexplicable, to Edwin, pieces of metal, hid the floor. Enough hammers, tongs, and other nasty-looking tools to equip an army were displayed on sooty walls. Jack himself sat on an anvil in the middle of the chaos. A long, heavy leather apron hung from his massive shoulders, but the forge was cold. He was drinking from a big metal mug. Cider, Edwin guessed.

Jack looked up bleary-eyed, then he spat on the floor. "What do you want with me?"

"Just a word."

"A word, eh? I'll be generous and give you two. Get out!"

For a moment Edwin regretted his snap decision. Jack was angry and sitting in the middle of dozens of potential weapons, not only the hammer he'd carried when Edwin ran into him before. "I want to help, Mr. Chapman."

Jack stared at him. "Help?" He looked genuinely puzzled.

"Yes. Help you. Help your daughter."

"Meddle, you mean."

"It strikes me that not enough effort is being made to find Isobel."

Suspicion hardened Jack's features. "Why should you care?"

"Why shouldn't I care? Why wouldn't anyone care?"

Jack set his mug down but made no effort to stand up. "It's Green put you up to this again, ain't it? Didn't find out what he wanted when he sent you to quiz me before. He thinks I killed her. Killed my own daughter!"

"He doesn't know I'm talking to you and he wouldn't be pleased. He doesn't seem to be doing much. It's almost as if he doesn't want to find out what's happened to her and the others." Edwin wasn't sure he should have voiced his doubts, but it got Jack's attention.

"Green don't want to know. You've got that right. What can I tell you I haven't told him?"

"I'm not sure. Do you have a photograph of Isobel?"

Jack's expression, which had softened, immediately twisted into that of a sneering gargoyle. "Now I see what you're up to. A pervert, are you?"

"Of course not. But everyone in the village is keeping an eye out for her while I don't even know what she looks like."

Jack grunted. Whether it signified that he accepted the explanation or considered it a transparent lie, Edwin couldn't tell. "Ain't got a picture of her. She weren't nothing to look at. Not that there weren't them that looked at her. Big for her age, you know."

"Would anyone have wanted to harm her or take advantage of her?"

"If anyone had tried I'd have killed him. She was just a child. She was a good girl. She arranged flowers at the church every week."

Edwin remembered Jack originally described Isobel as a bad girl who would have benefited from a beating. She'd killed her mother in childbirth, he had said. Was he a clumsy liar, trying to act the part of the loving father? Did he want to persuade people he hadn't hated his daughter because he actually had killed her, by accident or not? Or because he was afraid that's what people suspected him of doing, and what that might lead to?

Jack wiped tears off his cheeks with a meaty hand.

Perhaps he wasn't being devious. If the blacksmith attributed his wife's death to Isobel's birth, couldn't he love and hate his daughter at the same time? How would anyone handle that?

"Was Isobel acting differently than usual before she vanished?" Edwin ventured. "Were there any signs that she might run away?"

"If you mean did I give her a beating…"

"That's not what I mean. I know that's what people say. That's why I wanted to talk to you, to find out what you had to say yourself."

Jack shrugged. "I didn't notice anything different."

"Did she spend time with any of the others who are missing? Reggie Cox or the Finch boys?"

"She ran around with them Finch boys. She thought I didn't know. Issy wasn't the type to play with dolls. Looking for trouble with those boys suited her."

"Trouble?"

"Not real trouble. Smoking a fag on the sly, stealing sweets from Emily's shop. You know." The look Jack gave Edwin suggested the blacksmith thought that a retired professor probably did not know—had never known—what normal kids got up to when out of sight of their parents.

"And Reggie? I don't suppose he would have been much a playmate, being crippled."

"You really have no idea about Issy, do you? She visited Reggie every day, helped him out. She felt sorry for the poor lad. See, she was a good girl at heart—I mean she is a good girl." He lowered his head into his hands and sobbed. Edwin could see the man's pink scalp through his sparse, thinning hair.

He'd been a fool to think he could get anything useful out of Jack Chapman.

Jack suddenly straightened up. "I done my best by my daughter," he said. "You tell Green that, Professor. It's the father's job to see that a child gets discipline. I ain't her mother. I still see her mother. It's like she's no further away than you are right now. She tells me, Jack, you have to teach Isobel right from wrong, like a father's supposed to do. But you got to give her a mother's love too. And how does a man do that, Professor? After what she done to my wife? And that after how much Lilly wanted kids. All she wanted was kids of her own. Not hardly a lot to want out from the world, and she couldn't even have that."

"I'm sure you've raised Isobel as well as you could have. I'll insist Green investigate further. She's probably with the Finch boys. Three are easier found than one and I'm sure they'll be found soon." Edwin could almost convince himself. Could he convince himself that the blood-stained clothes were merely a ruse?

Almost.

"The Finch boys!" Jack shook his head and laughed. "Everyone's always worrying about them. You'd think they was each one half of the devil himself. I wish she'd spent all her time with them and never visited Martha Roper. If you're looking for a bad influence, look at that old bag, filling a girl's head up with all kinds of crazy ideas."

"What do you mean?"

Jack laughed again. "I don't know exactly and I don't want to know either. But whenever she came back after a visit to her she was awful restless. I reckon Martha put the idea of running away into her head."

Chapter Twenty-nine

Meg Gowdy's complaints greeted Edwin as he entered Grace's house. He recognized the grating tones of the publican's plump redheaded wife before he saw her seated with Martha at the kitchen table. Martha rubbed Meg's hand with a piece of bacon.

Was this a strange rural rite? It struck him as a waste of good bacon considering the difficulty in getting sufficient for a decent breakfast. Edwin's expression must have betrayed his thoughts.

"Get your notebook, Professor," Martha cackled. "Never heard of bacon curing warts, have you?"

Edwin admitted he had not and sat at the table.

Meg acknowledged him with a nod, took the cigarette from between her reddened lips, and spoke. "Don't like warts on my hand. Puts the customers off, but nothing I tried rid me of them so I came and asked Martha."

Edwin hadn't seen any warts when she'd served him breakfast. But then he tended not to notice things like that.

Martha beamed. "This'll do the trick, Meg. Now, you know that big ash tree behind the pub? Make a slit in its bark and slip this bit of bacon into it, see? Them warts will move right to that tree and your hand will be smooth as a baby's bottom."

Meg looked at the greasy back of her hand, and then at the bacon and gave Martha a dubious frown. "You mean that tree with all the bumps on it?"

"Them bumps is warts I cured. Been doing it for years, and it works every time."

Meg raised her eyebrows.

"Take a look at that tree. Right where the lowest branch comes out there's a big gnarled lump. That's the wart that was smack on the old vicar's nose, the vicar who was here before Mr. Wilson. He got the idea it looked like Satan. Weren't long before they retired the poor old chap, Satan on his nose or not," Martha said. "And over a ways you'll see three bumps like a triangle. Them was from a very private place on the widow Smythe, bless her departed soul. The most proper widow what ever lived or so she let on, but you could hardly see them little warts with a magnifying glass and they was in a place nobody would ever see anyway. But, oh my, she was anxious to give them to that ash tree."

Meg took a long drag on the remains of her cigarette. "Well, I don't care where my wart goes as long as it goes away. I'll do what you say. Thanks."

After she had gone, Martha gave a grim smile. "She's a regular devil to her husband. He's clapper clawed night and day. So who does she want a smooth hand for, I ask you?"

"Maybe it's just vanity. People will make fools of themselves to look beautiful."

"You don't think Meg's a fool for coming to me, do you?"

"It works, then?" Edwin asked with interest.

"'Course it works! There's a lot of good sense in old remedies, but you have to know what you're doing and if need be do it under the right moon. I mind the time years back when I helped a villager with a problem with her water. Used a special blend of broom plants and dandelion roots. Once she started to get better, she tried to make her own mixture but got it wrong and wound up spending a lot of time in her privy and serve her right."

Martha paused, reflecting. "It's not like I charge for my remedies. It's up to them as benefits if they want to give me something in return. It's a service to the village. My mother served Noddweir before me, and her mother before and right back for generations." A cloud passed over her face. "My persuasions will be missed when I'm gone, what with my stubborn granddaughter refusing to carry on."

"And what about your daughter?" Edwin ventured, recalling the photograph in the front room Martha had identified by a name he couldn't remember.

The cloud crossing Martha's face turned into a thunderhead. "Caught religion, she did." The old woman's anger was almost palpable.

"Well, I'm happy to hear you're so charitable, Martha." Edwin hastily changed the subject. He wondered what the vicar thought about Martha's old remedies and the need to prepare them at the right phase of the moon. Wilson had said he made an effort to accommodate country superstitions. Had he sought out Martha's assistance for his bad lungs? "About that wart remedy. Why put the bacon in that particular tree?"

The old woman smiled and tapped the side of her nose. "I'll not be giving you all my secrets, Professor."

That may have been true, but after he got his notebook she rambled on and on once again. Despite a great deal of repetition, he found plenty of new information to scribble down. Martha had not even begun to empty her well of wisdom during Edwin's initial interview.

"But you don't need to understand why it works," she told him at one point in response to his prodding. "Why are any of us alive and walking around? Do we understand it? But we get up and walk around anyway."

She fetched them tea from a pan on the stove. Edwin raised the cup to his face The brew smelled unusual. He set the drink down hastily.

"Don't fret," Martha said. She sipped from her own cup. "It ain't poison." She leaned toward him and whispered. "Nor a love potion."

Edwin lifted his cup again and essayed a taste. "Quite good."

"It's nettles. It purifies the blood."

Edwin almost choked. He imagined suddenly having a mouth full of stinging nettles. But there was no such sensation. Apparently the prickles were left out.

Martha's recounting of local lore had occupied his mind, but as he sipped tea, Edwin thought again about his conversation with Jack Chapman and how Jack said his dead wife appeared to him.

"Do you think there are ghosts, Martha?"

"Of course there are ghosts! The question is, what are ghosts? And here in the shadow of the stones—"

"Grandma been telling you stories, Edwin?" Grace, her nap over, came into the kitchen, yawning.

Martha gave a disdainful sniff, got up, and shuffled out to the front room.

Grace sat and rubbed her eyes. "It must be hard to adjust to rural ways after living in London and coming from America. What's Grandma been up to, aside from telling tales? When she avoids talking to me that's when she's been busy."

"She was curing a wart on Meg Gowdy's hand—with bacon."

Grace rolled her eyes. "Oh, and I was looking forward to having that bacon. It's not easy to get these days."

"It will be stuck under the bark of that ash tree behind the pub."

"I think I'll leave it there. Especially after it's been rubbed on Meg's hand. Probably tastes like a cigarette."

"Smoked bacon, then."

"You don't look like you believe in Grandma's cure, Edwin."

"Do you?"

Grace pursed her lips. "Mmmm. I'm not sure. You'd be surprised how many things she's right about."

"I'm surprised to hear you say that. Martha told me you refused to learn any of her secrets."

"Did she? Oh, she bent my ear when I was a little girl. I learned enough to know that my mother was right—there are things better left alone."

"It's hard for me to imagine you giving any credence to old wives' tales."

She tapped Edwin's notebook. "You're interested in such tales."

"Interested in it as folklore, not as fact. You're a sensible young woman. I don't understand what you mean."

"Sensible or not, we think differently here in the countryside. The countryside is different. Why would you disbelieve everything Grandma tells you after you've walked through the forest in the dark?"

"I don't see what you mean."

Grace smiled. "Isn't it obvious there's something out there in the dark forest, something you can't find in a city?"

Edwin wasn't sure if Grace was pulling his leg. "What, you mean fauns and satyrs and strange beings like that?"

She laughed, reached across the table, and patted his hand. "I always check paths nearest the village on my patrols. Come out with me tonight and you'll see what I mean."

Chapter Thirty

"I ask that free from peril, the hours of dark may be. I ask that free from peril, the hours of dark may be." Violet Gowdy tiptoed up the pub stairs singing a hymn under her breath. Her heart beat a tattoo of fright. She was afraid that the next second she would feel the sudden, shocking touch of the White Thing. Her back and arms tingled, as if sensing an unseen hand a fraction of an inch away.

About to make contact.

Now.

No, thank goodness, not yet.

She was always frightened when she visited the pub's privy in the dark, even though an oil lamp set on the well-scrubbed wooden bench seat burned all night. She feared bad, unseen things might grab her from behind as she passed down the short path in the back garden. Or perhaps the bad things would use her temporary absence to get inside the house and wait for her behind the back door.

As to what would happen after they grabbed her, Violet dared not speculate.

Except whatever happened would be very bad.

So she always ran out and back when the need arose and crept upstairs to her bedroom as quickly as she could.

Nothing had caught her so far.

But since the White Thing had begun to lurk, the journey was more terrifying than ever.

Recent events showed that her fear was not as silly as her parents tried to make out. Something was in fact taking children away and night would be the best time to catch a little girl alone outside.

A little girl called Violet.

Tonight, singing the hymn under her breath with a dim idea of holy protection, Violet had run back up the path. The moon washed the garden with a cold, blue light that deepened shadows among the bushes and trees.

Yes, anything could be hiding out there, waiting for Its chance.

But tonight It did not get one.

With a sigh of relief Violet reached the landing and crept past the open door of Tom Green's unoccupied room. Down the hallway she could hear her father snoring, a sound that usually kept her awake but tonight sounded comforting.

Safely in her bedroom, she turned the big key in the ornate lock and pushed a tilted chair under the doorknob.

At least the White Thing could not try to get in without her knowing. And when she heard the Thing she would scream and scream and her father would come running and save her from It. Her mother probably wouldn't bother to get out of bed.

There was something wrong between her parents. She could sense it. Her father often looked angry and her mother had become more short-tempered than usual. She had paid no attention to Violet that very morning when she tried to tell her what she'd seen. Indeed, she had been told at her age she should not be so daft, that there was nothing strange hanging about the pub despite its age, and besides how could anyone get in when the doors were locked at night?

Violet knew better.

The White Thing had somehow got in the night before.

Awakened by another row between her parents, she had lain, sleepless, for a time after silence fell. As she was about to drift off to sleep, she heard shuffling noises and, curious, got up to peer through her bedroom keyhole.

Because of the blackout the hallway had only a sliver of light along the top step, cast upwards by a lamp at the bottom of the stairs. Her father placed it there on retiring to avoid anyone falling in the dark. Then too, despite the fairly large keyhole, her vision was limited to a small stretch of hallway and the door to Green's room. However, she had glimpsed movement. Something white and formless creeping about in the dark.

It paused at Green's door. She didn't wait to see whether It entered his room. Terrified, she ran back into bed and burrowed under the blankets.

She waited and waited, listening for the sound of It at her own door, hearing only her own heart pounding. Finally she fell asleep.

Now she was snuggled down in her bed again, happy to be safe behind her locked door, with the chair propped against it.

Suddenly a thought struck her and she sat bolt upright, gasping in horror.

Was she really safe? Had she remembered to lock the back door just now?

What if she had forgotten in her hurry to get back to her bedroom?

It would be able to get in!

She was certain she had locked the back door.

At least, she thought she had.

But could she be certain?

Hadn't she better go and check? What if she hadn't? It might not come again but her parents would not be happy to find the door open tomorrow.

She might be sent up to her room all day.

At least she wouldn't have to go outside this time. Just down the stairs.

Her hand was on the chair to remove it from under her bedroom doorknob when her heart suddenly gave a leap.

Something was scratching at her door!

She didn't dare look through the keyhole. She was certain a huge, gleaming eye would be looking back at her if she did, and her heart would stop beating and she would fall down dead and her parents would be sorry for not listening to her.

But then it would be too late.

She backed away from the door and hid under the bed. She started to sing again, very low, "I ask that free from peril, the hours of dark may be."

Chapter Thirty-one

In the dark, Grace and Edwin walked around the sleeping village. Edwin was glad for the brisk pace Grace set. Despite it being midsummer the air had chilled the moment the sun vanished behind the mountains.

Having patrolled past the glimmering pond behind Susannah's cottage they were back to where the narrow way debouched into the High Street by the church. The only sounds disturbing the night were their footfalls and the occasional barking of a dog.

"There's something odd about being out at night when nobody is about and everyone is asleep. I feel as if I should whisper in case I wake them up," Edwin remarked.

"You are whispering." Grace smiled.

They continued on in companionable silence. The smell of earth and greenery, burnt away by the heat of day, filled the cool darkness. Insects sang in a monotonous cadence. Edwin was aware of Grace close beside him. From time to time her sleeve brushed his.

Had Grace really wanted his company during her rounds to show him the forest? If he were thirty years younger, or twenty, he might almost have allowed himself to imagine....

No, he refused to become a foolish old man.

Still, walking with her in the night like this, Edwin was reminded of walks with Elise. Grace was taller and sturdier than Elise, though. Nothing like her, even when Elise was the same age.

For a heart-stopping moment Edwin was afraid he was going to put his arm around Grace, lean over and kiss her cheek, as he had kissed Elise during those walks in the park.

Grace touched his elbow. "Did you see that? The light up there?"

They had reached the point where the High Street joined the road to the Wainmans' farm. Grace halted and looked toward the forest.

"No." Edwin didn't confess he had been looking at Grace.

"It's gone now. It was at the stone circle. We'd best go and see who it is." She stepped off the road. Edwin followed.

"Shouldn't we get hold of Green?"

"Probably, but whoever it is will be long gone by the time we drag Green out of bed. Maybe it's a tramp or a deserter. I can't think who else it could be."

Grace led Edwin up a steep path lined by black walls of vegetation.

This is madness, Edwin thought, toiling up behind. What if it's someone dangerous? A woman and an elderly man wouldn't be any match for a maniac. Still, he couldn't very well let Grace go on her own.

All the talk about supernatural events in the vicinity of the stones was so much nonsense. It was an interesting historical site but nothing more than that.

Or so Edwin tried to convince himself.

It was all he could do to keep up with Grace. To him the forest looked as black as a basement before you hit the light switch. He assumed she must be following a path but he couldn't see it. At long intervals Grace flicked her torch on for a second to orient herself. Mostly they plunged ahead through stygian darkness.

Grace had suggested he come out with her to see what the forest felt like at night. Now he knew. It felt like he was walking into danger. As they toiled upwards, his chest started to burn. He tried to stop himself from breathing in noisy, gasping breaths. He didn't want Grace to think he was…well…to think what? That he was older than her absent father?

They scrambled up the final steep incline, through a wall of blackberry bushes, and arrived at the stone circle.

"You can almost sense the stones thinking, brooding." Grace remarked.

The only entity Edwin could feel brooding was himself.

They stood and looked at the stones, nothing more than dark shapes barely discernible against the slightly paler grass and foxgloves around them.

Grace walked toward the circle and Edwin followed.

Despite not believing in the sentience of rocks, he felt a shudder of fear as he stepped into the center of the ring. *Don't be stupid*, he scolded himself.

Grace swung the torch around. It was she who noticed the trampled area within the circle but it was Edwin who pointed out markings on the stones.

"Those are new. I'm certain these ones weren't here when I was sketching yesterday."

"What do they say?"

"Nothing that I can make out. They're symbols."

"Tramps maybe?"

"The Guardians might be a place to pass on messages. A tramp's gazette." Edwin's attempt at humor sounded feeble even to himself.

Grace flicked on her torch and surveyed the circle again. "Someone was here, where that grass is trampled. A deer wouldn't bed down in the open. Whoever it was had that light we saw."

Edwin could feel the immensity of the starry dome of the sky open above him. He could almost admit to sensing a connection between the ancient stones and the depths overhead, receding into infinite silence.

"Nothing here," Grace said. "Let's go back by the path past the cliff."

They had taken what Grace called a shortcut on the way up. Now they went through another half-overgrown gap in the bushes and descended.

Passing the hazy glimmer that was the limestone cliff below the crest of the hill, Edwin stepped on something and stumbled. He grabbed a sapling to keep from falling.

Bending down he saw a torch on the path.

Grace shone her light around.

She gasped and broke into a run.

Edwin hobbled after her as fast as he could.

"Oh, dear God!" Grace stared down at a shadowy, lumpy shape.

It's Isobel, Edwin thought. Hadn't half of Noddweir expected to stumble across her body for days?

When he reached Grace's side she was shining her torch downwards. At the foot of the cliff, his neck at an unnatural angle, lay Special Constable Tom Green.

From the forest the observer can see the wooden sign above the village shop's window. It has been painted over but on closer approach there can be made out beneath the whitewash the ghost-like "O" of "Noddweir" and the phantasmal curve of the "S" in shop. Each pane in the big front window shows the moon's reflection, a cold spot of colorless light repeated twenty times. The blackout curtains behind the glass hide the shop's interior from view. There is no way to tell whether Emily Miller has left a lamp or a candle burning. She is almost certainly asleep at this hour. There is no dog guarding the shop. Perhaps she has chosen to sleep downstairs to guard the shop herself.

The faint crunch of footsteps on gravel, quieter than the noise of the night insects, will not wake her. The smaller window on the ground floor, which is sometimes cracked open during the day for ventilation, is closed now. There too, curtains conceal whatever lies inside. There are papers stuck to the bulletin board by the door beside the big window with its tiny reflected moons. The papers glow in the moonlight. The words on them are of no importance.

It is unlikely the front door has been left unlocked and is attached to a bell which jingles when a customer enters. This is not true of the back door. There is only cardboard stuck in the frame of the broken window beside that door, visible through the hollyhocks rising all along the back of the house.

The cardboard comes away easily, silently. A floorboard creaks underfoot. There is no sound in response.

Emily continues to sleep.

The village continues to sleep.

Chapter Thirty-two

Wednesday, June 18, 1941

"Cliffs and bad tickers can't be charged with murder," said Constable Harmon. "And yes, I'm unhappy—as you put it—about being dragged out here for two deaths from natural causes. The police are stretched to the breaking point these days, you know."

It was morning and the blackout curtains in Grace's front room were open but the nightmare continued. Constable Harmon, summoned by messenger from Craven Arms, lectured Grace as if she were a schoolgirl. Edwin guessed the man was barely older than Grace, of average size, with a bland face, untouched by experience. Looking at him, the main thing one noticed was the uniform.

Harmon picked irritably at the burrs that had stuck to his trousers during the walk through the forest to the cliff where Tom Green's body was found.

"I'm surprised at your attitude, Constable," Grace said evenly. "Especially after everything I've explained to you."

"About the evacuees running off?"

"Children gone missing."

The policeman sighed too loudly. "Semantics, Miss. And as for Constable Green's suspicious death...you said he was a city lad."

"Like yourself," Grace said. Her broad cheery face was chiseled by worry and exhaustion. The rosy cheeks were pale.

Harmon ignored her. "So this constable of yours, he obviously blundered through those thick shrubs in the dark and went straight over the cliff. Broke his neck. No fiendish killer there, Miss, just gravity. Not that gravity hasn't killed more than a few." He chuckled to himself, then frowned at the burr he'd detached from his trousers. He set it next to his notebook on the table by the armchair.

The man's demeanor exasperated Edwin. "Look, Constable Harmon, you haven't been living here in Noddweir the past few days. You don't know what it's been like. Emily Miller was frightened. And justifiably so, it turns out. As Grace told you, her shop was broken into. Her dog was killed. Burned to death."

"Of course she was upset," Harmon replied. "Bad for the ticker. A woman as elderly as she was. Is it surprising her ticker gave out? Her neighbor…" he picked up his notebook and consulted it. "Miss Radbone admitted that Miss Miller has a bad ticker."

"Heart!" Grace said. "Heart, for God's sake! You make her sound like she was a clock. And the way you act, as far as you're concerned, she might as well have been!"

"Let's not get emotional, Miss Baxter. Consider the situation reasonably." Harmon's gaze ran over his notes. "Miss Radbone stated that Miss Miller was always up with the sun, so she went to check on her very early this morning and found her dead on a cot in the shop. No signs of violence." He looked at his watch. "The ambulance will be here soon. Ambulances are in rather short supply at the moment."

Harmon, like the eager boy who was sent for him, had used a bicycle.

"What about the cardboard that was missing from the broken window at the back of Emily's house?" Grace asked.

"I assume it hadn't been secured very well. Fell out. Nothing gone from the shop. Or at least nothing that can be proved, because you admit you hadn't taken an inventory after the break-in and robbery."

Grace tensed visibly and glared at Harmon. "Emily was murdered."

"As a citizen, you can think anything you like, Miss Baxter. It isn't a crime. But as a policeman, I can't operate on beliefs."

Grace's clenched her hands. "Even if no one broke into the shop and killed her last night, it was the previous break-in and what was done to her poor dog that killed her. I insist that you take this seriously, Constable."

Edwin said, "And what about the markings we showed you on the stones? Don't you find that suspicious? All these deaths and those inexplicable scratchings, and—"

"Perhaps your constable was a secret Druid, Mr.....uh...?"

"Professor Carpenter," said Grace.

Harmon made a notation on his notebook. "You're not from around here, are you?"

Edwin persisted. "Don't you think there have been far too many unusual things happening to dismiss them all out of hand?"

"No, I don't think there has been anything unusual happening." Harmon stabbed his pen at his notebook as he ticked off the facts he'd recorded. "Four evacuees have disappeared. Len and Mike Finch, Reggie Cox, and Bert Holloway. Bert Holloway returned and said that he and the Finch boys had run off together. No doubt the boys broke into the shop to steal supplies before they left. A village girl—Isobel Chapman—previously ran away. Not surprising, is it? You told me yourself that everyone in the village knew her father beat her. She and the boys had probably all arranged to meet. Then your new constable, Tom Green, unfamiliar with the terrain, walked over the edge of a cliff in the dark and broke his neck, and an elderly woman with a heart problem—Miss Emily Miller—upset by recent events, died of a heart attack in her sleep." He looked up from his notes and raised his eyebrows. "Not a single one of those events is in the least bit unusual."

"But taken all together—"

Harmon cut Edwin off. "You're connecting dots in your imagination that don't have any connection in reality."

"What about the blood on Isobel's clothing?" Edwin struggled to keep his voice down.

"Worked a treat, didn't it? Kept you searching your backyards and annoying the constabulary while young Miss Chapman keeps getting further and further away. She's probably in London by now. If I had those clothes tested I'd lay a pound to a penny it would turn out to be chicken's blood. Or rabbit's."

"What do you mean 'if'? Surely you'll test them?" Grace put in.

"Do you know how many kids go missing these days?" Harmon paused. He tapped his lower lip with the end of his pen, as if making the calculation. "Let me guess. Quite apart from the abusive father, the little miss was the village tart. Liked hanging about with the boys. She's probably got herself into trouble and done a bunk. They're all at it these days."

Grace reddened. "You don't know what you're talking about!"

"Maybe you should make up your mind," snapped Edwin. "First she ran off because she was abused. Then she ran off because she was a tart. We're wrong to worry, because you have the answer, whatever it is."

Harmon shrugged. "Either way—"

He stopped abruptly.

There in the doorway stood Jack Chapman.

He was, Edwin thought, a terrible sight. His eyes glittered like glass. Black stubble stained his jaw. Other black stains spotted his gray shirt and leather apron. His huge arms hung at his sides. He looked borne down under a massive weight, heavy as death.

His voice came out in a hoarse whisper but it didn't matter. Edwin, Grace, and even Harmon, were stricken utterly silent. "I heard a policeman were here. My daughter's gone. I want you to look into her disappearance."

Harmon found his voice. "I'm sure you do." He consulted his notebook. "Mr. Chapman, isn't it? With all the unhappy evacuees we have running around these days, there are more missing children in the country than there are policemen. I was sent here about Constable Green. I am not authorized to take time to look into your daughter's running off."

"Green's dead. My daughter may still be alive." Jack shuffled forward ponderously. He looked even larger in Grace's small front room than he had in his smithy.

Harmon stood up. "Girls go off all the time." His tone was more conciliatory. "You'd be surprised how many we pick up every week. Usually they come back of their own accord, like—" He started to lift his notebook to his eyes but then apparently thought better of removing his gaze from Jack, who took another few steps forward. "Like the boy, who came back. What's-his-name. Not to mention she hasn't been officially reported as missing and until she is, well...."

"I'm reporting it to you now!" Jack's voice sounded like a rasp drawn against a horseshoe. "Take this down."

Harmon closed his notebook. "I'm here on other business. You'll have to go to the station in town to file a missing persons report. And I advise you to speak more respectfully when you do."

Jack took one more step forward and without a word struck Harmon on the jaw. The constable crumpled back into his chair, a puppet that had its strings cut.

For an instant Jack loomed over the man, then, thankfully, turned and walked slowly out.

When Edwin saw that Harmon was not dead, but blinking and groggily shaking his head, he turned to Grace and smiled.

She smiled back.

Chapter Thirty-three

"What now?" asked Duncan Gowdy. He had taken his accustomed position behind the bar, though the villagers crowded into the Guardians pub were not there for refreshment. "If a town copper refuses to take us seriously, should we go to his superior?"

"I don't know that would help," Grace said. She stood in front of the bar and had finished summarizing Constable Harmon's visit. She glared at Jack Chapman, who lounged against the fireplace. "Assaulting a policeman isn't going to win us any friends amongst the constabulary."

Jack spat on the flagstones.

Edwin reckoned it was a comment on the constabulary rather than Grace. Despite the crowded conditions, each person, hunched in a chair, leaning against a wall, or simply standing with arms folded, was surrounded to a more noticeable degree than usual by that individual space loved by the British, an almost visible border around every person. The air between the spaces was thick with suspicion.

Grace took no notice of Jack's disrespect. "What we need to do," she continued, "is organize a larger night patrol. We could base it on the bobby's beat model, you know, each person patrols a stretch of street, both ends touching other beats. That way, every street in the village will be covered numerous times a night."

"Have we got enough men to do it?" asked Duncan. "It's not women's work."

"Rubbish!" said Susannah Radbone. "A woman can blow a whistle as well as any man!"

Edwin thought Susannah must have an iron will to have shown up at the meeting, devastated as she was by her friend Emily's death.

Grace said, "You're right, Susannah. We'll have to draw up a list of volunteers for certain hours."

Duncan reached under the bar and produced a pad and pencil.

"But what we supposed to be looking out for, Grace?" The question came from a slight young woman with a face as faded as the dress she wore with its ghost of a floral pattern. "It's like we're being tormented by something," Her voice shook. "I daren't let my children out my sight. I wouldn't be here right now if me mum wasn't keeping an eye on them."

A murmur of assent swept through the stifling room. "Is it tramps what's responsible?" asked another woman. "Skulking about in the forest, like?

"Or tinkers?" suggested an elderly man. "Folks calling themselves tinkers, I mean. Gives them an excuse to roam about and get up to no good."

"Might it be deserters?" ventured a stout middle-aged woman. "Once they go on dog's leave they get vicious, and they're armed."

Grace shrugged. "Could be any of them. On the other hand—"

"Witches is what it is." The speaker was Martha's acolyte Polly. She had placed herself on a chair in the middle of the room, hands on her big hips, elbows thrust out as if daring anyone to get near to her. "Saw the manes of the Wainmans' horses matted something fierce when I passed by their field this morning. Them's witch's stirrups. Witches have been riding them horses. Last night the witches was riding."

The faded young woman who had spoken earlier turned so pale it appeared she might vanish into air.

Heads turn immediately from Polly to Martha.

Martha met the unfriendly stares with a steady gaze and then cackled. "Could it be fairies stealing the kids?" she jeered. "Or should we look for cloven hoof prints up there—?" She jerked her head in the general direction of the stone circle. "You're all fools!"

"I would have reckoned you to agree with Polly," Duncan said. "She got her crazy ideas from you, after all."

Grace flushed. Was she supposed to defend her grandmother's irrational fancies?

Martha laughed again, sounding like an aged crow. "You won't listen to me when I give you fair warning. Why should I help any of you? Maybe you ought to be looking at those that commune with the bottle? There's as much evil in the bottom of a bottle as there is up on top of the hill." She looked straight at Jack Chapman.

Jack stiffened. "What d'you mean? You hinting at me knowing about these missing kids?"

A farmer put his hand on Jack's arm. "Never mind about that. The old witch is looking to cause trouble." He raised his voice. "What about Haywood? We all know he's peddling illegal goods. He deals with you, Duncan."

The publican leaned forward over the bar. "What do you mean by that?"

"Obvious, isn't it?" came the reply. "You notice he's not here tonight. Flogging stuff on the black market attracts a bad element...."

Several men shouted at once and Grace hammered on the bar with a heavy glass ashtray, calling for silence. "Yes, Duncan deals with Haywood. But so do a lot of us. So does the vicar—excuse me, Mr. Wilson, these are desperate times—does that mean the vicar is responsible for these outrages?"

Edwin glanced at the minister, who faced Grace with a slight, pained smile as if to acknowledge the justice of her statement. Of course everyone already knew about his business and that of all their neighbors, it was simply never spoken of out loud. Oddly enough, the one person everyone was sure didn't deal with Haywood was Emily, despite her keeping the village shop. She was probably the only person in the village harmed rather than benefited by Haywood's lawbreaking. Did that mean anything?

Jack growled, "And what about Martha there? She wanders around at night."

"I do no such thing," Martha declared emphatically.

"But you do," Susannah said. "I've seen you wandering up and down the High Street at all hours of the night!"

"And what was you doing up at all hours looking out of windows, spying on your neighbors?" Martha snapped back. "Or was you up in the forest looking down on Noddweir when you saw me stretching me legs when I couldn't sleep? Look at yourself. A broom to ride would suit you a treat, it would."

"Who are you to throw accusations around, Martha?" shouted Jack. "How do we know you haven't been up there messing about in those stones? You filled my daughter's head with rubbish and worse than rubbish. Where's she gone? What do you know about it?"

Edwin thought if it was not for the press of bodies in the room Jack would have attacked Martha as he had attacked the policeman in Grace's front room. His eyes were feral. Like an animal, he reacted by instinct rather than reason. Edwin found the man frightening.

"What do you know, Jack Chapman?" squawked Polly coming to Martha's aid.

Martha rose and drew her shawl tighter around her shoulders. "I'm not staying here to be insulted by this huffle-footed fool, Grace. I'm going home."

"That's right, Martha," Polly put in. "You tell 'em."

"She says she's going home." Jack emphasized the second word, "but is she—or is she planning more mischief?"

Edwin stood up. "I'll escort you back, Martha." He took her elbow, noting Grace's little nod of thanks.

"And who is vouching for you?" Jack demanded. "You're not one of us. How do we know what you're up to?"

"I can vouch for the professor," the vicar said in mild tones. "We have been in correspondence for a long time."

"Did he ever put a snapshot in this correspondence?" Jack asked "For all we know, he bumped off the real professor and took his identity. Nobody ever seen him before, did they? He could be anyone."

"That's nonsense," Wilson said.

"Maybe so, but the devil can appear in a familiar shape."

"True enough, Mr. Chapman," the vicar said. "But what we have to agree is that the devil is indeed abroad in Noddweir. Can't you see he's turning us against each other? We must stick together, look out for each other and especially the children, otherwise who knows how it will end?"

"You're a regular Churchill," someone muttered.

Susannah got to her feet and rapped on a table. "This squabbling is accomplishing nothing! Let's get back to business. Grace's idea of extended night patrols is excellent. I'll be first to volunteer. Put my name down, Duncan. Any hour will do."

"She's got no authority to organize patrols or anything else," sniffed Meg Gowdy from the end of the bar. "Would have been much better if your father was here, Grace. I mean, he's a real constable, or I should say was, now he's joined up. I don't suppose you know where he's serving?"

"Certainly not. They're not allowed to say."

"But surely—?"

"I don't know." Her tone had turned sharp. "Duncan, put me down too. We can work out the hours once we know how many volunteers we have. Edwin, I'll take Grandma home if you want to stay."

"That's fine, I'll go with you," Edwin replied. "Let me know when I'll be on patrol, Duncan." As he said it Edwin couldn't help thinking how odd it was to be volunteering to patrol the midnight streets of a place he hadn't set eyes on a week before.

The trio left the pub. Grace looked grim. They walked a short way in silence and finally Grace said, "About my father, Edwin..."

Edwin gave her a puzzled look.

"Don't pretend you weren't curious. I could see you were."

"Well, I couldn't help but notice you seemed....well..."

"It's not just that we're not supposed to ask where our family members are serving. And no, before you ask, I haven't tried to find out or arrange a simple code to use in letters."

"Oh?" Edwin felt adrift. There were obviously things the British, under siege, took for granted as common knowledge of which he had no inkling at all.

"No," Grace replied. "What I'm afraid of is that my father's in trouble and hasn't joined up at all."

Chapter Thirty-four

The deserter ran a dirty, calloused finger over the incomprehensible carvings in the eroded stone. As if he would be able to decipher them by touch when they meant nothing to his eyes. Signs made by tramps, he guessed. And the tramps might still be nearby. The shallow scratchings were fresh. Automatically he felt for the revolver stuck in his belt. He had nothing to fear from tramps, did he? Besides, why would they bother him? He was now a tramp himself.

He examined the marks again. One resembled a malformed swastika. Maybe. There was another that looked like a crab, but almost surely wasn't. Muttering a curse, he straightened up.

The deserter—or tramp—ambled over to one of the larger stones, moving soundlessly as had become second nature to him. He had wandered for months through silent places. He wasn't sure what the date was but he knew the forest.

Pulling off his haversack, he sat down in the stone's shadow. Leaning back he felt roughness through his worn shirt. The shadow was remarkably cooler than the sunlight. He took a drink from his canteen and water dribbled into his beard.

He was enveloped by the scent of grass and the electric hum of bees. He watched a fat bumblebee crawl into a foxglove a foot from his face. The foxglove nodded with the bee's weight, swallowed it up, and grinned at him. He moved his gaze to the pale blue sky.

He didn't want to think. Mostly he wanted to forget. So many things he wanted to forget and so few he wanted to remember. He lifted the canteen again, gulping the contents down as if it was a good pint of ale though it was merely warm, brackish water.

The countryside was alive with tramps when he was a lad. He and his friends regarded them with a confused mixture of fear, contempt, and envy. They knocked at the back door and his mother gave them a few biscuits and a cup of milk. He always feared that one day she would open the door and find a knife at her throat.

The tramps were always present, though seldom seen. If a shed burned down, or chickens went missing, or clothes vanished from a line, it was said to be the work of tramps. Not a particular tramp, of course, because they were nameless and forever moving through. An elemental force like the wind, like evil.

When he and his friends saw the dusty men hiking down the main road they pelted them with pebbles and then ran, in delicious terror, knowing full well that their young legs could easily outdistance any vagabond who chose to pursue them. None did, although they screamed imprecations. Simply playing their part, he reflected later in life. More amused than tormented?

Yet at times, when he caught sight of a tramp cutting across a field, attired in a fabulous, multicolored plumage of unmatched rags, free as a fox, coming from who knows where, heading for the unknown, he almost wished he could abandon his comfortable house for the feral life.

And now he had.

He opened his eyes and felt the sun beat down. His lank, heavy hair might as well have been on fire. The shadow had crept off him. How long had he been unconscious?

He suffered odd spells lately. Abruptly he would be awake without any memory of what had happened immediately before. At times he found himself in a different place than he last remembered, without any idea how or why he had been there. Living off the land was taking a heavy toll.

There came to him the feeling he was being watched. He struggled to his feet and blinked at the stone circle. The eroded rocks might have been rotten, broken teeth arranged around a great, round maw, ready to gape open and swallow him. He saw nothing else.

As he moved, his shirt stuck to his skin. He was sweating profusely.

No. Not sweat. He looked down at his chest, numbly, unable to assimilate what he saw.

He ran a finger down the sodden shirt front. His finger came away red.

Blood.

He was soaked with blood.

The man who deserves to die looks surprised. He has run his fingers through the ritual blood and over the magic symbols on the stone. Yet his expression displays no hint of understanding. His startled gaze turns to the thick tangle of blackberry bushes surrounding the clearing. To him they make a solid wall, concealing anything behind them.

Shading his eyes he looks toward the sun, as if judging the time.

For him it no longer matters what the hour is.

Time stands still, on Guardians Hill.

For the dead.

He paces around inside the sacred circle. Finally he stops. He turns his back, and relieves himself against the tallest stone.

For that sacrilege he will suffer even more.

He whirls around suddenly. Puzzled. Frightened. Reaching for the gun at his belt. Then he appears to calm himself and walks back to where he slept, picks up his haversack.

He couldn't have heard such soft laughter, could he?

He leaves the circle.

No doubt he thinks he is leaving the hill.

Chapter Thirty-five

Muttering his annoyance, Edwin answered the rapid tattoo on the front door. He and Grace hadn't been back from the meeting at the pub long enough to sit down. He was surprised to see one of the woman he had overheard arguing in front of Emily's shop.

She gave no sign of recognizing him. She looked distraught. "I have to talk to the constable…to Grace, I mean…"

"Don't you think you should be talking to—?" Edwin almost said "Constable Green" then remembered and stopped short. Who could villagers turn to other than Grace?

The de facto constable appeared from the kitchen. "Oh, good God! Now what?"

She led the woman, who had begun to tremble, to a chair and sat her down. "What is it, Betty? What's happened?"

"It's me boys, Patrick and Jim," the woman blurted. "They've gone! Disappeared!" She looked at Grace wide-eyed and started crying.

Grace patted her shoulder. "Try to calm down. Tell me what's happened, and we'll see what can be done."

The woman subsided into hiccupping sobs. "Me twins! Gone!" Her voice rose into a wail. "They just…went…"

"When did you see them last?"

"Right before bedtime. They went the usual time. And that's the last I seen of them!"

"But it's the middle of the afternoon. You only just noticed they were gone?"

Betty dabbed at her eyes. "There's all the others, you know. The girls and the other boys. It's enough not to trip over them while doing housework, never mind counting them."

Edwin had sat down on a chair by the door and tried to remain unobtrusive. He recalled Betty's supposed friend railing about how many kids she had.

"What makes you imagine they're gone? Probably they went out to play."

"And miss breakfast and dinner too?" Betty snuffled. "Anyway, I checked their room and the window was wide open. They must have gone out it so as not to be heard."

"No one heard them leave?"

"Me mum's room's next to theirs but she's deaf as an adder."

"All right. We'll organize a search party right away. You go home for now."

◇◇◇

Three hours later Grace and Edwin conferred in the kitchen. No trace of the twins was found and nobody had seen them. The villagers searched dutifully through forest and fields but it was easy to see they no longer expected to find anything. The spirit had gone out of everyone.

Grace left off searching to rest before her evening patrol, giving orders to the searchers to report back to her by dusk. She had no authority but most of Noddweir was inclined to take orders from her, nonetheless.

She boiled water for tea. "The question is did the boys run off? Or were they taken? "

"Taken from their bedroom? Wouldn't they have kicked up a devil of a row?"

"Not to mention these are village children, not evacuees."

"Isobel was from the village."

"She's the only one who seems to have come to grief."

"There isn't any pattern."

Grace swirled bubbling water round the teapot to warm it, drained the pot, and made tea. "No. It doesn't make any sense, does it?" She handed a cup to Edwin.

Edwin lowered his face to his cup. The tea was too hot. It burned his lip. He blew on it and the rising steam misted his eyeglasses. "Here's a theory. Let's say Isobel bragged about how she planned to take off for the big city. However, something else happened to her before she had a chance to run away."

"Something to do with her father," Grace said sourly.

"Not necessarily." Edwin stared through his foggy lenses into his cup. "Whatever happened to Isobel, when she went missing the other kids thought she'd made good on her promise, so they followed her. Or thought they were following her."

Grace said nothing for a moment, staring thoughtfully out the window. "The Finch brothers, I can see. And maybe Bert and Reggie. They all spent a lot of time together. But Betty's twins…they can't be twelve yet."

"They weren't friends with the others?"

"Not that I know about. They're so young. Why would they imagine they could run off and survive on their own?"

"At that age it's nothing but a game. As soon as the sun starts to go down they will be back with their tails between their legs."

"A nice thought. If they've stayed that close why haven't we found them?"

Edwin tried his tea again. "What's your idea then, Grace? You know people here better than I do."

"I'm trying not to form any opinions. I don't want to cut off a line of investigation because of my own preconceptions about the solution."

"You sound like a detective. Did you pick up a few tips from your father?"

Grace's face clouded. "Hardly. From detective books. By the way, you left your copy of *Brighton Rock* in the front room. Right vicious little bugger, that Pinkie."

"Do you suppose there's an adult Pinkie in Noddweir?"

She hesitated. "A person as evil as that?"

"Hitler, for example."

"Well, yes, but not here in Noddweir. Can you see Hitler

goose-stepping down the High Street? Ordering a pint at the pub? But Pinkie now. What he did to that poor—?"

Edwin raised his hand. "Please. Don't tell me how it turns out."

Immediately he saw the incongruity. Why should he care how Graham Greene's invented story ended when he was faced with a potentially more tragic and unresolved real life situation?

Grace lifted her cup, swirled tea around. "I don't think people like them are actually human. They look human on the outside, but what's inside isn't anything like you or me, like normal decent people."

"I appreciate the compliment."

"I can see you think that's silly. But there's definitely evil in the world. Darkest evil."

Martha appeared in the doorway. "You're right. There's evil abroad. And it's been in this very house."

"Grandma! Have you been eavesdropping? And what do you mean by evil in the house?"

"Somebody's been stealing my things," she grumbled.

"Things?"

"My herbal headache necklace and rheumatics liniment for a start. And my false teeth."

"Oh, Grandma. You're always forgetting where you put them! Why would anybody want your false teeth?"

"Same reason I bought them secondhand years ago, of course. So's they could eat solid food."

"And the other things?" Grace searched the kitchen, looking into drawers and the pantry.

"Them with the knowledge can find other uses for what I makes them from."

The bread bin's enamel lid rattled. Grace reached in and produced a set of false teeth. "The rest will turn up soon enough." She handed the dentures to Martha, who took them gingerly, as if they might bite. Then she shuffled out.

Grace closed her eyes and exhaled slowly. "Grandma can be a real problem."

"You have too much on your plate," Edwin said. Should he try to help or mind his own business?

He didn't have time to weigh the options before there was yet another knock on the door.

"Oh, for..." Grace turned to go to answer it, then stopped. "Come in," she called out. "Door's on the latch."

In a moment Harry Wainman blocked the kitchen doorway, looking more infuriated than ever.

"How's the search going?" Grace asked.

The corner of Wainman's tightly compressed lips twitched before he spoke. "Wouldn't know. Bert's gone again. He wasn't in his room this morning. His clothes are gone too. And good riddance says I, but the wife, you know, softhearted bugger, said I should report it."

Grace rubbed her eyes wearily. "Consider it reported."

Wainman hesitated at the door. "Should I turn in his ration book?"

"No, hold it for now. But don't use it."

Wainman nodded curtly. "I won't be taking the little bugger back. Enough is enough."

Edwin watched the farmer's broad back as he stalked away. If only enough were, in fact, enough.

Chapter Thirty-six

Susannah Radbone did not know how much more she could endure. It was not like her to acknowledge the possibility of defeat. That she could not help but do so as she completed her solitary patrol of Noddweir's night-shrouded streets frightened her.

She would have preferred to be out with a partner but, predictably, more villagers approved the patrol scheme than cared to volunteer. Given another day or so, things might be better organized. In the meantime she went out on her own.

She succeeded only in discouraging herself. With the blackout curtains drawn, the streets were inky corridors. Most residents were in bed. Susannah might as have passing through rows of mausoleums. Beyond the village the mountains rose up forebodingly, darker than the star-specked night sky.

What might be hiding out there?

Susannah stopped beside a gate leading into a narrow field fronting the forest and lit a cigarette.

The air smelled of dust and grass and throbbed with insect sounds.

Was her discouragement a result of old age? Was she simply worn down by all the years of contending with life? All the troubled students. All the disappointments. There were triumphs too. But even the promising pupils usually stepped straight from school into a lifelong cage formed of family, poverty, factory, and drink.

For those the war wasn't such a bad thing, uprooting them from the impoverished surroundings which would have trapped them otherwise.

Susannah took a drag on her cigarette and blew the smoke out through her nostrils. There had once been a young man who said she did that like a film star. She had never married. She would have had to give up too much of herself. Now she wondered if she had given up more by not marrying.

She had always been entirely self-sufficient but the loss of her friend Emily had taken something from her that she did not have it within herself to replace. The disappearance of Reggie had stolen something as well.

If she were still in Newcastle she would be able to find tutoring jobs. She missed working with children.

Had it been a mistake to retire to the countryside? What did she care about making jam she found barely palatable? Years ago the idea of country living sounded appealing. But she was a city girl. Night in the countryside unnerved her. The racket made by insects was nothing like the scattered voices and sounds of vehicles one heard in the city. The noise from the insects was inhuman, mechanical. The random chirps and ratchetings blended into rhythmic waves, a trick of the mind. What stealthy sounds were being obscured?

She drew more smoke into her lungs and shuddered. How did the saying go? A goose just walked over my grave?

The dark mountains radiated malevolence.

It was nothing but her imagination. Merely the environment acting on her nervous system at a subconscious level. No wonder country people were superstitious. No wonder a doddering, half-senile old woman like Martha had her followers and everyone in the village slavishly paid obeisance to the fairy tales pawned off on them by the vicar. It was all environment.

Whether city or countryside, people ended up enslaved by their environment. In Newcastle people were enslaved by the poverty surrounding them, here it was these damned spooky mountains.

She tossed the cigarette butt down, ground it underfoot, and strode homeward.

She was approaching the church when she noticed movement further down the street.

Her heart sped up.

What exactly was she supposed to do anyway?

She forced herself to walk faster, toward where she had glimpsed the movement. Now she could see nothing. Had it been her imagination?

A high hedge grew before her cottage. Her chest tightened with apprehension as she walked past hurriedly. Someone might well be lurking behind it.

"Don't be an old fool," she chided herself. "You're acting like a schoolgirl."

Across the street Emily's shop looked the same as always. Her friend could have been inside finishing *Treasure Island*. Except Susannah knew better. She realized she would think of Emily every time she passed the shop.

But it had been a heart attack, hadn't it? Everyone got old and died. Why did Emily's death feel so wrong to Susannah?

She went in and locked her front door. A faint noise came from the kitchen. A scratching. Scratching at the kitchen door.

For an instant she had the impulse to turn and run. But where? And how far would she get at her age?

She edged into the kitchen and took the largest carving knife out of the rack by the sink.

The scratching continued.

Susannah felt dizzy with fear. She raised the knife shakily.

Who was about to break in?

Or what, she suddenly thought.

Then there came a distinct meow.

"Blackie!"

Susannah closed her eyes for an instant and exhaled with relief. Then she threw open the door without looking out.

The black cat trotted in, dropped a tiny bloody bundle of fur at her feet, looked up, and gave a loud meow.

"The great hunter makes an offering," Susannah muttered to herself. Her smile was faint and her lips trembled.

Chapter Thirty-seven

Thursday, June 19, 1941

Long morning shadows reached toward Guardians Hill, visible above slate rooftops, when Edwin set out for the vicarage. A week had passed since Isobel Chapman went missing.

As Edwin approached the vine-covered house a small girl came racing out from the back as if the devil were after her. "Hold on!" He put a hand into her path. "What's the matter?"

The girl stopped and looked up at him wide-eyed. "Nothing's the matter. The vicar's going to have a parade!"

She clutched a sheaf of papers. She handed him one and he saw penciled in childish letters:

PARADE
Saturday, 21 June
MEETING at CHURCH
Tonight, 7 pm

"I'm to take these to Mr. Gowdy so he can let everyone know," the girl said excitedly.

"What a good idea. Well, off with you then."

"There'll be prizes too," the girl called back as she ran.

Edwin found Timothy Wilson in the vicarage garden, seated in one of those low-slung chairs cobbled together from a few lengths of wood and a piece of canvas. Several small girls were busy pulling weeds from a vegetable patch which ran up to the churchyard. The vicar took books from a carton at his feet and placed them on the small table beside him.

At Wilson's invitation Edwin lowered himself gingerly into an identical chair. To his surprise he found it more comfortable than he'd imagined.

He picked a book from the pile. *The Wind in the Willows*. "Prizes?" Edwin guessed.

"Yes. How did you know?"

"I ran into your little Mercury on the way over. A parade's an excellent idea to take the children's minds off everything that's going on."

"I hope it will take the parents' minds off our troubles too," Wilson said. "Finding ways to outfit the children will give everyone something different to think about. We must continue to give the children as normal a life as possible."

He lifted a ponderous tome with a dark cover from the box, scowled, and set it in the grass by his chair.

Edwin gave him a questioning look.

"*Pilgrim's Progress*. Not sure how that got in there." He carefully hacked into a handkerchief.

Edwin glanced away and studied the spines of books piled on the table while Wilson's coughing fit subsided. He made out Beatrix Potter, A.A. Milne, *The Railway Children*. "You don't want to save these for your own charges?" He nodded at the girls in the garden who were intent on extracting an earthworm from the roots of weed they had pulled. They had taken great care to plop themselves squarely in the dirt.

Wilson stuffed the handkerchief into his pocket. "Oh, I have plenty more books to amuse my temporary guests."

Edwin frowned sharply. What was the vicar, an unmarried man with no children, doing with children's books anyway?

Maybe Wilson realized what he was thinking because he explained that between the wars he had administered spiritual guidance to an orphanage and been given a few boxes of books when he left to take up his new post in Noddweir.

Edwin felt ashamed he had, for a second, almost suspected his friend of what was better left unsaid. It was all the terrible events that had taken place. The very air they breathed was poisoned. After a while nothing seemed impossible, no matter how unthinkable. He waved *The Wind in the Willows* before replacing it on the pile. "Too bad we all can't get along famously like Mole and Ratty."

"Unfortunately, the world is filled with weasels. And let's not forget that Mr. Toad was a bit of a loose cannon." Wilson paused, studying the book he'd picked up and then placed it on top of *Pilgrim's Progress*. "Biggles," he explained. "I don't believe in war books for children. War is so much worse than depicted. Even so, Biggles is too realistic for the little ones."

While a new war raged, many still suffered from the last war to settle everything once and for all. Others who weren't yet born when the last war was fought suffered, thanks to it as well. Isobel Chapman for example, if the villagers were to be believed. Abused by her father because his mind as well as his body was damaged in the trenches.

"By the way," Wilson went on. "Did you hear Susannah Radbone has left?"

"Left? Why, no. Did she tell you?"

"Hardly. My cleaning lady said she was on her way to the vicarage when she ran into Susannah. Had her bicycle out in front of her cottage. Told her she's too upset to stay in Nod-dweir, between Reggie vanishing and Emily's death. She's gone to stay with her sister for a while. In Aston on Clun, I think. She'll make arrangements for Emily's funeral from there and let us know so those who wish to can attend."

"I'm surprised. I'd have thought if anyone I've met here would stick it out, Miss Radbone would."

"A tough old bird, but we all have our limits."

"And what about you, Timothy? You don't sound well." Edwin had intended to ask the minister to elucidate more clearly what he intended at certain spots on his map, but now he decided to keep it firmly in his pocket.

Wilson shrugged his coat hanger shoulders. "I'm fine. The difference is that Susannah's alone and I'm not."

"You have your charges to look after." Nodding toward the garden Edwin saw the girls busily collecting earthworms, their battle against weeds forgotten.

"True, but that's not what I meant. It's that as a man of God—but I shouldn't get into that."

"With an atheist like me, you mean? I wouldn't mind being able to believe. I'm afraid I simply lack any sense of the divine. Elise believed in God and an afterlife, but we never discussed it."

"Maybe she's right, Edwin, and will be waiting for you."

"Yes, well…"

"At least you won't depart Noddweir and make a rude gesture in my direction as Susannah Radbone probably did as she left!"

There was a blood-curdling shriek from the other end of the garden.

One of the girls hopped up and down, frantically slapping at her dress.

"They're throwing worms! They're throwing worms! Where did it go?"

Two other girls rolled in the dirt, yanking each other's hair.

Wilson levered himself out of his chair. He looked white as a ghost. "Pardon me, Edwin, while I sort this out." He smiled wanly. "Satan never sleeps."

Chapter Thirty-eight

"Violet, don't you want your tea?" Meg Gowdy asked her daughter. "You always like shepherd's pie. What's wrong with it?"

The girl looked up from pushing her food listlessly around her plate and shook her head. "Not hungry, mum."

"But you always like shepherd's pie!" Meg repeated. "Do you feel all right? You look pale."

"Don't go on at her, Meg." Duncan spoke through a mouthful of bread and margarine. "If she don't want to eat what's on her plate, I will. No sense wasting good food."

An irrational flash of anger hit Meg like a lightning bolt. "Greedy pig! Finish your own and go and clean the windows like you said you would." Shaking, she went to the sink to rinse her plate. How she hated the man!

"Yes, your majesty." Duncan crammed the remaining bread into his mouth, got up, and stamped down the hallway.

Meg turned to Violet. The girl had pushed her plate away, leaned her head on her hand, and drew patterns in the tablecloth with her fork.

"Violet, are you sure you're not sickening for something? God, I hope not. We're sailing close to the wind with the bills as it is. Thank heavens you've already had measles. I don't think any of the village kids has chicken pox. Surely we would have been told?"

"No, mum, really. I'm just a bit tired."

Meg sat down again. What could a child know about being tired? Tired of a useless husband, a pathetic little village, a wasted life. "Not sleeping well?" She tried to make her tone sympathetic. "Upset stomach? Had to go to the loo during the night? Broken sleep can be very tiring."

Surely her daughter was still too young for the onset of the monthly curse?

Violet bit her lip and then blurted out. "Mum, I seen Bert!"

"Violet!"

"No, really I did."

"When was this? And where?"

The girl lowered her gaze and began drawing patterns again. "It was Tuesday night. He was here."

"Here? Violet, you must have been dreaming! How could he get in—no, wait a minute. I've told your father a hundred times about leaving the spare key under the doormat out back! But then again, it was a dream, surely?"

As much as she relished the idea of more proof of Duncan's fecklessness, she hated the idea of Violet being upset.

"I seen him," Violet persisted. "Something come scratching on my door, but I wouldn't let it in. And then after a bit I heard Bert whispering, and he came in and we talked."

"In the middle of the night? In your bedroom?" Meg's face reddened.

"It was all right, mum, we're friends."

"What did he want? Is he in trouble? Why didn't you call me or your dad?"

Violet sighed. "He said not to. He came to tell me he wasn't dead. But he knew something he couldn't tell anyone. He wanted someone to talk to because he was scared."

Meg stared at her daughter, amazed. She could always tell when Violet was lying. And she wasn't. "This was on Tuesday night?"

"Yes. He said he'd come back last night but he didn't. I stayed awake all night waiting for him."

So that explained why Violet was tired. Meg rubbed her forehead. What did it all mean?

Duncan stuck his head in the doorway and spoke hurriedly. "I have to go out. If I'm not back, you can open up."

"Well, isn't that nice? And what about the windows?"

"If you want the windows cleaned, you clean them. There's a fire not far from the Wainmans' farm!"

When Duncan arrived on the scene, Wainman and several villagers had already given up what was obviously a fruitless attempt to save Haywood's house. He joined them in using shovels to beat out small fires that threatened to set the surrounding shrubbery ablaze.

Duncan beckoned Harry Wainman aside. "Sorry about the old place. Louisa's bound to be upset."

"No concern of mine," Wainman growled. "Good thing we shifted it. Good riddance, I say."

Already the house was in a fair way to being reduced to a black skeleton sagging over a pile of ashes and burnt wood.

"Seen a fire move that fast once." Duncan leaned on his shovel. "In Scotland, it was. When I was a boy. A local farmer burnt down his neighbor's barn over a silly quarrel about a missing cow."

Wainman frowned. "You mean you think this was deliberate?"

"Possibly," Duncan said quietly.

Wainman grunted. "Could be he was storing petrol in there. That would account for it going up so fast."

"More importantly, where's Haywood?"

Wainman stared at the ruins. "You don't mean you think what remains of him might be under that lot?"

Chapter Thirty-nine

The sturdy wooden door of Noddweir's church stood open, allowing the evening sun to stream into the interior, warming the stone-flagged floor. Dust motes danced in the light but the ceiling beams remained in shadows. Lamps set on the altar struggled against the dark pools above.

It was as if the shadow on the village was creeping into the church, Timothy Wilson thought as he entered the pulpit and surveyed his congregation. He delayed the meeting about the parade to allow those who dealt with the fire at Haywood's house to attend. It was impossible to make the simplest plans any more without having them disrupted by whatever was stalking Noddweir.

He had not planned on holding any kind of service but several women insisted. He hoped the unbelievers who had come about the parade would not feel ambushed. There were those in the village whose beliefs were pagan. He glanced up to the colored representation of Saint Winnoc endlessly grinding corn.

Weren't all beliefs an attempt to make sense of the unknowable?

He rubbed his eyes, exhausted from lack of sleep, and the strained, white faces with purple smudges under the eyes turned up toward him from the pews showed he was not the only one who had spent recent nights tossing and turning.

What was he to say to them, his poor flock wandering in the fields with wolves cutting their young out of their pack?

"My friends," he began in a husky voice that barely reached the church door despite the utter silence brooding in the building, "it has been suggested that we pray for help as we travel along this hard road."

There came to him the travelers' psalm, the song of pilgrims on the road to Jerusalem. It was dear to him, for his own road was hard and his destination still far away. "…The Lord is thy keeper: the Lord is thy shade upon thy right hand. The sun shall not smite thee by day, nor the moon by night…"

He sensed the wariness between his parishioners. "Let us remember always that we must stay together and protect each other. Oh, I know there has been much drawing away from each other…" He glanced around the spread-out congregation, which looked uneasily at its neighbors. "…and it's understandable, but as Mark cautioned us in the Gospel, if a house be divided against itself that house cannot stand. So now, let us pray together—"

"I don't hold with all this praying business, Vicar!"

A man lounging in a back pew stood up. The vicar was surprised to see it was Jack Chapman. The entire congregation twisted round to see what Chapman had to say, and one or two were already whispering to their companions.

"Instead of praying, we should be patrolling with guns at all hours." Chapman continued.

"We need to patrol but we need to pray too," Wilson replied. "The psalm tells us that unless the Lord keeps the city, the watchman remains awake in vain."

"Jack's right!" came a shout. "Anyone with no business what's caught on the street after dark should be arrested and—"

"We got no constable here," Chapman pointed out, "unless you count Grace, and I don't."

"We don't need a constable," said a farmer in a front pew. "Anyone causes trouble, scrag 'em and worry about the law later. Sorry, vicar, but we have to fight fire with fire."

"The devil's abroad in Noddweir!" a woman added. "Fire's his natural home!"

A piercing demonic yowl stopped her cold.

Heads swiveled to see Martha standing in the church doorway, silhouetted by the sunlight, her wild, white hair a radiant mist. She clutched a black cat which spat and clawed and yowled.

Martha hobbled down the aisle. "Susannah's cat come home! I got it off her doorstep. Susannah wouldn't go without Blackie!"

"You ought not to bring it into church, Martha, it's not the place for it," Wilson remonstrated almost inaudibly. He'd let things get out of hand.

"Quiet, you stupid thing!" Martha shouted.

Was she addressing Wilson or the cat?

She grasped the cat by the neck and held the spitting creature at arm's length. "Where's Susannah? That's what I want to know! You all ought to be out looking for her!"

"Get that old witch out of here!" Chapman roared, lunging at her and getting a clawed face for his pains.

"Please, please, remember where you are," Wilson pleaded.

Two men jumped up and grabbed Martha, who dropped the cat. It bolted from the building. There were screams.

Martha was marched out. She babbled in a fury. "It's them stones. You'll see. You'll see!"

The congregation was in an uproar. Wilson tried vainly to calm them with calls for respectful behavior in the Lord's house. His faint voice was drowned out.

It was a handicap not to be able to shout people down.

As the sun slid behind the mountains, red-gold light touched the topmost branches of the forest pressing in on both sides of the narrow dirt road. A smoky smell hung on the air and a deep stillness. The trees looked ready to spring on those unwise enough to be out in this lonely place after dark.

Edwin and Grace, for instance.

Edwin shivered though the air was still warm. "I don't think there's much point in continuing, Grace. It'll be too dark to see before long, and it's best not to be out here when night falls."

"Just a little further."

They walked on in silence and around a sharp bend. The dying sunlight's gilding faded.

Grace suddenly halted and grabbed Edwin's arm. "There!" She pointed to a black mass of bushes. "See that glint?"

Edwin adjusted his eyeglasses. "No."

Grace dragged him forward.

A bicycle lay tucked under the thick foliage. The stray beam of sunlight that had fingered the bell on its handle died as Grace spoke. "Just in time! We'd have missed it otherwise, tonight at least."

Edwin pulled the machine onto the road.

"It's Susannah's," Grace said. "It's the only red bike in the village. See the cat carrier and the suitcase tied to the front?"

Edwin looked around. The sun was almost gone and a light wind was rising. "But where is she? How did the cat escape?"

Grace frowned. "The carrier lid's loose. It appears he ran into the forest."

"He did?"

"You don't think Susannah hid her bike in the bushes unless there was a good reason, do you?"

"It'll soon be too dark to go in there looking—not to mention far too dangerous. We'll have to organize a search party tomorrow morning." The words stuck in his throat. Yet another pointless search party.

Grace flicked on her torch. "Susannah could still be nearby." She found a gap in the bushes and stepped into the forest. Edwin followed reluctantly.

Twilight enveloped them. Grace played her light over a chaos of tree trunks, ferns, rocks, all flashing into view and vanishing as she swung around. Susannah could be six feet away and invisible to them, as could her attacker.

There must have been an attacker.

"I don't see any signs anyone came through here. No footprints..." Grace waved her torch, letting its beam dance crazily in the treetops. "Susannah!" she yelled. "Susannah! Can you hear me?"

No reply. The forest swallowed up the sound.

"We should go back."

"Not much further," Grace said. "It feels like we're not alone. What if Susannah is hurt? She could be lying unconscious nearby."

The old man and the woman stop where the path passes through a thick stand of laurel, now nothing but a solid mass of shadow in the darkening forest. The man is closest to the bushes blocking the narrow way. They exchange words. The man sounds afraid. His eyeglasses catch a glint of the last light as he shakes his head. The woman points down the path. They are only a few steps from the laurel.

The torch swings around again, licking over glossy, concealing leaves.

"What if Susannah is hurt?" the woman says distinctly.

The old man's reply is unclear.

The forest is filling up with night, trees and bushes vanishing, the sky drained of color. The searchers' expressions cannot be discerned.

The man says something else, too low to be heard. The woman steps around him to continue along the path.

Chapter Forty

Reflexively Edwin reached out and put his hand on Grace's shoulder. For an irrational instant he had a sinking feeling as if he'd suddenly, inappropriately, touched one of his students. He immediately regretted it. What right did he have? However, Grace stopped arguing.

"It's far too dangerous," he said. "There's nothing the two of us can do. Except blunder into an ambush, as Susannah must have done."

"You're right, Edwin. It looks as if people are being actively prevented from leaving the village."

The road, glimmering in the dusk, looked bright by comparison to the forest. They started back and after a couple of minutes Grace moved closer and put her arm through his. Was the gesture meaningful, Edwin wondered?

By the time they reached Noddweir, blackout curtains were closed as dusk purpled into darkness.

"Black as a coalman's hat," Grace remarked. Several rooks cawed overhead on their way to their roost, breaking the silence lying over the village. "Or as black as the heart of whoever's responsible for the current situation," she added, opening her front door. Before entering her gaze swept the street. A figure approached the pub. "Go in, Edwin. I want to talk to someone."

Edwin had followed her gaze. "Don't you think I should come with you?"

"It's Louisa Wainman," Grace said. "She shouldn't be here this time of night. Be a dear and make us tea."

Happy to have got Edwin safely back into the house, Grace hurried down the street. She intercepted Louisa, who carried a suitcase.

"I'm leaving Harry," Louisa announced defiantly. "Tonight I'm staying at the pub. Tomorrow I'm gone."

"What happened? Where will you go?"

"Birmingham or Newcastle. Maybe Birmingham. Lots of factory jobs, good paying ones. I'll be all right."

"You walked from the farm by yourself? That wasn't wise."

"You were out walking too. I saw you coming in with your lodger. Nice man, that, for a Yank." She gave Grace a meaningful smile.

"Don't change the subject. I don't think you'd up and run off right now, considering everything that's happening here."

Louisa smiled grimly. "I'll be glad to see the back of the place. I'm a bag of nerves." She sighed. "You know, Harry was hoarding petrol. Kept it in the barn. It's gone."

"Stolen, you think? Dear God, surely we're not in for more arson?"

Louisa shook her head. "No. I suspect Harry used it to help the blaze along at Haywood's place."

"But why? It makes no sense!"

"Does anything make sense? Now mind, I have an idea. I think it was to make it seem like we're under siege here."

Grace observed further proof was hardly necessary. Hadn't Louisa heard about Susannah?

"Ah, but that wasn't the only reason," Louisa continued. "Harry's a cunning bugger, or at least likes to think he is. The fire was part of his scheme to cover up. He killed Issy, Grace, I am as certain of it as I am I stand here." She gave a bitter laugh. "Don't look so shocked. I've known for a while now they were having an affair—"

"Louisa! She's only a child!"

"Don't matter to certain men, and it didn't matter to him. They met in the church when she was arranging the flowers. Imagine that. The filthy swine! In a church! Was bound to be noticed sooner or later. But he couldn't pull the wool over my eyes for long. I told him I knew about it. He denied it a couple of days ago."

Louisa gave a sob, her expression changing from anger to grief. "I feel it in my bones, Grace. They started to meet elsewhere. I think it was at Haywood's house. He killed that girl to stop her blabbing about them or else it was an accident. Then he set fire to the house to get rid of the body. People will write it off as just another of the terrible things that have been happening. Caused by the bogeyman they're all imagining."

"But the fire was only today. Where's he hidden Issy in the meantime?"

"Plenty of places round here. An entire forest. The farm's outbuildings."

"The ruins will have to be gone over carefully, in any case," Grace replied. "We'll know more then. And for that matter, where's Haywood?"

"Probably in Craven Arms picking up more little comforts for the good folk of Noddweir. Won't he be surprised when he comes back and finds he's been put out of business by losing all his stock?"

Although relieved to be back inside, Edwin regretted that his walk with Grace had ended. He put water on for tea, then sat at the kitchen table, chin on hand, trying to forget the warmth of the much younger woman walking close beside him in the nighttime chill, the pressure of her arm against his, the way her hips brushed him every so often.

She had said villagers were being prevented from leaving. But surely that didn't follow simply because one elderly woman, out alone, was attacked?

Martha wasn't about, he was glad to see. He recalled her babbling about the Guardian Stones' malign influence as she'd been escorted from the church. He cast his memory back over supernatural legends connected with standing stones. It was his experience that when traced to source, there was a prosaic explanation for impossible events, like magic tricks, where sleight of hand and clever misdirection produced apparently miraculous results.

Magicians could make people disappear, mystifying and delighting audiences. But the people they caused to vanish always returned.

When Grace came in she was crying.

She dropped into the chair beside him and sniffled and wiped at her eyes. Her shoulders shook.

Edwin almost put a comforting hand on her arm, then decided against it. He felt acutely awkward, not sure what he should do to alleviate the distress of this woman he didn't really know, although he felt he did. "What is it?"

"It's father."

"You haven't had bad news?"

"No, but I'm afraid of it." She looked at him with wet eyes. "I'm worried about him."

"I'm sure he'll be fine."

Grace glared at him. Now there was anger in her eyes. "I said I was worried about him, not for him."

"But what does Louisa Wainman have to do with it? You don't think he and she—"

"Nothing like that." Grace described her conversation with Louisa.

Edwin shook his head. The idea of the coarse middle-aged farmer and a child Isobel's age repelled him. "I still don't understand what it has to do with your father, Grace."

"You can be as thick as pea soup at times, Edwin! Issy was always over here having her ear bent by Martha. Everyone knew that. But a week or so before father left, the wretched girl started dropping hints that the two were carrying on."

Edwin sat back in his chair. "Grace!"

"Never mind. There's nothing that can be said. Do you know since I found out I haven't managed to force myself to pray for his black soul? God help me. I burnt the only photo of him we had and the filthy note Issy left and said nothing. I tried not to believe it. Issy's always had a vicious tongue and liked to cause trouble. But then, suddenly, out of the blue, he joined up. Or claimed he was joining up. When Louisa started talking about Harry silencing Issy, I thought what if it wasn't Harry, what if it was my father who came back to shut her up?"

Chapter Forty-one

"You suspect your father of murdering Isobel?" Edwin heard his voice rise.

"If you knew him—"

"But what about everything else that's happened? Emily and Constable Green being killed, all the others gone missing, the fire at Haywood's house?"

"There doesn't appear to be a common thread, I admit. But my father is an evil man." Grace clenched her eyes shut. "I pray to God I haven't inherited any of his evil."

"I…I'm sure you haven't, Grace." Edwin immediately felt stupid. What did he know about inherited evil? And what did Grace mean about her father being evil? Only that he had molested Isobel? Or was there more?

Grace put her face in her hands. Edwin leaned over impetuously and put an arm around her. She laid her head on his shoulder and shook with sobs.

Edwin didn't know what to say. How could a tiny village conceal secrets of such enormity? He remembered his initial sight of Noddweir from the cart. Looking down the High Street he had seen the well-kept public house, the ancient church, the slate-roofed houses with their neat gardens. But he also recalled the dirt road into the village, the forest pressing in toward the narrow way as if to cradle it in dark green fingers. In retrospect perhaps the forest had its claws fastened onto the road and Noddweir to keep anyone from escaping.

And forests hid secrets.

Grace cried until Edwin felt her tears soaking through his shirt. Although he realized with a pang it was totally inappropriate under the circumstances, he couldn't help enjoying her so near to him.

Finally she raised her head, snuffled, and gave him a sheepish look. "I'm sorry. I'm probably imagining things. Maybe I'm no better than Grandma, convinced the Guardian Stones are to blame. Imagine them stumping down the High Street, intent on mischief!" She forced a smile.

Edwin thought it best not to mention old tales about stone circles coming alive at midnight to prowl the forests or lumber to a brook to drink.

Grace kept talking. "He never was much of a father. Drank too much, especially for a policeman. It was an easy job then, before the war. The occasional bit of poaching was about the worst he had to deal with. Half the men in the village go out of a night to do it. They'd slip him a rabbit or two and never get caught."

"Village men go out in the forest at night, you say? Who in particular?"

"Means nothing. There was never any reason not to be out at night. Grandma occasionally wanders about at night. In fact, she's out right now."

Edwin asked what Martha did when she went out after dark.

"Gathers herbs and roots," Grace replied. "You have to pick certain plants at the right phase of the moon to get the best results, or at least according to the old ways. I expect you know a bit about that?"

Edwin nodded. "I've read about that belief a number of times, but Martha is the first person I've met who actually does it."

"You can't suspect Grandma?" Grace said.

"No. Certainly not," Edwin said quickly and not altogether truthfully. "But there are others who..."

"...think she's mad? That's true. More than one villager thinks she's mad. Who knows what lunatics do when the moon's right!"

Tears flowed again and she wiped her face. "Cursed on both sides of the family, I am. My evil father, my crazy grandmother."

"You aren't like your grandmother. Or her mother, from what Martha told me."

"Oh yes, she says she's from a long line of wise women. Not witches, mind you. She complained I refused to follow in her footsteps, didn't she?"

"Well—"

"She was stuck with Polly, the only one in the village willing to learn. Unfortunately Polly's a half-wit. Hardly suitable. Then Isobel took an interest."

"Isobel?"

Grace made a noise between a sob and a laugh. "Amazing how evil works, isn't it? How Satan plots against us. Why, if I hadn't agreed to look after Grandma, she would never have brought Issy into the house to tell her about her persuasions, and if she hadn't brought Issy into the house, Father would never have—"

"He might have anyway. Look at Harry Wainman."

Grace glared. "Is that supposed to make me feel better?"

"Better than seeing everything as a plot by satanic forces. Evil isn't a force, it's an attraction. It can't control anyone who chooses to resist its attraction." Edwin felt awkward, finding himself talking about evil forces.

"It wasn't me who broke away," Grace said. "It was Mum. Grandma would try to teach me her secrets and Mum would read to me from the Bible. Not that I was old enough to understand much of it. But I could understand the difference between right and wrong."

"You owe a lot to your mother, then," Edwin said, although he believed that giving up Martha's wisdom for the Bible's was simply trading one set of superstitions for another.

"I can barely remember Mum. One day she was simply gone." Grace got up suddenly to rummage in the pantry. She brought out a rifle and a box of ammunition and laid them on the table.

"Father's rook rifle," she told him. "Telling you about poaching reminded me. He used to hunt rabbits mostly. It's time I made sure it was still in working order."

"Don't tell me you know how to use that?"

"Father taught me to shoot rabbits practically before I could read."

"You killed rabbits? When you were a little girl? You must have been horrified when you realized what you'd done."

Grace hefted the gun. "Why would I be? They're nasty pests, even if they do make a decent stew. They'll destroy your whole garden if you let them. I was proud of being a good shot."

Not long afterward, Edwin sat in bed unable either to sleep or switch his mind off. He had tried to look over his notes but couldn't concentrate. Grace suspected her father of murder? Grace's father was molesting Isobel? Grace described it as "carrying on" as if it were an affair, but when a grown man did that to a child, it was nothing but molestation, wasn't it?

The *Light of the World* print struck Edwin as grotesquely ironic. Where was the light in Noddweir? Every knock on the door brought more bad news. It would never be Jesus at the door with a lantern. If He ever did arrive, He'd knock in vain. Everyone would be far too frightened to open up.

He had an uneasy vision of Grace kneeling beside her bed not far away and praying to her unseen and apparently uncaring God. Did she kneel to pray? Why would he think of such a thing anyway? Did his treacherous imagination want to see her in her bedroom? When he had put a comforting arm around her she had not shrugged it off. How had it happened he accompanied her on her night patrol? Surely he was not any real help. Did she simply enjoy his company?

What's the matter with me? Edwin asked himself. I should know better at my age. Grace could be my daughter. It was almost as bad as Grace's father or Harry Wainman with Isobel.

His wife's photograph smiled at him from the table.

And how could he be thinking about a young woman he hardly knew while Elise looked on? It was a betrayal of his wife's memory. The very fact Edwin continued to live was a betrayal.

Yet he was only doing what the two of them had planned all along. And very soon, when he reached the end of what they had planned, he would roll to a stop and that would be that.

"I am sorry, Elise," he murmured. He removed his glasses and set them on the table and his wife's face blurred like a fading memory.

Chapter Forty-two

Friday, June 20, 1941

"That's that then!" Joe Haywood spat into the blackened ashes where his house had stood.

At least his wallet was full, thanks to the deals he'd done while away. Had someone destroyed all his stock because they had it in for him? A jealous villager? A business rival?

It was getting too risky to continue trading here anyway he decided, poking at what remained of a sofa with a large stick. He couldn't find the envelope stuffed with cash. Probably it burnt, though it was possible the place was robbed and then set alight.

Some called it black marketeering, but he preferred to think of it as helping buyers obtain desirable goods which happened to be in short supply. And why not? The poor buggers worked hard enough with little by way of recreation except a game of darts at the pub and singing hymns on Sundays.

A shame he had to move on so soon. The isolated village was out of the way of uniformed snoopers on the lookout for resourceful businessmen or those who had better things to do than take orders and march around. Both descriptions fitted Haywood. His claim of being a conscientious objector had worked well enough so far but the current series of events in Noddweir was attracting far too much attention, including that of a regular constable from Craven Arms. He didn't need anyone checking into his background.

Better to get out before he was arrested for one reason or another.

It could be whoever had set fire to the house had done him a favor. If everyone assumed he'd died in the flames he should be able to disappear before they found out he wasn't dead, if they ever did.

There was only one problem.

She had red hair and sweet lips. Could he convince Meg to come away with him?

He laughed harshly at himself. Was he getting soft? No matter where he set up shop next there'd be women. And the moment he flashed a handful of pound notes in the local pub they'd be around him, drawn as moths to a flame.

Besides, he could always send for Meg if he wanted. After a few weeks without him she'd be all the more eager to escape that feckless lump of a husband.

The decision made, Haywood decided to cut through the forest to the main road and hitchhike back to Craven Arms. From there he could catch a train. He didn't want to run into anyone while he was leaving.

It was surprisingly dark under the canopy of trees. He passed through a stand of pines, their trunks rising branchless almost to their crowns, columns in a cathedral tossed together by a mad god. Twice he tripped over roots and fell. Dried pine needles stuck in his palms. He cursed. At this rate his trousers would be ruined by the time he got to the road.

There were sounds too. Rustlings. Birds maybe, or rabbits, or whatever the hell else lived in the forest.

A loud snort brought him to a halt. A deer emerged from the vegetation. It looked straight at him with huge eyes, then bounded off.

He shivered. Christ! Those big buggers made him break out into a muck sweat every time he glimpsed one. They were worse than cows. At least cows were confined behind fences.

As he continued on, his thoughts turned to the disappearances that had bedeviled Noddweir. The villagers were afraid there was a criminal lurking in these forest. Haywood dismissed the idea. The only criminal in the forest right now—"criminal," technically speaking—was Joe Haywood.

No wonder the villagers acted weird, surrounded by dark forests with that damned stone circle brooding over everything. You wouldn't find him anywhere near those stones, even if all the talk about them was nothing but superstitious nonsense. Luckily, to reach the main road without being seen, he only needed to skirt the hill, which was in fact what he was currently navigating.

There was an evil atmosphere about the circle. If he was honest—and he reckoned he was, with himself at any rate—he'd admit it frightened him.

Through the trees ahead he could see light. Had he reached the road already? No, as it turned out. He'd come upon one of those abandoned charcoal-burning platforms. He'd seen them often enough to have found out what they were. However, he'd never seen one before with a crude cross made of large dead limbs in the center.

His foot touched something soft concealed in long weeds. Bending down he saw it was a haversack. He started to utter a curse and stopped himself. The owner was probably lurking nearby.

He looked into the clearing. A big crow perched on the one arm of the cross, moving jerkily, a wind-up toy, pecking. At what? A ripe stench filled the air.

Haywood didn't linger. He skirted around the clearing. When he reached the far side he glanced back, curious to see what had kept the crow busy.

Joe Haywood had not spent his life in genteel surroundings. He had got up to dirty business in his time and seen rough sights, many of which he'd taken a hand in creating. But what hung on the cross caused him to fall to his knees instantly and vomit onto the moss until his sides ached.

When he had finished, wiped his mouth, and got dizzily to his feet, he realized he was being watched.

He didn't have the impression he was being watched. He was certain.

A twig cracked in the trees to his right. Turning, he could see nothing.

Leaves rustled. The sound came from behind him. Nothing there either that he could see. The faint rustling might have come from anywhere in the surrounding thick undergrowth. He wasn't used to forests. Maybe the mountains created an echo.

Another noise.

In front of him?

"Bloody hell." He couldn't tell what direction sounds came from in this damned forest. What could be everywhere at once?

In the next second, he found out.

Chapter Forty-three

It was time he got in touch with Joe Haywood, Timothy Wilson thought as he searched through almost-empty kitchen cupboards. Then he remembered Haywood's house had burnt down. Had all his illegal wares gone with it?

Finally he found a tin containing a handful of broken biscuits. What else did he have to offer his visitor? Emily Miller had given him a jar of gooseberry jam. Did anyone really like gooseberry jam?

It might not be strictly proper for a vicar to deal with a black marketeer, but when parishioners sought Wilson out for counseling, advice, and comfort, they naturally expected a cup of tea. Or so he thought.

He had set cups and a plate of biscuits—the largest of the remaining pieces—on the side table in the parlor when one of his resident evacuees showed in Violet Gowdy. He directed her to a chair. Perched on it with her auburn hair neatly braided, wearing her Sunday best pink-flowered dress she resembled a Victorian china-doll waiting for the tea party to begin.

Wilson served the tea and biscuits while Violet looked at him, solemn and silent. He leaned back in his chair. "Well now, Violet." His voice was especially weak this morning, a ragged croak. "Your mother asked me to talk to you. What seems to be the problem?"

She looked at him suspiciously. "There's something bad stealing children. Everyone knows that."

"There are those who think that. Others think the children are running away. Copycats, you see."

Her mouth full of biscuit, Violet scowled at him. Talking with children was not the vicar's forte. He'd never married and had children of his own. He was comfortable teaching them in a group, but speaking with youngsters individually about personal matters made him feel awkward. He didn't speak quite the same language.

"Mum told me she prayed to Jesus to keep me safe," Violet stated. "But I saw the White Thing! I did! And Bert never came back neither."

"You can be sure your mother's prayer will be answered, Violet. Jesus is everywhere."

"Even in Noddweir?"

"Of course."

"Then he knows where Bert and the other children are. So why doesn't he send them back or tell us where to look?"

Wilson sipped his tea slowly to give his voice a rest and his mind time to work. The trouble with children was they hadn't yet learned to pretend to accept platitudes as answers. "Violet, your mother is concerned about you. She doesn't want you to be afraid. You know from your Bible lessons that Jesus walks beside us. He's right here in this room with us."

Violet's expression darkened. "I saw the White Thing going to Constable Green's room and he got killed. I never saw Jesus. Except one time after church my friend Patrick claimed he saw him in a cloud, only it didn't look like Jesus to me. It looked more like a tiger. And now Patrick's gone too."

What was this "White Thing" she was so convinced she had seen? Wilson decided it would be better not to inquire. "Haven't you ever felt Jesus was near to you?" he asked instead.

"At times I sing a hymn and I feel…something…" Her tone suggested she was trying to get the answer correct rather than from any conviction.

"See. What a good idea. Singing a hymn is a way to feel Jesus protecting you."

"But why didn't Jesus protect the other children?"

"We don't know that he didn't. They may all have got back to their homes by now."

"Not Issy or Patrick and Jim. They live here."

"And how do we know they aren't going to return safe and sound?"

Violet had finished her biscuits. She still resembled a china-doll, a sullen china-doll with crumbs around her perfect cupid's bow mouth. Wilson had to clear his throat before speaking. "No one is more precious to Jesus than children. Remember how He said suffer them to come to Him?'"

"If Jesus loved children why would He want them to suffer?"

"When He said *suffer*, He meant allow them to come to Him."

"My mum is always telling Dad he makes her suffer."

Wilson tried to suppress a cough and failed. He covered his mouth with his handkerchief and hacked uncontrollably until his eyes streamed. He could see Violet staring at him with alarm. He was supposed to be offering the child comfort. A right mess he was making of it. Finally the spasms subsided and he forced his lips into what he hoped was a reassuring smile but suspected was a frightening rictus.

When Violet left, Wilson went to the church.

Although people were in and out the past few days, the church was deserted at the moment. Light streamed in through the stained glass windows, scattering rainbow colors across the empty pews. Should he have spoken with Violet here, where the grace of God was more evident than in his gloomy parlor? He had continued to talk to the child but doubted whether his efforts had helped her. His words had sounded feeble even to himself.

His own beliefs were complicated, intellectual, not anything he could convey to a child. Not as comforting as simple beliefs.

He knelt before the altar and prayed.

He had assured Violet that Jesus was always close at hand but this morning it felt as if He were far away.

Wilson spoke easily to others about the presence of Jesus but he was not certain he could feel that presence himself. Or not so strongly as a man of the cloth should. Certainly he had experienced a sense of the divine during services, as Saint Winnoc looked down and the light coming through the colored windows suffused the worshipers' rapt faces with a warm glow. At night, in the quiet hours when he studied the Bible, trying to parse out the meaning of a particularly troublesome verse, a stack of exegeses beside him, the presence was there also.

But was it Jesus he felt swelling within his chest during these times or merely beauty and intellectual challenge, a sense not of the divine but of the heights of human endeavor?

Colleagues, when he had had contact with colleagues, claimed that Jesus spoke in their ear, that they knew He was there as surely as they knew Wilson was sitting across from them. Did they? Or did they say so because they thought they should? Or did they merely interpret whatever they did feel in the manner they supposed appropriate? And what did they feel? Was it different from what he felt or were they simply being dishonest about it or interpreting it differently?

Not that Wilson needed to hear the voice of Jesus to believe. He believed in his own way, because he had heard the fading voices of soldiers on the battlefield, young men dying in hope rather than despair, thanks to the sacred teachings. Didn't that alone justify it all?

What, in the end, would be the point of not believing, of having no hope?

He clasped his hands and closed his eyes. He prayed again, but could not convince himself that his words were escaping past the devil looming over Noddweir.

Violet walked home feeling cross after her visit with the vicar. An excruciating experience, like having to sit through a church service all by herself and not being able to daydream. The biscuits were stale too. She ate them because her mother ordered her to be polite and act like a young lady.

She was never sure what to make of it when adults talked about Jesus and God being up in the sky but walking around on earth like ghosts too. Did her mum really believe that? Did Violet? She kind-of did and she kind-of didn't. She scuffled slowly along the High Street, happy the day was young and that she wouldn't need to worry about the night for many hours yet. She didn't notice Martha approaching until the old woman called to her.

"Violet, my child, I've made something for you."

Martha was too close for Violet to pretend not to see her so she stopped and waited. When Martha got close Violet could smell her old lady scent, faded flowers in a dim, musty room.

She held out to Violet what appeared to be a small doll.

Violet peered at the object. It was shaped like a person yet on closer inspection its humanity vanished. There was nothing but dead entwined twigs, dried grass, and bits of bark, all bound together with string.

"It's a charm," Martha told her. "It's to protect you from what's coming to Noddweir."

A chill ran down Violet's back. She bit her lip. One second Martha was holding a doll, the next it was a bunch of dead sticks.

"Go on, take it," Martha urged. "Keep it near you all the time. Then bad things won't be able to get at you."

Violet took a step backwards, confused. What scared her about a bunch of sticks tied together?

She looked at Martha. With her wrinkled, dried-apple face and wild hair she suddenly looked like the witch many villagers claimed she was.

Don't be silly, Violet told herself. It's only old Martha. You know Martha.

Issy had known Martha too, hadn't she? Spent hours with her, and where was Issy now?

Violet felt panic rising.

The witch pushed the hideous stick man toward her.

Violet turned and ran home to the Guardians pub as fast as she could, without looking back.

Chapter Forty-four

Leaving the house, Edwin met Martha. Stamping along, muttering to herself and looking disgruntled, she didn't acknowledge his greeting.

Grace had already left when Edwin got up. He'd felt vaguely disappointed when he found the kitchen deserted. It was early. There was still a chill in the air. Had she raced off to avoid seeing him after her confessions the night before?

He had jam and toast and made tea. Although he lingered, Grace didn't return. Edwin knew he ought to be pursuing his studies, but when he sat down with his notes and tried to go over them they didn't seem important, everything considered. Visiting the stones or rambling around the forest alone probably wasn't a good idea. Even if one assumed Emily Miller had died of a heart attack, Susannah Radbone's disappearance indicated that whoever or whatever was preying on Noddweir's children had now turned its attention to adults.

Or was he being an alarmist? There was no evidence Susannah had come to grief. Perhaps her bicycle had broken down and she had left it and hitchhiked to town. She had struck him as the stubborn type who would do such a thing. Possibly the bicycle was damaged in an accident, not that he and Grace had noticed any sign of one.

But supposing his theory was correct, why had she left her belongings and the cat-carrier?

There was no point sitting around waiting for Grace and brooding. He'd walk around the village. He told himself he wasn't really hoping to run into Grace, merely getting a little fresh air while it was still cool. With sunlight sparkling on quaint cottages and birds singing, it was difficult to believe in distant war, let alone murders at home.

Could there really be an evil creature lurking in the forest, beneath the very trees from which birds called so cheerily? Suddenly there was a dreadful howl of excruciating pain.

Looking around he saw a black cat—Susannah's cat—sitting before the closed door of her cottage, tail flicking in annoyance.

When he walked over, the cat looked at him, back at the door, and yowled. "I'm afraid your mistress isn't home."

Would Timothy's young charges like a cat? He tried the door. It was unlocked. The cat trotted inside, tail raised high, went straight into the kitchen, and resumed caterwauling.

Edwin followed. There was a faintly unpleasant smell in the air. "Waiting to eat, are you?"

He'd visit Timothy right away. If one of his girls wanted a cat she could take him back to the vicarage.

The cat circled Edwin's legs, making pitiful noises. When he moved, it made no effort to avoid his feet.

"I won't be able to get you anything if you trip me up and I crack my skull," Edwin chided. The words had as much effect as his remonstrances had on his duller students.

Feeling guilty, he poked around. The first jug of milk he found had soured, accounting for the smell. Another jug had not yet soured. He poured it into a saucer and watched the cat lap greedily. Would Susannah be so extravagant?

He poured the soured milk down the drain in the sink. The odor lingered behind.

The kitchen looked in perfect order, with no dirty dishes waiting to be washed, no sign that Susannah had left in undue haste. Jars of gooseberry jam marched in neat rows across the counter.

Might there be a clue to Susannah's departure in the house?

Not that Edwin had any inkling of what it could be. Susannah had simply become disenchanted with Noddweir following the death of her friend Emily and decided to leave. It was understandable, wasn't it?

On the other hand, Grace couldn't be expected to investigate everything at once. Edwin could help.

He'd already scanned the kitchen and seen nothing unusual. Although what did he expect to find? A reminder note? "Leave Noddweir tomorrow?"

He left the cat working at the milk in the saucer—Edwin was overgenerous—and went down the hall. A cramped, starkly furnished bedroom on one side he guessed was Reggie's.

He hesitated before going upstairs but finally did, finding a larger room with lace curtains that was obviously Susannah's bedroom.

Edwin paused in the doorway. On a small round-topped table inside lay two books. Russell's *The Problems of Philosophy* and Virginia Woolf's *Mrs. Dalloway*. He could see himself in the dressing table mirror, his image that of a graying burglar with eyeglasses slipping down his nose.

What was he thinking? He couldn't go snooping through Susannah Radbone's possessions. He shouldn't be here.

Shaking his head, he turned to leave. The smell was stronger here than in the kitchen. A foul odor. Not sour milk then? A few steps further down the hall, the stench increased. He had come to what must be a closet door. He pulled it open. A cloud of flies exploded into his face.

Several fat bodies smacked against his forehead and cheeks, obscene raindrops.

He backed away, cursing and waving his hands at the disgusting insects.

Now he could definitely smell decay.

His heart raced as he peered into the dim closet filled with brooms and mops and hanging coats. Several cardboard boxes sat on the floor. Bending, Edwin saw those in front contained canning jars.

He pushed them aside and pulled out the box in the back.

More flies.

A tea towel was loosely draped over the box. Edwin lifted the towel.

In the bottom of the box, alive with glistening flies, sat an unidentifiable object about half the size of his hand. Was it a scrap of meat or the remains of a small animal a cat would drag in? It was too badly rotted to identify. He gagged and tasted bile.

Beside the putrescent mass was a jumble of kitchen utensils—knives of all sizes.

All displayed rust-colored stains.

Edwin and Grace stood at the edge of the pond behind Susannah's house, watching Jack Chapman wade around and probe the water with a long metal rod.

Edwin shook his head. "You can't really suspect Susannah murdered all those children and hid the bodies in the pond? Surely after a certain time they would—"

"I know it sounds ludicrous, but considering what's happened here lately…"

"I suppose she is an outsider by Noddweir standards."

"That's nothing to do with it." Grace sounded exasperated. "Well, maybe something to do with it. Of course I don't believe a word of it, but if I look into the possibility it might stop the talk. You can't tell with strangers. Who knows what she got up to before she arrived. That's the sort of thing they're already saying."

Chapman worked his way methodically across the pond. Water rose over his waist, then to his chest. Dragonflies flashed in the sunlight. Spindly-legged bugs skittered across the water. What was beneath that placid surface?

The water came nearly up to Chapman's shoulders now. Edwin shuddered, imagining himself wading out there, setting his feet down blindly into muck and weeds. Finding his leg caught suddenly in….what? A tangle of branches or the ribcage of a half-decayed torso?

"What was it in the box, Grace?"

She shrugged. "Couldn't tell. Nothing left but a badly decayed chunk of flesh." She didn't speculate on the knives' significance.

"I can see what you mean about gossip," Edwin said. "Saying Susannah only came here because she planned to kill the children. Hid the bodies in the pond. Mad, you see. Her friend Emily became suspicious so Emily had to die too. But then the fiend was afraid Emily might already have talked, so it was time to depart."

"Something like that. She'd be a suitably unlikely suspect in a mystery."

Edwin guessed she was right. What did he really know about Susannah Radbone, whom he'd only met a handful of days ago? What did he know about anyone in Noddweir, when he came down to it?

Shielding his eyes against the sun, he watched Chapman work on the other side of the pond. The big man's shirt was plastered to his broad chest. When Grace had gone to the smithy to borrow a suitable rod for the job, he'd immediately volunteered to do it. Was it because if any victims were to be found, Issy was the most likely?

Chapman paused and felt around with the rod, as if prodding at an object concealed in the mud. He jammed the rod down, letting it stand upright. Clearly he'd found something.

The buzzing of insects sounded suddenly louder as Chapman bent and reached into the water. When he straightened up he held a rusted, muck-filled biscuit tin.

Edwin could see relief on Chapman's face.

"If Susannah didn't reach her sister's home, what happened to her?" Edwin asked Grace as the blacksmith resumed his search.

"I'm hoping she walked out to the main road and got a ride. And while her cat apparently escaped, what worries me is she left her suitcase."

"Maybe she's planning on hiring someone to bring her back for it." Edwin realized it sounded silly.

Chapman waded back toward them, coming around the pond's edge where it was shallower. "Checked it all, Grace. Nothing."

"Thank God," Grace murmured. "I appreciate your help, Jack."

As Chapman approached he suddenly looked down, leaned over, and reached into a clump of vegetation.

He bellowed in pain as he yanked his hand away.

A tiny gray shape clung to his finger.

Chapman cursed and shook his hand. Whatever had hold of his finger refused to let go. He stumbled onto the land and slammed his hand on the ground until his miniature assailant relented.

Edwin saw a small, limp, furry form. "Looks like Mole from *The Wind in the Willows,*" he muttered.

Chapman wrapped his wounded finger in a grubby handkerchief. Blood soaked through the fabric.

"Water shrew," Grace explained. "They're not a fit animal for children's stories. They'll give you a nasty bite."

Chapman saw Edwin's distress. "Don't worry. It won't kill me. Hurts like hell, though. The movement caught my eye. Serves me right, looking with my hand."

Grace clucked with sympathy. "You'd better go home and clean it off well, Jack."

Chapman stared down at the tiny corpse. For a moment Edwin thought he was going to kick it, but he turned away and walked off.

"He's embarrassed such a little beast gave him such a big tussle," Grace observed. "He'll have bad pain and a bit of swelling, but he should be all right."

Edwin shook his head. "A venomous shrew. Who would've guessed?"

Grace grinned bleakly. "We're full of surprises in Noddweir, aren't we?"

Chapter Forty-five

Edwin was in his room changing his muddy trousers when the shouting started. He rushed downstairs into the kitchen without putting on his shoes. A rotund, red-faced little woman was loudly haranguing Grace, who sat wearily at the table.

"Are you sure that Alan is gone, Harriet?" Grace asked the woman, who looked to Edwin like an enraged garden gnome.

He started back, but Grace gestured him in urgently. "Harriet, this is my lodger, Professor Carpenter. Professor, Harriet Lamb."

Harriet nodded curtly as Edwin took a chair beside Grace. Harriet lowered her voice in deference to the newcomer but her words were no less vehement. "Am I a liar, Grace Baxter? I had to borrow sugar from Nellie Atkinson and you know how she gossips. When I got back Alan wasn't in the house."

Grace leaned back in her chair, perturbed as well as tired. "And he was there this morning?"

"His door was still closed, didn't I already tell you?"

"But it's afternoon. What makes you think he didn't get up and go out to meet his friends?"

"With the devil stalking the streets? Besides, I've told him not to go out on his own."

"I saw Alan and a couple of other boys playing by the pond yesterday."

"Did you know? Are you hinting I can't control my own son?"

"Why don't you wait a bit, Harriet? If he doesn't come home for his tea—"

"Wait! There's a fine thing. My boy gone and all you can do is tell me to wait."

Edwin forced himself to sit in silence. He didn't want to give Grace the idea he thought she couldn't handle her unofficial job.

"We're doing as much as we can." Grace's voice was tight with irritation. "Where would you suggest we look for him?"

Harriet remained planted stolidly where she was. She crossed her big arms and scowled. "If I was in charge I'd be questioning the vicar!"

"What? Do you think Mr. Wilson—"

"He's a deep one, that vicar, if you ask me. What's he always doting on the children for? This parade he's arranged and all those little girls he keeps in the vicarage and him not married, as Nellie pointed out to—"

Edwin couldn't restrain himself. "That's absurd," he snapped. "Besides, he can barely manage to cross the street after what the Germans did to his lungs."

"You know the vicar better than we do then?" sniffed Harriet. "He can get around better than he lets on."

"I know him as well as you do, Harriet," Grace put in, "and I agree with Professor Carpenter."

The glare Harriet gave them both could only be described as malevolent.

"How about all them boxes of books?" The way Harriet spit out 'books' made it sound like a dirty word. "Children's books. What's a grown man without a family, an unmarried man, doing with boxes of children's books? Bait, that's what I call them. Bait to lure the innocent. All them wild tales. Fairies and pirates and such. Useless they are, putting ideas into kids' heads. The only book we need's the Good Book."

Grace stood. "I will send someone to look for Alan as soon as I can, Harriet. Now I must get back to this report I'm working on, so if you'll excuse me…." Her glare convinced Harriet to stump out, ungraciously muttering over her shoulder about how deep the vicar was and it was a disgrace nothing was done about it.

Grace slumped back down in her chair. "Grace is in disgrace," she suddenly giggled. The dark concavities under her eyes made her look older.

"You should rest, Grace."

"I wish I could." She took a deep breath. "But there's work to be done."

"You don't think the boy is actually missing?"

"I don't think so. It's possible, of course." She shrugged. "Mothers are afraid to let their children out of their sight. I can't say I blame them."

Edwin tapped the pad on which he could make out Grace's neat, schoolgirl's handwriting. "What's this report? Can I help?"

"Thanks, but no. I'm summarizing what's happened here this past week. I intend to make sure the authorities take notice and send help."

"You're not thinking of going to Craven Arms yourself after what happened to Susannah?"

"We don't know that anything happened to Susannah."

"We're under siege here, Grace. I think it's time we stop pretending otherwise."

Grace pulled the pad over and scanned it. "Everyone's on edge. Losing their tempers. Scared."

"With good reason." Edwin stared intently at her. She was trying not to meet his gaze. "You can't try to go into town by yourself. I'll go."

She turned a puzzled face toward him. "You? But Edwin, why would—"

"I'm very fond of you, Grace. I couldn't bear it if anything happened to you."

There, he'd said it.

She looked at him in confusion. "I…"

Had he made a fool of himself? An old fool? He started talking again, as if that was going to help matters. "When we were out walking last night, I could sense that you….well…"

Grace bit her lip.

She put her hand on his arm. "Edwin, I'm very fond of you. You're like the father I never really had."

Chapter Forty-six

He'd failed as a father.

Jack Chapman sat brooding on the anvil beside his cold forge and downed yet another mug of cider.

A real father would have knocked sense into his daughter's head. A father who was doing his duty would have beaten the badness out of Issy. Never mind what the rest of the village might think. They weren't living with evil like Jack was.

The cider—made by a local farmer—burned the back of his throat and churned his stomach.

Jack started drinking to kill the throbbing pain from the shrew bite as soon as he returned home from searching the pond. Nasty little buggers, those water shrews.

Drinking soothed the physical pain but didn't ease the agony in his soul. Or wouldn't until he drank enough to lose consciousness, his usual method of getting to sleep at night.

Through the forge's open doors he could see past the junk-strewn yard into the field across the road. He was dizzy from the cider or from the shrew's venomous bite. It wasn't dangerous but the effects were unpleasant while they lasted.

When he and Lilly were courting they strolled the fields at twilight. That was after the war. The first war.

He had returned wounded in his mind. You couldn't see the world the same way after you had turned to speak to a colleague and found he no longer had a head, after you tried to pull your hand out the mud after a barrage only to discover you'd been up to your elbow in your best friend's intestines. How could there be any good in a world like that?

No, the place he found himself after those experiences was nothing but a hell, populated by demons who claimed to be human.

When he was back in Noddweir a year he got to know Lilly. She was a sudden, undreamt-of light in a world where all the lights had been extinguished. She gave Jack a reason to live again. To believe there was still good beyond all the evil. They had married and planned a family.

And Issy had killed her, ripped her apart in the act of being born, the young heifer.

Jack was sure he would never see anything as horrific as what he had seen in the trenches. He was wrong. The lifeless face of the woman he loved was much, much worse.

So vivid was the pale, still image it seemed to materialize out of the darkness before his eyes. Untouched by the years that had passed. The features young, delicate. So unlike their coarse daughter. How could Lilly have given birth to such a monster?

"What have you done to our daughter?" Lilly asked him in a susurration as sad as the wind rustling the flowers on a child's grave. "You promised me you would take care of her and look what's happened."

Tears welled up in Jack's eyes, blurring the phantom visage.

"Lilly…I did my best…."

Then he was lying on the ground on his stomach.

He rolled over feeling grit under his back. He must have passed out.

Staring upward he could dimly make out the rafters of his forge. Dawn must be approaching. He pushed himself up to his knees and the smoke stained walls spun around. He realized he was far from sober. He remembered the vision of his dead wife.

"Lilly?"

No answer.

His right arm felt sticky. It looked wet in the gray light. He smelled the coppery odor of blood.

What had he been doing? Stumbling around the smithy and injured his arm?

"Do you believe that?" a voice whispered.

"Lilly?"

He staggered to his feet and took a few wobbling steps in the direction from which the voice had come and out into the yard.

Above the treetops, in the graying sky, hung a sharp crescent of moon, a horned moon. His daughter was born under the dark influence of a horned moon. He should have drowned the child immediately.

"And whose fault is your daughter, Father? Not Mother's. Not such a good woman as Mother."

Jack closed his eyes tightly. Forced himself back to his senses. He was still drunk. The world wouldn't stop spinning.

When he opened his eyes Issy stood in front of him, a misty ghost in the pallid light pooled in the yard.

"Devil!" he breathed.

The apparition laughed. "Who's the devil, Father? Did I ask to be born? Did I ask for the beatings you gave me?"

"I never beat you. Never."

"So you tell everyone. Liar!"

"You lie! The devil lies!"

"It is time to stop lying, Father. It's time to do what has to be done."

Jack saw that the ghost held in its hand a coil of heavy rope.

Chapter Forty-seven

Saturday, June 21, 1941

By mid-morning it was already sweltering—weather British newspapers would doubtless call a "scorcher," Edwin thought. The younger children among those gathered at the church door for the parade were fretful.

He felt unsettled himself, acutely embarrassed by his confession to Grace, or more honestly, by her reaction. He had run into her briefly that morning as she went out on patrol. They exchanged awkward greetings. He wasn't sure how he was going to face her now. Lucklly the parade gave him something else to occupy his mind.

Edwin scanned the crowd, mostly women with a sprinkling of farmworkers who had taken an hour off to see the parade. Mothers hushed their children's excited chatter when the vicar announced the arrangements.

"We shall form a line and Professor Carpenter and I will lead the children round the village so everyone can see them."

Edwin glanced up the High Street. Villagers stood at their garden gates, many holding small flags. A lump rose into his throat at the sight. This was not his country, but he and Elise had always admired Britain. Besides which, a sincere show of patriotism was undeniably moving, notwithstanding that it was called the last refuge of scoundrels. He hastily turned his attention toward Timothy Wilson, who continued speaking in a labored whisper.

"We shall stop at the top of the High Street, where I'll present each entrant and everyone can get a good look at them. Every child will receive a book and the winner will receive two."

"Three cheers for the vicar!" came a yell and the crowd obliged, despite remonstrations from Wilson.

Mothers marshaled the children into a ragged line and Edwin and Wilson led them away, followed by the adults.

Cheers and waving flags greeted the children as they progressed up the dusty street. They might have been a conquering army returning from the wars. Even the smallest child, a little girl pushing what Edwin deduced to be the family dog in a doll's pram—nobody was quite sure what she was meant to be—was caught up in the excitement. A happy grin illuminated her face as she trundled along beside her mother.

"It's remarkable how inventive people can be using whatever is to hand," Edwin remarked. "I never thought I'd see Britannia wearing a colander helmet and carrying a dustbin lid shield and garden fork trident!"

Wilson smiled. "A splendid effort. But I'm afraid the lady who does the cleaning for me will be annoyed when she finds the feather duster has been destroyed for the tail of the baby duck."

Edwin glanced back. The oldest evacuee billeted with Wilson was leading her youngest sister, who was dressed as a duck in a yellow pullover, cardboard beak held in place with string, and a bundle of feathers tied to her back. "The children will enjoy the attention," he said, "not to mention the books."

"Yes." The word came out as a long wheeze.

"Do you think you should walk this much, Timothy?"

"I'll be fine."

Edwin hoped his friend wasn't overestimating his strength. From what he was told, he wouldn't have expected Wilson capable of a continuous walk around the village, especially on such a hot morning. Shading his eyes, he glanced at the sky where scattered clouds avoided the sun's blazing orb. He couldn't help noticing the knob of Guardians Hill.

Wilson must have seen the direction of Edwin's lingering gaze. "It's strange that we're having our jamboree on the summer solstice. Celebrations in the old days were a lot more, shall we say, robust?"

"So Harry Wainman was telling me." Edwin recalled the surly farmer's account of naked dancers among the stones.

Wilson stopped and turned to address the children. "In a moment each of you will walk round the line so everyone can get a close look. My friend the professor here has agreed to be judge for the best costume, having—as Americans say—no horse in the race. And then we shall parade back to the church for the prize-giving."

The first contestant to break away from the others was an older village boy, whom the vicar described as a sandwich board man, pointing out the slogan urging everyone to Dig For Victory daubed on cardboard oblongs worn front and back. "And as you see, John has been digging for victory and has a basket full of vegetables to show for it."

"I grew 'em myself and they're better'n anyfink you'd pick up in town," the patriotic lad boasted as he moved to one side.

"Next, we have a representative of our gallant allies the French, ground under the Nazi boot but still fighting," Wilson went on as a boy wearing a black beret took a hasty circuit. Edwin did not have the heart to mention he heard the boy tell the sandwich board brother that he thought it was a stupid idea to pretend to be a famous painter with no brushes, only a beret.

Wilson next described the baby duck's trio of siblings. "They are, as you see, swathed in brown paper and string, and I understand this represents parcels. Let's hope there's no postage due!"

Despite the laughter, several women wiped away tears. Were they thinking about parcels of little comforts they sent to their sons and husbands overseas?

A tow-headed boy dressed in his blue Sunday suit, shiny with wear, though well cared for if a little short in the legs, came next.

He carried a homemade wooden airplane and made zooming noises as he paraded around the line. "As you see, Albert is an RAF pilot like his father, now posted as missing and for whose safe return we pray."

A special round of applause greeted his remarks. Again Edwin felt a lump in his throat. How could these people go on trying to live normal lives when they could never be sure from one day to the next what might happen? Then again, wasn't he living here with them, coping with the same situation? Hadn't he gone on despite Elise's death? What else could you do?

Now three village boys pranced along together in the guise of a butcher, a baker, and a candlestick maker, carrying a large knife, a mixing bowl, and a tin candlestick. The next entrant brought several frowns. It was an evacuee with a lock of hair stuck to his forehead and a burnt cork mustache. His goose-stepping effort was spoiled by his wellingtons and a ripple of laughter broke out, mixed with vigorous booing.

Several other children had their turn in the spotlight, most dressed as such old favorites as gypsies wearing a shawl and paste jewelry or mice with string tails and brown paper ears attached to headbands. Wilson kept up his commentary, pausing to cough occasionally, his voice reduced to a near whisper.

Edwin imagined him as a young man, lending what aid and comfort he could in the hell of the trenches. Who could guess that so many years later he would be offering solace to others caught up in evil closer to home?

Violet was the last to parade, tripping over her long skirt and wearing a cardboard crown and feather boa. Described by the vicar as "our gracious queen, may God bless her and King George," Violet smiled on all and sundry in regal fashion, the effect marred by her need to keep adjusting her crown and muttering "bother the thing."

Edwin guessed that her costume was her mother Meg's idea.

There was a hearty round of applause and Wilson asked Edwin to name the winner.

Edwin adjusted his glasses. He didn't mind handing out grades to his university students, but judging these hopeful and excited children made him uncomfortable. "It was a really difficult decision," he finally said, adopting his best academic tones. "But as a representative of British spirit and inventiveness, I think Britannia should be awarded first prize."

Britannia whacked her shield with her trident and yelled in triumph. Everyone laughed. Then the vicar said "Now for the prize-giving!"

The two men led the parade back down the High Street to the church door. Edwin wondered if Wilson would make it to the end of the parade route. Despite having almost lost his voice during his commentary, Wilson moved at a steady if slow pace. Edwin remembered Harriet's claim that the vicar could move better than he let on. Feeling guilty, he dismissed the thought. That Wilson kept walking by sheer force of will was hardly a cause for suspicion.

The sun burnishing the landscape vanished suddenly behind fast-moving clouds. For a moment the contrast darkened the world. The temperature dropped.

"The box of books is inside the door, Edwin. If you would oblige?" Wilson looked dead on his feet.

"Of course. The key?"

"We never lock the church during the day. Spiritual comfort is everyone's right and they may seek it within."

Edwin turned the iron ring handle on the worm-eaten door. The box of books sat nearby and as he picked it up the sun came out again, filling the church with multi-hued light.

At the base of the altar, bathed in colored light from the stained glass window behind it, lay the mutilated corpse of Joe Haywood.

Snatches of muted cheering drifted to Grace's ears while she patrolled. Twice, through gaps between cottages, she caught sight of the ragtag parade marching along. She felt isolated, a lonely ghost wandering empty streets, though they were abandoned only temporarily by those watching the festivities. She told herself she needed to make certain nobody got up to mischief while householders were elsewhere. But in truth she also wanted to avoid Edwin.

How could he think she cared for him? Surely she couldn't have given that impression? Or had she? Living in a tiny village, she rarely dealt with people she did not know and who did not, at least to an extent, know her. Maybe among strangers in London, or in Rochester in the United States, her normal, unguarded friendliness would convey more than it did in the close-knit community of Noddweir.

Stupid of her. Edwin was such a nice man. He had suffered so much and yet was not hardened or bitter, only sad. She hated to hurt him more. She sensed an innocence about Edwin, which was strange since he was a highly educated man from a big city as compared to the country folk here in Noddweir. But in the country one grew up closer to the world's harsh realities, even if your father wasn't abusive.

Too bad her father hadn't been more like Edwin.

And after all it was too bad Edwin was old enough to be her father.

Her gaze darted from side to side as she walked briskly along the High Street, alert for furtive movement. She spotted only a cat slinking past the front of Emily's closed shop.

The cat rushed over to her, meowing. She bent over to scratch its ears. "Sorry. I can't offer you anything."

She straightened up, checking the pocket of her blouse, making sure her report to the Craven Arms constabulary hadn't fallen out. She hadn't wanted to leave it at the house. Grandma was acting strangely of late, Grace wasn't sure anything left in the house with her would be safe.

She wondered how Jack Chapman was faring with his shrew bite. He was another man who had suffered, but unlike Edwin he had turned mean and bitter. Of course Jack had lived with his loss for far longer than Edwin had. As the lonely years went by would Edwin finally succumb to despair?

Her knock on Jack's door elicited no response so she went around to the smithy in the back.

Walking into the shadeless yard was like stepping into an oven. The hard-packed dirt radiated heat.

"Jack?"

No answer.

Grace strode past the wagon parts littering the yard. The long rod Jack had used to probe the pond leaned against the smithy's brick wall.

He must have drunk himself into a stupor to dull the pain. It was a good excuse, not that he usually needed one.

"Jack. It's Grace."

She paused in the doorway, dazzled by sunlight and blinked into darkness, which gradually lightened as her eyes adjusted. An unseen fly buzzed loudly.

It took her mind a second to register what she saw, so unexpected was it.

In the far corner, at the end of a rope tied to a rafter, hung Jack Chapman.

Chapter Forty-eight

"No! Oh, God no! No! No!" Meg Gowdy pounded both fists on the bar in the Guardians pub.

Louisa Wainman tried to put an arm around her but Meg pulled away violently, smacking Louisa in the mouth with an errant elbow.

"Get a hold of yourself, Meg!" shouted Duncan.

Violet, still wearing the cardboard crown and feather boa from the parade, clung to her father's side, looking from him to her mother, eyes wide, mouth trembling on the verge of sobs.

"I have to see him! I have to see Joe!" Meg took a few running steps toward the door before Grace blocked her way.

"You don't want to see him, Meg."

"Let her go," said Duncan. "Let her get a good look at her fancy man. Serve her right!"

Meg turned on her husband. "Bastard! Worm! Spineless failure!"

Violet's mouth moved convulsively but only strangled sounds emerged. Her face was so white she might have been in shock.

"Better than being a whore," Duncan replied.

Louisa dabbed at her bleeding lip. "At least if Meg were to leave you it would be for another adult. How do you think I feel, playing second fiddle to a babe in arms?"

Duncan said nothing. All hell had broken loose when Edwin found what was left of Joe Haywood. What had seemed like all hell hadn't been quite all, because a few minutes later Grace came racing to the church with the news that Jack Chapman had hung himself.

Later Grace returned to the pub with Meg and him and Violet. He must have told her she needed a drink. Didn't they all? Not to mention new lives.

Duncan experienced a weird calm. He became an observer. His life had been a tottering ruin for years. It was almost a relief to see it finally fall down. So this is actually the end, he thought, as he watched Meg pace and curse and blubber over Joe Haywood. Thank God. At least it's over.

Louisa took Meg by the arm. "Get packed. We can leave together. I'm afraid Harry's going to come after me any minute."

"It's too dangerous to try to leave," Grace said. "Remember Susannah."

"You don't accept it was Jack Chapman did it then?" Duncan asked. "Strikes me as obvious. He killed his daughter, tried to cover up, and finally the guilt was too much." Duncan suddenly remembered his own daughter, reaching down to pat her head, knocking her cardboard crown onto the flagstones.

Grace shook her head. "Jack wasn't clever enough to get away with everything that's happened here. I'm going into town right away. The authorities have to pay attention and send immediate help."

Duncan reached under the bar and pulled out his rifle. "I'll go, Grace. I want to get out of here anyway."

"No, Duncan. It's not a good idea." Grace looked meaningfully toward Violet.

Meg laughed. "What? You think I can't take care of my daughter by myself? She'll be better off without that pathetic excuse for a father."

Duncan hefted his weapon and walked around the bar. "I'll stick to the fields beyond the village, in case the maniac is watching the road."

He walked past Grace to the door. What if there was someone out there watching and waiting? He might never make it into town.

Maybe that would be for the best.

Shaken and sick to his stomach, Edwin returned to his lodgings and found Martha in the kitchen.

She glanced up from a mass of twigs piled on the table. "You look poorly, Professor. Is it the heat? I can give you a potion."

"I'll get a drink of water."

"You need anything to settle your stomach?" Martha's arthritic fingers moved slowly and with obvious effort plaited the twigs together.

He filled a glass at the sink. He sipped the water slowly, half choking on it. His whole insides were in turmoil. He kept seeing the ruin of Haywood.

Martha stared at him for a second or two. "It's not just the heat? Something else has happened?"

Edwin sighed. "Yes. It's bad. Very bad. Haywood is…" He trailed off. He couldn't very well describe the hideous mutilations to the old woman.

"Dead?" Martha smiled grimly. "Not surprised. Never been popular round here. A shifty sort. Where'd he get that stuff he sold? Stole it, I'm certain. Came on him and Duncan Gowdy shouting at each other at the pub one morning. A regular broggil, it was."

Edwin would have guessed most villagers were happy to have Haywood and his black market goods around. But then, what did he really know about this place? Obviously somebody hadn't liked Haywood. Had hated him, in fact, with a savage, animalistic hatred, judging from the display in the church.

Was it Haywood's illicit dealings? Had Noddweir been caught up in a war between black marketeers? He tried to shift his mind away from Haywood's murder. "Speaking of stealing," he said, "were you able to find those other things you had, er, mislaid, Martha?"

She gave him a keen look. "No, I haven't found them. I don't expect to now. That's why I'm making these charms."

"Charms?" The inquiry came automatically. What did he really care about charms right now?

"Yes." Tears welled up in her eyes. "I should never have talked so much about my persuasions. Oh, almost everybody who hears about them laughs. They don't know what I know, what my mother and her mother before her knew. There's terrible danger for Noddweir right now."

"But Martha—" Edwin began gently.

"You don't know, Professor. You can't. If there's a horned moon on the summer solstice, if you use the right persuasions you can find the gateway to hell in the middle of them stones."

Edwin blinked in surprise. Martha's voice was as matter of fact as if she were talking about the price of eggs. She really was—well, not mad, exactly—but senile.

Before he could respond she pointed a gnarled finger at him. "Blood is needed for them persuasions. And so's vervain and henbane and those herbs are in the headache necklace and rheumatics liniment what got stolen."

"But who...? I mean...you said nobody took your persuasions seriously."

Martha lifted what she was working on to examine it more closely. Apparently satisfied with the little figure made of entwined sticks, she set it on the table. "I said almost everybody laughs at what I tell them. I wish now there wasn't them who took it seriously."

Edwin stared at her, speechless.

She gave him a sly smile. "I'm not mad, you know. Only an old woman who made a mistake and intends to put it right."

Standing amidst the stones on Guardians Hill is like standing in front of a blazing forge. The grass that at sunrise was damp with dew has withered in the monstrous heat. The stones are hot to the touch. Unnaturally hot. The foxgloves bow their heads.

Though the sun is a molten orb, the horned moon is faintly visible in the washed-out blue of the sky.

From the clearing's edge the whole of Noddweir can be seen, the huddled cottages, the surrounding fields and farm buildings, the line of the narrow road escaping the constricted valley.

A solitary figure moves along the edge of a field at the base of the hill. His form melts, stretches, and twists like something seen at the bottom of a boiling pot of water. He carries a rifle. He is moving away from Noddweir.

He will not succeed in stopping what is about to happen.

The time has almost arrived.

Chapter Forty-nine

Grace closed the blackout curtains, shutting out the honey-colored sunlight that had filled the room. It was almost sunset and Duncan still hadn't returned with help.

"It's a long walk to Craven Arms," Edwin said. He'd been sitting with a book in his hand when she'd come in to close the curtains.

"Not that long. Surely he would have been able to get a ride once he got to the main road?"

"Maybe there wasn't an ambulance available? They'll send an ambulance for the bodies and he could come back with it."

Jack Chapman and Joe Haywood were now lying in the back of the locked smithy. Grace and Edwin both realized nobody would be coming for them today.

"I should have gone," Grace said.

"If you had tried to get to town, it would be you who was… gone." Edwin stared into the dimness enveloping them, not looking at Grace. For most of the afternoon, while they waited for help that never arrived, they had avoided one another, moving from room to room in an elaborate dance, each finding an excuse to be where the other was not. He put his book down.

"Grace, I'm afraid this last week…everything that's happened…has been too much for me on top of the journey here. I haven't been myself. I would never have said—"

"It's all right, Edwin. It's not as if I was insulted."

"Ah, well...that's a good start at least...or rather..." Edwin stood up abruptly. The air was stifling. "I'm going to talk to the vicar. I've puzzled over everything and there are questions I want to ask."

"Be careful."

"Yes. Anyway, it isn't quite dark yet."

After he had hurried off, Grace muttered another prayer. She wouldn't have prayed in front of Edwin. Maybe he was right, with his learned disbelief. Had her prayers achieved anything? The whole village had prayed, and to what end? The mothers whose children had vanished had beseeched God for help. Betty never missed church and now both her boys were missing. The vicar certainly had prayed and if anyone had God's ear it would be the vicar. It was easy enough to say that what happened in the world, both good and evil, was all part of God's mysterious plan, until it was you or yours being sacrificed for reasons beyond human comprehension.

Martha had her own beliefs. All day long she'd puttered around in the kitchen, working on her persuasions, going out to the back garden to pick plants from time to time, leaving briefly once to see Polly, who grew those Martha had a difficult time propagating. The house smelled of herbs boiling on the stove.

Grace was happy not to interfere. It kept her grandmother occupied and out of trouble.

The old woman was awfully quiet, Grace now realized.

The kitchen was deserted. A pot with a sticky residue in the bottom sat on the stove. The table was cleared of all but a few stray twigs and leaves.

Grace checked the garden. Martha wasn't there. A huge orange sun sat low in the sky, sending impossibly long shadows from the trees at the back of the garden up the house walls.

Going quickly to the privy, Grace knocked. "Grandma!"

No answer.

When she'd questioned Martha about her labors the explanations were confused. Grace thought her grandmother was having one her bad days. Or was she being purposefully evasive?

If anyone would know what Martha was up to, it would be Polly.

The cottage of Martha's devoted pupil sat alone at the end of a short cul de sac. Left to decay since her husband had died decades ago, the house was half hidden behind a garden that had run wild. Bushes reached up the eaves. Grace's knock at the front door elicited no response. Tall spikes of hollyhocks by the porch swayed ominously in an unfelt breeze.

After a short search she found Polly weeding an herb bed concealed in the wilderness. She looked nervous when Grace asked about Martha.

"Let's see. Your grandma came by this afternoon at least once."

"What about this evening?"

"Can't say as I recall her visiting since tea time."

"Don't lie to me, Polly. I can tell you're lying. Did she tell you to?"

"Now, Grace. You know how it is with an old woman's memory."

"You saw her not long ago, didn't you?"

Polly scrunched up her face as if she were trying to squeeze the memory out. "Might've needed one last ingredient for one persuasion or other."

"And where is she now?"

Polly licked her lips and said nothing but Grace noted how her gaze flickered toward Guardians Hill.

"She's gone up to the stones, hasn't she?"

"Well..."

Grace didn't wait for the reply. She was already running back in the direction of the High Street. She should've guessed what Martha was working at all day. Magic to counteract the evil she insisted hung about the stones.

Grace would have to go after her but first she must get her father's rifle. Whatever evil was out in the forest, a weapon would be more effective against it than Martha's persuasions.

◇◇◇

Edwin sat with Timothy Wilson in the vicarage garden and watched the swollen and malevolent sun squat for a moment on the mountain top. Then it slid out of sight, so quickly the movement was almost discernible, drawing harsh, red light out of the sky with it and leaving only a glow like that of a burning city.

"You don't mind staying outside, do you, Edwin? I can hardly breathe indoors with the blackout curtains closed."

"Is it necessary to keep the windows completely blocked so far out in the countryside? Considering your condition—"

"We all need to make sacrifices."

Edwin thought that his friend had made sufficient sacrifice in the last war but didn't say so.

"I've been giving a lot of thought to the stone circle myself." Wilson's quiet voice was almost masked by the chattering and shrilling of insects. "They can be places of power, especially at certain times such as the solstice. Evil power from a Christian viewpoint, of course. But as far as finding specific information about the Guardians, I can't tell you any more than Harry Wainman did."

"Naked corybants that no one alive has seen?"

"I'll bet Wainman didn't use the term 'corybant,' Edwin! You don't believe these old superstitions, I take it?"

"No. It isn't what I believe, it's what other people might believe."

"Beliefs are real to the believer," Wilson pointed out, "even if the thing believed in isn't real."

"Indeed. And that has effects in the real world. Look at Hitler and his murderous notions."

"None of which is very helpful to you. I'm sorry I can't offer more information, Edwin."

"Was Isobel Chapman going through puberty?"

Wilson paused before replying, startled. "I suppose so. She was big for her age. Well developed. One couldn't help noticing. Not that I—"

Edwin waved his hand. "Don't worry. We can't help noticing." Even when a woman is young enough to be your daughter, he thought ruefully. "So she might have been on the verge of menarche, if she hadn't begun already?"

"Oh...that's not the sort of thing a young girl would confide to the vicar."

"You've read *The Golden Bough*, among other things. Primitive people harbored a dread of menstrual blood, and in particular the first blood. They considered there was evil power inherent in the condition, which is why they often placed restrictions on a woman who had reached that time. One tribe confined her to a hammock slung up under the roof, so she couldn't touch the ground or see the sun. Suspended between heaven and earth, she couldn't cause any mischief."

Wilson looked thoughtful. "Issy's blood-stained clothes... have we been looking in the wrong direction?"

Edwin's heart skipped a beat when he found Grace's front room empty. There was no one in the kitchen either. He called up the stairs. No reply.

He looked into the kitchen again. Martha's persuasions and charms were no longer there. Had she put them away? Taken them somewhere? All day long she had talked about the Guardian Stones.

He looked in the pantry. The rifle was gone.

Martha must have gone to the Guardian Stones, but hoping to do what? Grace must have gone after her. Why else would she have taken the rifle unless she was going into the forest?

He ran out the door after them. If he had believed in a god, Edwin would have prayed he would not be too late.

Chapter Fifty

The Lord is thy keeper. The Lord is thy shade upon thy right hand. The sun shall not smite thee by day, nor the moon by night.

The psalm the vicar recited came back to Grace as she made her way deeper into the forest.

...nor the moon by night....

The moon had long since set.

The horned moon, Grandma had called it.

The horned moon had gone to ground behind the mountains but not before placing its evil imprint on the night.

Grace followed the rut of a path, forcing herself to move deliberately. She didn't dare turn on her torch. She didn't want to alert whatever might be out there in the darkness. Whatever had sprung upon Susannah and Joe Haywood and most likely had ambushed Duncan Gowdy and the children as well.

She followed the lesser darkness where the path formed a gap between trees and bushes pressing in on either side.

Grandma must have come this way. It was the most direct route to the hilltop. But she hadn't caught up to her yet. Had the old woman wandered off the path and become lost?

It might be better than her reaching the Guardian Stones.

Grace felt the ground rising. Her breath came harder, not from exertion but fear. Grandma couldn't be far ahead now. If only Grace could risk calling out, not that the stubborn old woman would pay any attention.

Grace pushed on. Thorny brushes across the path might have been claws fastening on her. The touch of thick, heavy laurel leaves felt like the fingers of murderous hands. She pushed overhanging limbs aside with the rifle and ducked under them, trying not to make too much noise.

What was that?

She paused and peered into the suffocating night.

Beyond the path she discerned only gradations of black, hinting at trees and the bulky shapes of shrubbery, merging at a short distance into an utter void.

She had the uncanny sensation she was not alone. It was the panicked feeling she had upon awakening from a nightmare convinced a nameless something stood beside her bed. Now, here, the freezing fog of terror did not evaporate into wakefulness.

The Lord shall preserve thee from all evil, she muttered to herself. He shall preserve thy soul.

There. She heard it.

Voices.

She looked upwards.

An orange nimbus glowed over the summit.

Isobel Chapman stood silhouetted against the bonfire blazing in the stone circle atop Guardians Hill.

Draped in a ragged, blood-stained sheet, her hair wildly tangled with twigs and leaves, her face daubed with blood and ashes, she bore no resemblance to the young girl for which the villagers had mistaken her.

She threw another gobbet of flesh into the flames. As it hissed and popped, she raised her arms to the sky. Her band of naked children smeared with dirt circled the fire anti-clockwise, then halted and drew closer together, staring into the sparks that swirled upwards as if being drawn into a celestial whirlpool. Firelight and shadows played over demonic faces with the snouts of animals.

Isobel chanted words learned from the old woman.

The old woman didn't understand the knowledge passed down through the generations. Like everyone in Noddweir, she was blind. The villagers had mocked Isobel because she was not like them. How could she be? They were human. The ignorant, pitiful brute of a father, the weakling mother too frail to survive the performance of her only purpose, were not her true parents.

She was born of the Guardian Stones and the horned moon.

For thousands of years the stones had ruled the land, until their worshipers betrayed them. Then they slept fitfully, waiting.

What was a sleep of slow centuries to gods?

After they had borne her, they had whispered her destiny in dreams. Told her secrets. The old witch, unknowingly, had passed on the knowledge necessary to avenge the ancient betrayal. At the coming of Isobel's power in the metamorphosis of blood, the Guardians called her to them.

The Guardians dwell in deepest hell, went the rhyme Martha had taught her. Did the old hag not realize it was literally true?

Above the crackling flames she heard a boy crying for his mother.

Isobel pivoted and jabbed a finger at the child, who immediately subsided into quiet weeping. A bigger, chubby boy put his arm around the child.

"Bert," the child sniffled, "can't you take me home, Bert?"

"Quiet! Don't let her hear you!"

But Isobel, senses grown preternaturally sharp, heard every word. She had no use for little snivelers or soft boys who showed them kindness. She would instruct Len Finch to slit their throats.

Afterward.

Isobel tilted her head back to address the sky and babbled in a high-pitched voice. "Wake, lord of the underworld! Hear me! I was yours from birth, favored, born under a horned moon. Ruler and protector of the wicked, lover of all evil, we bow to you as master."

A bat materialized out of the night, tumbled through the rising sparks, and was gone.

Isobel's voice rose. "We have done all you asked. We have lied and stolen. We have killed and offered blood and torture to you. We have carved the magic life-beckoning symbols into the stones."

By now her voice had risen to a shriek. "Come, lord of darkness, horned god, destroy! Kill them all! None are worthy to live! Torment them with long agonies! Make their children writhe in agony! Send your sacred fire to cleanse the earth of every trace of them!"

Isobel paused, panting, and threw the sheet she wore into the fire. It fluttered like a great bird, then caught fire and disintegrated. Heat beat against her skin like the black wing of a fiery demon. Sparks settled on her arms, burning pinpoints.

She knelt, naked, and screamed at the sky. "Blood and fire and death and pain! And if any live, give them to the dark gods of Hell men call cancer and pox and deaths of babies unborn!"

Long shadows radiated outwards from the ancient stones, gyrating in the lighting from the surging flames. Were the stones dancing too? Did they shift and move to pull themselves up from the ground? Each stone flung a shaft of darkness upwards, darker than the night.

Isobel clawed at the dirt, ripped up earth and grass and foxgloves and flung them into the flames.

The foxgloves shrieked as they withered.

Isobel leapt up and danced and her followers danced with her, frolicked in a temple abandoned by worshipers for thousands of years, circled by infinite pillars of darkness.

Again the sinister words of Martha's rhyme came back to her. Circle round, unholy ground.

She danced until she was giddy with exhaustion, until the fire in her lungs was indistinguishable from the fiery heat assaulting her flesh, her hair smoldering as sparks flew out, caressing kisses of fire. She threw her head back and gazed upwards.

She sensed a trickle of blood run down the inside of her thigh.

Already alive with newfound strength, Isobel was ready to receive the ultimate power.

She felt it.

A vibration.

A buzzing. As of enormous flies.

Chapter Fifty-one

Lightning bolts of pain ran through Martha's chest as she labored to the top of Guardians Hill. Normally she would have sat down, but now it didn't matter. She paused to rest many times as she made her slow, roundabout way upwards to avoid detection.

As if a force held her back.

She would not sit down again.

Struggling on, she heard Isobel's demonic chant grow louder.

She touched the effigy made of twisted sticks dangling on string around her neck. A cross formed from the gnarled roots of herbs hung there too. The persuasions she spent the day concocting were sewn into her shapeless, flowered dress in packets and stoppered medicine bottles.

Martha called her concoctions "persuasions." However, those she carried tonight were not meant to persuade, but rather to command. Far removed from her usual cosmetic lotions and herbal remedies, these required a sacrifice.

She stopped at the clearing's edge where the stone circle stood and watched the demon child with her animalistic tribe dance recklessly before the flames. Their long shadows flickered across the old woman who waited still, unseen, gathering up what little strength she had left.

How had she failed to see Isobel for what she was?

Had the ancient stones blinded her?

In recent years people began to call Martha senile. She heard them when they thought she wasn't listening. It was true, words skittered out of her grasp when she sought them, things went missing, she forgot what happened ten minutes before, or found herself somewhere and couldn't recall how or why she'd got there.

Yet as her mind disengaged from the familiar world, she saw more clearly the world hidden beneath what people called reality. Saw the shadow hanging over Noddweir, felt the icy rivulets of evil oozing from Guardians Hill, heard the circled stones murmuring to each other in the night as they came awake after thousands of years.

Finally she understood fully certain pieces of wisdom passed down to her.

The demon child threw back her head and gazed into the sky.

Martha stepped out into the firelight.

Edwin crashed blindly through the trees. He was being followed.

He'd lost the path. It didn't matter. His destination was the hilltop. He simply needed to keep climbing.

And hope whatever followed didn't catch up.

A low-hanging branch raked his face. He grabbed at his eyeglasses, barely saving them from being knocked off.

He wasn't certain how he could help if he did overtake Grace, but he had to try.

How many nights since Elise's accident had he lain awake replaying the scene outside the theater? Could he have acted like men in movies who took the chance to be heroes? He could have done whatever was necessary if Fate had played fairly with him. It seldom did in real life.

He shoved his eyeglasses back into place. There was a rustling not far off. He looked over his shoulder.

Did that sapling move?

There was no wind.

Edwin turned and struggled on, eyes narrowed, toward the hill top. The lurid glow of fire rose into the sky. It did not penetrate down the hillside into the trees.

Something grabbed his face. Invisible. Clinging to his nose and mouth.

A spider web.

He flailed at it, momentarily, stupidly, panicked at the thought of the bulbous spider that must have woven it and might now be crawling in his hair or down the neck of his shirt. He took a few steps backwards, tried to wipe the web off his hands.

His foot found nothing but space. He rolled down a dirt bank into a muddy puddle, his heart pounding as if it were about to explode.

Stygian darkness pressed on all sides. Only directly overhead hung a hint of the lighter night sky.

The crater. He must have fallen into the bomb crater he'd seen on his first day in Noddweir.

He was fortunate he hadn't broken anything. Or at least it didn't feel as if anything was broken, though one knee throbbed. His fingers clutched a large stone sticking up from the muck. That must have been the culprit.

He pushed himself to his feet.

From above came a demented shriek, more animal than human. Weight smashed into Edwin's back, drove him down again. The thing on top of him snarled, clawed, and bit.

Edwin's shoulder blazed with pain.

Reaching around, his hand found a face. He shoved and the teeth let go. His assailant dived for his neck. Edwin tried to throw the attacker off and failed. The thing moved with inhuman speed, strength, and ferocity.

He remembered the rock, grabbed it. Struck backwards to dislodge the clinging monster.

To Edwin's horror the rock clanged ineffectually on metal.

When Martha approached the bonfire, Isobel looked away from the sky. The tribe fell silent. Crouching, sub-human shapes, their gas masks gave them the appearance of gargoyles or monstrous frogs.

Passing between two ancient stones surmounted now by towering pillars of darkness, Martha touched the charms around her neck and murmured words she had never understood until this night. Tentacles of shadow which sought to bar her writhed away. Now… at last…she was fully aware of the reality which had eluded her for a lifetime.

Isobel's eyes shone wolf-like in the firelight. "Stupid old woman! What do you think you're going to do?" She laughed. The sound was ancient, hollow, echoing up from a corridor reaching thousands of years into the past.

Gooseflesh rose on Martha's arms. "I'm going to put an end to your wickedness, Isobel." She couldn't stop her voice from quavering. "I know how. I was your teacher, remember, Goddess forgive me."

Isobel's lips curved in a gargoyle's smile. Smoke curled up from her tangled hair where sparks landed. "I should have had you killed after I left, old woman. Len, Mike. Throw her into the fire!"

Martha stroked a hand over her dress, feeling the packets and bottles of persuasions fastened inside. She clutched the charms hanging from her neck.

Two demons loped toward her, filthy hands outstretched.

There must be a sacrifice, but she could not bear to be touched by those vile things.

She stepped toward the conflagration. The heat roasted the skin of her face red. Another step and the white cloud of hair around her head exploded into flame. She started to chant. The chant rose into a scream as she took a final step into the flames. Sparks licked the hem of her dress, then raced up its sides, and spread. A bottle exploded.

Over the roar of the blaze, the buzzing of a monstrous fly grew louder.

Edwin lashed backwards with the rock once more and again it rang on metal. He felt skin being torn from his throat. The horror clinging to him fought with superhuman strength as he tried futilely to push it off or squirm out of its grasp.

Then abruptly the pressure ended.

The weight fell away.

He heard a thump.

"Edwin! Are you all right?"

Grace's voice.

Turning over, he could barely make out the motion as she brought the rifle butt down with another thump on the featureless shape beside him.

A torch flicked on for long enough to reveal Reggie Cox sprawled out, naked and covered in dirt. The light glinted off the metal brace on his leg.

Grace turned the torch off and knelt down. Her fingers found the wound on Edwin's neck. "It isn't bleeding badly. He missed the artery, thank God."

"Martha," Edwin managed to say. "Did you find Martha?"

Grace's lips tightened. "Not yet. When I heard the commotion I turned back. A good thing I did, too."

Edwin got up unsteadily as Grace scrambled up the side of the crater. When she reached the top she stopped, looked upwards, and came sliding back in an avalanche of earth and stones.

"Oh my God! Get down Edwin! Get down!"

He looked up at the sky before Grace yanked him off his feet.

Something dark was moving across the stars.

◇◇◇

As the old witch burned, her screaming chant rose into an ear-piercing screech, rose until it left the range of human hearing.

Weirdly colored flames burst from her fiery clothes, sending serpentine coils of smoke charging upwards between the infinite shadow pillars. The demons leapt and howled and shook their fists.

The air vibrated with a monstrous buzzing.

Martha burned furiously, with preternatural speed. In a moment she was nothing more than a flaming, silent totem.

Isobel stepped as close to the fire as she dared, exulting as the blistering heat caressed her.

She gazed upwards, toward a dark shape approaching.

She heard an eerie whistling roar and another and another, louder, ever louder.

Isobel raised her arms to greet the coming of the power.

Epilogue

"We're trying to identify the remains but there's not much left." Constable Harmon gave a hopeless shrug.

Edwin, seated across from Harmon's desk at the Craven Arms police station, remembered crouching in the old crater with Grace, deafened by thunderous explosions, blinded by a rain of dirt and rocks, while the earth shook as if trying to throw them off into eternity. When the bombs stopped falling and the plane's throbbing faded until it was lost in the sounds of night insects, they climbed to the top of Guardians Hill.

No sign of the stone circle remained, nor any hint of life. The clearing was a cauldron of fire and smoke, ashes and sparks whirling upward in a titanic column. Edwin and Grace might have been looking into a volcano or the gateway to hell.

Harmon stared, grey and tired, at the folder in his hand as if it might suddenly tell him anything new. His manner was no longer as supercilious as during his visit to Noddweir when he'd refused to treat the deaths of Emily Miller and Tom Green as anything out of the ordinary. Nevertheless, although the constable now acknowledged that something terrible had happened, it was plain he wasn't sure exactly what it was or how it related to his law enforcement duties.

"Not only haven't we been able to identify any remains yet," he said, "we haven't found any bodies elsewhere except for the crucified deserter, Baxter. He would have been better off fighting the Krauts."

Harmon glanced up and abruptly bit off his words. Turning slightly, Edwin saw Grace in the doorway.

"It's all right." She crossed to the desk and took a chair beside Edwin. "Father wasn't a good man and it finally caught up to him. They've released the body. I'll arrange to have it sent back to Noddweir for burial." She took a cigarette out of her purse and lit it. "Reggie's been talking?"

Harmon pushed an ashtray toward her. "Oh, yes. Cunning little bugger. He didn't do anything. Except what the others forced him to do. To hear him tell it, he had to go along. He was no match for them, with that brace on his leg."

Grace blew out a cloud of smoke. "So he says. He'll be released from hospital soon, won't he?"

"Yes, and in a few years he'll be in prison or an asylum for the criminally insane."

"Was it Reggie who killed Emily's dog?" Grace asked.

"Yes. Sleeping downstairs as he did it was easy enough for him to sneak out of the house, despite the brace on his leg. He confessed he strangled the dog first because he loved it and didn't want it to suffer."

"A strange kind of love, but logical in a twisted way," Edwin observed.

"He set the dog on fire because Isobel promised to cure his leg if he did. He says he was afraid of retribution if he refused," Harmon continued. "He's still very angry about it. His leg remains the same and he reckons it was because he gave the dog a merciful death compared to what Isobel had in mind. Her magic didn't work."

"Poor Patch trusted Reggie because the little monster gave him treats," said Grace. "No wonder he didn't bark when the children broke into Emily's shop."

"But what about Emily?" Edwin put in.

"The little swine claims she had a heart attack after he and Isobel and the Finch boys reached through the broken window to unlatch the door and get into the shop. Not surprising really, given he says they threatened to set her on fire like her dog."

"And Special Constable Green was doubtless helped over the cliff." Grace gave Harmon an accusatory look.

The constable massaged his temple as if he had a terrific headache. "In retrospect, Miss Baxter, I can see how those two deaths fit into the larger pattern, but at the time..."

"At the time you should have paid more attention to what we were telling you! And what else did Reggie get up to? What about the dead thing and the knives in Susannah's cupboard?"

"It was a frog. The boy dotes on frogs...in his own way. It was planted with the knives to make trouble for Miss Radbone. She had already left Noddweir, which would make it look still worse."

"And you've found no trace of her?" asked Edwin.

"No. And nothing of Duncan Gowdy either, although considering what happened to the other adults the kids got hold of it's easy enough to guess their fate."

Edwin wondered whether Grace should be hearing these details so soon after recent events. After all, she would have to return to Noddweir to live by herself. "The children had a remarkably easy time creeping about in secret," he said. "Breaking into houses, carrying out abductions."

"Not abductions. They enticed others to join them willingly," Harmon corrected.

"Nevertheless—"

"Doesn't surprise me." Grace flicked ashes into the ashtray. "Issy's lot were mostly hardened city kids. Children in the country aren't quite so tough in the way they are. And Issy knew the forest like the back of her hand, so it was easy to find hiding places."

Harmon riffled through the papers in his file, scanning them.

"If you can believe him, Reggie gave an explanation for everything," he said. "It says here they discovered Harry Wainman hoarded petrol. They used it to set fire to Joe Haywood's house after stealing from his stores. They proposed to camp out all winter and we found a cache of tinned food and a couple of tin openers where Reggie told us to look."

"Utter madness," Grace declared. "They'd freeze to death."

Harmon shrugged and continued to turn over pages. "They transferred Haywood's body into the church while the kids' parade was at the far end of the village. Knew the parade was planned, you see, and were ready for it. They constantly observed, listened, watched for people trying to leave the village."

Edwin shook his head. "So when I felt the back of my neck prickling, I was in fact being watched."

Grace shivered. "To think they were in my house when they stole Grandma's herbs and such."

"Yes, there is that aspect," Harmon said slowly. "Reggie swears they were assisted by supernatural forces associated with that stone circle, forces controlled by Isobel."

Grace gave a harsh laugh. "Grandma filled that girl's head with nonsense and it got Grandma and a lot of others killed."

"Martha couldn't have known Isobel was the way she was," Edwin protested.

"No? You think not? How could she have missed it? The girl was pure evil!"

"I wouldn't blame your grandmother," Harmon put in hastily. "Isobel Chapman wasn't right in the head, in my opinion. I've gone over everything you told me, Professor Carpenter, as well as Miss Baxter's statement and the vicar's, not to mention everything we've got out of Reggie, and it's pretty clear what happened, if not why."

He paused for a moment to gather his thoughts. "Correct me if you think I'm wrong. The blood on Isobel's clothing was human. She hadn't been murdered, she was menstruating. She'd got hold of the idea that with that came real power. Does that sound right?"

Grace said nothing. She sat smoking, stony-faced.

Edwin nodded. "It has been claimed, and especially if it was the first."

"Isobel began recruiting followers," Harmon continued. "Whether the other children actually believed her tales or merely liked the idea of living in the forest and raising hell is irrelevant. We know what they did, if not the details of how they did it. For example, Violet, the Gowdy's daughter, said she saw a white thing approaching Green's room. Reggie claims Isobel left a note supposedly from you, Miss Baxter, in Green's room to lure him up to the Guardian Stones."

"Shows what a fool he was," snapped Grace. "If I wanted to meet him up there I wouldn't have sneaked into the pub to leave a note. I'd have simply asked him. To think he imagined…" Her face reddened.

"Yes…well…" Harmon muttered. "At any rate, Reggie also says the night Jack Chapman was killed, Isobel left them saying she was going to Noddweir to deal with her father."

"Didn't he hang himself?" Grace asked.

"We found a wound on the back of his head. Our theory is Isobel found him drunk, knocked him out and hung him. She was strong enough to handle the body."

"But what was the point of terrorizing the village?" Edwin asked. "Why would they kill people who'd done nothing to them?"

Grace stubbed out her cigarette. "Evil doesn't need a reason."

As Grace waited on the railway platform to see Edwin safely away, she lit another cigarette.

Edwin frowned. "I didn't know you smoked."

"I don't very often. Grandma didn't like me to." She blew out a particularly large cloud of smoke and looked down the track. "It's really no concern of yours, Edwin."

"No, I suppose not. Will you be all right now, living by yourself?"

"After all that's happened, you mean? Of course. Is it any worse than what's happening in Europe and elsewhere? One day the war will end and the survivors will simply rebuild and try to get on with their lives."

"You're a practical young woman, Grace. I don't know I could resume life in the same place after what went on."

"I plan to leave soon. Maybe I'll go to Birmingham, find work where I can contribute more to the war effort."

"You won't be the only one to go. By the time the war's over there won't be anyone left in the village."

"Polly will still be there. She's the wise woman now, for those who believe in things like Grandma's persuasions. As far as they're concerned she possesses the same knowledge that saved Noddweir."

"She owes her reputation to your grandmother's sacrifice. I notice Polly didn't go up to the stones with Martha."

"She claims she had an attack of the rheumatics and couldn't climb. Not that she could have helped. What happened wasn't Grandma's doing either. Can you start to believe in God now, Edwin?"

"Why would what happened make me believe in God?"

"Who was it brought the bombs down on those accursed stones?"

"Some young German pilot on his way to Wales getting confused by the bonfire and thinking it was something worth bombing, mistaking it as the result of another plane's bombs."

"You don't think it might have been the hand of God?"

"Your God? Or Martha's? Or Isobel's? Or the god worshiped by the builders of the circle?"

Grace smiled bleakly. "Oh, Edwin!"

"If anything, what's happened might make me believe there's evil forces at work in the world. Why was Isobel the way she was? Reggie says she told him her father never beat or abused her. He claims the bruises you and others saw were self-inflicted. Was she simply born evil? Was Martha right, did the stone circle exert a malign influence over Noddweir? Was it because Isobel ate blackberries in October and invited the devil's attention? Or was it because she was born under a horned moon? Yes, I might believe in evil forces if I were superstitious, which I'm not."

"Do professors always engage in intellectual arguments when they are standing on railway platforms saying farewell?"

Edwin felt his face flush. "I apologize. I haven't exactly distinguished myself during my stay here."

"You saved my life, racing into the forest after me."

"I remember it was you who knocked Reggie off my back."

"But if I hadn't turned back to help you I would have reached the top of the hill as the bombs started falling."

"You might have reached Martha in time."

"No, I would have been too late. She didn't want to be reached. She wanted to confront Issy. Maybe she did help put an end to the horror."

Edwin's reply was cut off by the sound of a train whistle.

"I know you intended to stay longer," Grace said. "You don't need to cut your visit short."

"There's nothing left for me to study."

"The barrows are still there. You never got to examine them closely."

"It's a difficult time for Noddweir. You don't need a foreigner underfoot."

"What will you do?"

"I don't know." He was surprised to hear himself admit it. He couldn't recall a time in his life when he did not know exactly what he was going to do next. He felt a sudden rush of panic and elation.

"Don't look behind you, said Death, but we're being followed." Edwin recalled Emily Miller's words on his first day in Noddweir.

"That's a local expression, Edwin. I've never been certain what it meant."

"Maybe it means we spend too much time looking over our shoulders for death, while death is always right beside us, a fact of life. We ought to pay more attention to things we could do something about. Then again…"

The roar of the approaching train drowned him out.

Grace flipped her cigarette toward the tracks, leaned over and kissed Edwin on the cheek, then pivoted and strode quickly away. He averted his gaze from her retreating back and turned to watch the train arrive.

To receive a free catalog of Poisoned Pen Press titles, please provide your name, address, and email address in one of the following ways:

Phone: 1-800-421-3976
Facsimile: 1-480-949-1707
Email: info@poisonedpenpress.com
Website: www.poisonedpenpress.com

Poisoned Pen Press
6962 E. First Ave. Ste 103
Scottsdale, AZ 85251